PRAISE FOR DAVID F. ROSS

'A twisted love letter to Glasgow at her finest and worst, shot through with an eye for 1970s detail and an awareness of our current, complex ills. This is hardboiled Tartan Noir with a musical edge, streetwise intelligence and exactly the sense of humour you'd hope to find as showbiz meets Duke Street and high-society enforcers battle gentlemen of the Sarry Heid and graduates of the Bar L' A L Kennedy

'Ross brings his ever-so-dark humour and caustic eye to 1970s Glasgow, and it proves to be the perfect pairing. *Welcome to the Heady Heights* is where the famous Williams, Connolly and McIlvanney meet, using the city's "No Mean City" reputation as the backdrop to a story that lifts the lid on the worlds of showbusiness and politics, and finds that the contents are rotten' Alistair Braidwood, Scots Whay Hae

'A solid gold hit of a book!' Colin McCredie

'Full of comedy, pathos and great tunes' Hardeep Singh Kohli

'Warm, funny and evocative' Chris Brookmyre

'If you lived through the early eighties this book is essential. If you didn't it's simply a brilliant debut novel' John Niven

'Dark, hilarious, funny and heart-breaking all at the same time, a book that sums up the spirit of an era and a country in a way that will make you wince and laugh' Muriel Gray

'A madcap romp through the 1980s with Ayrshire's greatest band. It captures a world of indie rock and fucking wallopers with hilarious élan' Stuart Cosgrove

'As warm and authentic as Roddy Doyle at his very best' Nick Quantrill

'Took me back to an almost forgotten time, when vengeance was still in vogue and young DJs remained wilfully "uncool". Just brilliant' Bobby Bluebell

'Ross levers the various plot twists and turns effectively. He also knows his music and the numerous references give the book authenticity. You will be thumbing through old records (or the modern-day equivalent) as a result of reading this novel' Danny Rhodes

'Ross's social commentary, however, is applied as judiciously as his humour ... More than just a nostalgic recreation of the author's youth, it's a compassionate, affecting story of a family in crisis at a time of upheaval and transformation, when disco wasn't the only thing whose days were numbered' *Herald Scotland*

'The final novel in Ross's "Disco Days" trilogy, this work is a warm, funny consideration of reconciliation between middle-aged friends and a celebration of music's healing powers. Suggest to fans of Nick Hornby' *Library Journal*

'By turn hilarious and heartbreaking, more than anything Ross creates beautifully rounded characters full of humanity and, perhaps most of all, hope. It will make you laugh. It will make you cry. It's rude, keenly observed and candidly down to earth' Liam Rudden, *Scotsman*

'The result is a mounting sense of tension as the book moves towards its conclusion ... it stands on its own merits and can be highly recommended on that basis' *Undiscovered Scotland*

'The novel succeeds on the strength of the characters, with the band themselves a well-drawn and sympathetic creation, while their manager Max Mojo, a hoodlum recreating himself as a Malcolm McLaren-style impresario, will live long in the memory' David Kerr, *Press & Journal*

'Ross has a brave and distinctive voice, which is sure to appeal to men and woman across the country' Culture for Kicks

'Ross's trilogy is one of the most interesting and original recent publishing debuts and as someone growing up in the late 1970s and early 1980s, I find it nostalgic – but also tender, realistic and hopeful' Blue Book Balloon

'The dark humour in these books paints a truthful and perceptive portrait of Scottish men of a certain age, and the blend of humour and poignancy hits just the right balance' On-the-Shelf Books

'A tale of consequences, with heart and soul, a coming-of-age tale set in difficult times, David Ross has written a terrific story that will have you laughing out loud one moment and sobbing into your pillow the next' Liz Loves Books

'There are some deeply moving and genuinely heartbreaking moments but the power of friendship and a love for music runs strong throughout, and for all of life's sucker punches and poignancy, this is ultimately an uplifting story of hope. And a bloody funny one at that' Mumbling about...

'It's a cracking tale and I've thoroughly enjoyed being along for the ride ... with music and a huge dose of Scottish wit' The Book Trail

'Brutally honest, the language is stark, and often blue, but this adds to the absolute realism and authenticity. This is Glasgow after all, it's the music business, it's middle-aged guys with regrets. Lets not try to gloss over this life. This is humanity at its toughest. This is excellent' Random Things through My Letter Box

'I love a book that can make me laugh out loud in one chapter and make me an emotional wreck in the next ... this has had this effect on me' Segnalibro

'Heartbreaking, poignant, and ferociously funny' Espresso Coco

'If you like Irvine Welsh you need to read David F. Ross, not as much grit but certainly of the same calibre ... absolutely I will be reading this author again' Always Reading

'This book evoked such intense emotions – I had a lump in my throat, tears in my eyes and a giggle in my belly' Chapter in My Life

'I cannot wait for what David Ross decides to do next. I'm sure I'm not the only one thinking that' Christopher Clark

'David Ross definitely has a way of putting the human into his characters; they live and breathe, and you feel every emotion with them ... The humour in amongst the sadness; the wit and charm; the music – everywhere the music; but above all the love, tenderness and friendship' Reading Writes

'I love the way David weaves the strands together and keeps you turning the pages. His ear for dialogue remains as acute as ever ... This isn't another *Tutti Frutti*, there's so much more to this story than that' Gordon Hunt

'It is funny, fresh and damned entertaining. Plus there is the music – always the music and the forgotten songs, the trivia and the sheer depth of knowledge David Ross brings to his books; reading them is so very enjoyable. Fabulous, funny and frequently foul-mouthed' Grab this Book

'The brilliance of David F. Ross is his ability to plunge us into 1980s Ayrshire in all its madness, violence and despair (with a smattering of hope) ... It's a vivid and colourful world and could only have been created by someone who was there ... The dialogue is muscular and spot-on, the locations come alive and the characters are believably flawed' Words To Terrify

'Ross demonstrates a gift for expressing life that surely has more to give. There is a real empathy for people of all kinds in the pages, there are "good" people doing bad things and "bad" people doing good things, because people are not good or bad, they are just people dealing with what is in front of them, imperfectly. This book is worth reading for that truth alone, but it also takes you on an emotional journey that reminds you what it is to be human, a fabulous debut' Live Many Lives

'Very much a story of nostalgia. As soon as I started reading it I was transported back to the eighties with memories of *Top of the Pops* and getting ready with my tape recorder to record my favourite songs that were in the top forty' By-the-Letter Book Reviews

'The writing in this book excels because it takes what would ordinarily be page upon page of humour and one-liners, keeps them, embraces them and yet at the same time the story is poignantly crafted, the wit balanced out with pure, genuine emotion' Reviewed the Book

'The whole vibe is spot on ... For all the wannabe musicians/band members this shows how tough the whole scene can be and the elation if the pinnacle is reached' Cancer Sucks

'There is a certain rollicking, cinematographic quality to both books' Mumble Words

'This novel was a revelation for me, a breath of fresh air and I can honestly say I have never read anything like it' My Chestnut Reading Tree

'I really enjoyed this book, and the effective manner in which David Ross controls the humour, emotion and tragedy in equal measure. His characters are likeable, the comedy moments are genuinely funny, and the emotion isn't over the top or exaggerated. This is a high-quality, extremely well-drawn and assured debut from this new author' Books and Pals Blog

'The humour is well pitched and executed, in places even sublime – but David F. Ross has a talent for social angst, and it's this I'd love to see more of in the future' A Novel Book

'It strikes the perfect balance between weighty socio-political commentary and witty observation. I laughed out loud a great many times and shrunk in sadness during the harder moments. A tragic comedy of deep family difficulties and comedic coping mechanisms, it makes for a strikingly authentic and enjoyable read' Publish Things

'Ross has written a great coming-of-age novel that is full of wonderful prose and characters who are instantly likeable' Literature for Lads

'Ross is particularly adept at world-building. His gritty and authentic depiction of Scottish life in the 1980s is particularly hard hitting, and is very clearly rooted in the author's own teenage years. Because of this, the novel itself is imbued with an acute sense of reality, feeling in parts almost like a legitimate memoir' Cuckoo Writers

Welcome to the Heady Heights

ABOUT THE AUTHOR

David F. Ross was born in Glasgow in 1964. His debut novel, *The Last Days of Disco*, was long-listed for the Best First Novel Award by the Author's Club of London. National Theatre Scotland acquired dramatic rights for the book in 2015. He has written pieces for *Nutmeg* and *Razur Cuts* magazines, and in December 2018 was chosen to contribute a poem commemorating the 16th anniversary of the death of Joe Strummer for the publication *Ashes to Activists*.

Follow David on Twitter *@dfr10* and visit his website: *http://www. davidfross.co.uk*.

Welcome to the Heady Heights

David F. Ross

**ORENDA
BOOKS**

Orenda Books
16 Carson Road
West Dulwich
London SE21 8HU
www.orendabooks.co.uk

First published in the United Kingdom in 2019 by Orenda Books

ISBN 978-1-912374-61-8
eISBN 978-1-912374-62-5

Typeset in Garamond by MacGuru Ltd
Printed and bound by CPI Group (UK) Ltd, Croydon CR0 4YY

For sales and distribution, please contact *info@orendabooks.co.uk*

Welcome to the Heady Heights

For my dad

'Glasgow's a bit like Nashville; it doesn't care much for the living, but it really looks after the dead.'

—*Billy Connolly*

July 1976

The city shimmered in a ridiculous heat. *Hottest summer since records began,* claimed those who knew about such things. At other times of the year, the smog from hundreds of factory chimneys would have totally obscured the urban terrain from this elevated perspective. It was the end of the Glasgow Fair fortnight; the city air's annual break from the relentless industrial processes that employed many of its citizens.

Archie loved the Necropolis. The Molendinar Burn running below it was where St Mungo had founded his church; the seed of Glasgow. It now represented where East End *bampottery* stopped and the city centre began. A 'civilian' had to be wary, of course. The Necropolis was understood to be where Glasgow gangsters liked to pass instructions to their enforcers. Those activities apart, it was a tiered hill of calmness and serenity. He often came up here to look down across the city of his birth, to try to understand his place in the wider scheme of Glaswegian things; and to get pissed in peace, almost always in that order. Even allowing for the liquidity of the light, a man could orientate himself from here. Archie could see the physical punctuation marks that signposted the locations of various social groupings. Away in the distance, the soaring Glasgow University spire marked where the cultured West End started; across the dirty grey Clyde to his left, the Caledonia Road Church indicated the edge of the decayed urban wastelands of the Gorbals. And finally – to his right as he slowly rotated his head – beneath the blackened soot and the smoke stains was the muscularity and crafted beauty of the cathedral's stonework.

As he pondered the pace with which the decade's grains of sand were disappearing, Archie was gradually working his way towards personal objective number three. He was accompanied by his regular companions: Madeline, Lucy and Sandra, who regarded him seductively from their prized place on the side of three Tennent's lager cans. Madeline lay to his right, crumpled and spent. He had Lucy in the palm of his left hand now.

Archie was fifty-two years old. One of life's natural procrastinators, he was aware that life was passing him by. It was happening slowly, and without any real abrasion, but even in his positive moments, he acknowledged that he should do something about it. There were essentially four routes for his kind: the factory shift worker, the Corporation transport worker, the gangster, or the alcoholic waster. Occasionally someone managed to break free – to move up west where the air was cleaner and the prospects more obvious. It might be through raw talent at football, honed in the back courts or on the uneven streets, or a lucky pools win. But in every case Archie was aware of, the booze or the bookies dragged them back. Escaping the fate of the East End weegie was harder than breaking out of Colditz Castle.

All the routes open to a male carried a life expectancy that was almost Dickensian. And Archie had already passed the point where the home straight statistically began. The hereditary odds were stacked against him too, but perhaps unusually, his father's heart had outlasted his mother's. It was an accepted truth that the men of Glasgow's East End passed before the women; a life of toil outside the home was perceived as harder than the daily drudgery in it. But Archie thought another life was out there, even for him. He could visualise it; it was tantalisingly close, just beyond the Trongate's awkward, loose cobbles.

Archie Blunt was funny, or so he thought. At least as funny as Connolly; *and look at him now* – mates with Parky, forgetting all about *his ain folk*. Archie had met him and his manager in a Duke Street pub a few years ago when the Big Yin was singing and playing his banjo. Archie bought them both a pint and opportunistically told an old joke about three men from Calton. It had made Connolly laugh, but apparently not enough to buy Archie a drink back ... or to offer a credit when the *Cop Yer Whack For This* LP came out, with its opening song, 'Three Men Fae Carntyne'.

Archie Blunt had that kind of luck: constantly in the right place, but seemingly always at the wrong time. He had successful trials with Celtic as a youngster, but then Adolf intervened, and competitive football was suspended. Along with most of his young, barely literate team-mates, he signed up. By the time the war ended, and normal service was resumed, Archie was pushing twenty-three. Not old for a footballer admittedly, but a disadvantage for a skinny one who hadn't played for five years and was trying to find a new club. So he looked for other work. But, like everyone else he knew, Archie had left St Mark's School at fourteen, and without an education to speak of, doors remained firmly closed.

Archie had had some happiness. He had married. But in the five years since Betty had been gone, he hadn't been with another woman. This perplexed him. He had his own place in Tennyson Drive. He'd taken over the rent when his ma passed away and his old dad went into a sheltered housing complex. The council were planning to rename it *Elizabeth Street* in preparation for the Queen's Silver Jubilee. They weren't to know, but for Archie it was yet another ironic twist of the knife. He didn't smile much in public now, not since losing the teeth, but then too much smiling only drew attention, suggesting a big win on the horses, or a full-house bingo windfall. Better not to have people speculating about public displays of sober happiness, just in case. Emaciated frames and bulging, yellowy eyes were the usual characteristics of East End males but Archie, while still slight, now looked like his larder was always reasonably well stocked. All in all, he thought he was some type of catch. So why was he alone? And unfulfilled. Sitting up here night after night with just the pigeons for company?

But even in such moments of self-doubt, Archie Blunt remained a stoical son of Glasgow; an unrequited optimist. Like the city itself, he couldn't be kept down for long. There was always opportunity waiting around every second Glaswegian corner. Admittedly, some wee bam with a blade was often around the third, but these were decent odds for a bottle-half-full merchant. Something new and potentially exciting was always just a random pub conversation away. It was a little over a month since he had finally been dismissed from the Corporation, after nearly six months of unexpected Transport & General Workers Union blocks and threats on his behalf. Even though his pocket couldn't really stretch to it, he'd headed over to The Marquis for a swift half. And, as Glaswegian luck would have it, Chib Charnley was there canvassing for a new driver. The fact that Chib and his fearsome boss, Wullie Dunne, were indirectly responsible for Archie losing his Corporation job mattered not a jot right now. Being a driver for a dodgy firm wasn't the life-changing opening he craved and moving over into the precarious and nefarious world of the man known as the Wigwam was dangerous in many ways, but Archie couldn't ignore the sound of opportunity knocking, and after a 'purchased recommendation', Archie was back in business.

Now, the City of Eternal Optimists glistened and sparkled below him. He wiped his mouth on his jacket sleeve, stood up and stretched. Better head back home to sleep, he reckoned. 'Dinnae want tae be late on the first day,' he said aloud to the seated Charles Tennant: eighteenth-century chemist, and renowned champion of those less fortunate.

Refreshed and renewed, Archie's heart pulsed with pride that he was a part of this place. It was exciting, amazing, uplifting. Its succour truly *was* perpetual. At times like this he felt pity and not envy for the tiny few who had left it. Glasgow's generosity, its relentless pursuit of better things, the *gallusness* of its people, who would give you the very shirt off their ba—

'Gie's a wee swally, eh son?' A frail, ghostly jakey-voice wafted in from the shadows, interrupting the stream.

'Nae bother,' shouted Archie, into the descending gloom. 'Here, have a swig ae Sandra. It's aw nae bother at all, pal.'

ONE

Glasgow Belongs Tae Me...

∏ine month/ earlier...

He waited and waited and waited, becoming increasingly agitated. It was early morning and bitterly cold; the hurricane had now done its worst according to Michael Fish, but Glasgow didn't seem to be listening. The storm-force winds were still battering the boarded-up shopfronts and rattling the few panes of glass left in the three tenement floors above them. And the bus was late. And so was Chib Charnley.

He'd observed Chib hirpling along the street. The wind was behind him, but he still moved like a man of twice his age.

'Where the fuck've you been? *Jesus,* Chib!'

'Ah'm sorry, boss,' said Chib. 'It's my hip. Man, it's absolutely heavin'.'

'Aye, well.' Wullie Dunne sighed. 'Get it looked at properly then.'

Wullie found it hard to lambast Chib Charnley. He'd taken a bullet for his boss, after all, and although that had been more than a decade ago, Wullie would always look after his minder. It was the least he could do. He wasn't going to be like other bosses, who went through hired muscle like Richard Nixon went through tape recorders.

'Finally!' sighed Wullie as the bus pulled up for them. It wasn't a recognised stop, but the driver and conductor were both on a modest cut for making the weekly Thursday morning exception.

Things were going through a rough cycle. Everybody was having to rein in the expenditure, which was why Wullie Dunne had been using the top deck of the number 61 bus for 'business meetings' every Thursday morning for almost a year. It was the route used by Tollcross residents to get home on giro day. Since he had collections to make from most of them, it seemed like common sense to combine the two

– saving on the escalating cost of the petrol. The Arab oil embargo might've taken its time in getting here, but it was now well and truly hitting the streets and petrol stations of Shettleston.

'Sorry, Mister Dunne,' said Archie Blunt. He held out a hand to assist Wullie onto the bus's back platform, even though Chib was the one who needed help. 'Duke Street was blocked off. A Milanda bread van was on its side. The wind blew it over. The stuff was everywhere, like. Christ, ah've never seen so many seagulls! An' they're aw fightin' with the dossers for the scraps. Mental, so it was! Just like that Hitchcock movie.'

'Fuck sake, Ah'm frozen stiff, here! Let us on an' gie it a rest with the film reviews, eh? Didnae expect Barry Norman tae be takin' the fares this mornin'.'

Amid rasping splutters and clouds of diesel fumes, the aging Corporation bus pulled way, chugging through the sideways rain like a glistening Irish tricolour. Archie held onto his pole, leaned out, peaked cap at a suitably jaunty angle, and looked ahead. A man he recognised gesticulated at him. It was Bobby Souness. Archie's finger was poised over the bell. The bells were rarely used; most drivers preferred to control all movement by use of their mirrors. Regular crews often employed coded, choreographed clouts on the ceiling of the driver's cab. But Archie's new driver was still learning the ropes. Archie had the power – the final *say-so* on whether or not the bus should make any unscheduled halts. The bell remained silent. At that moment the bus swerved in closer to the kerb and ploughed through a large puddle. A comedy spray enveloped Bobby Souness. He hadn't been sharp enough to jump back. The young driver hadn't intended this outcome, he was simply pulling in to let an ambulance pass, but Archie applauded him anyway.

'Ya fucken walloper, ye!' yelled Bobby Souness, shivering. Freezing water dripped from his bearded chin, down his neck and inside his shirt. He heard the triple ring of the bell, and the bus slowed again. Archie Blunt glared out from the open rear access.

Bobby Souness had never quite understood why Archie Blunt hated him. As he ran towards the still-moving bus, he couldn't recall any slight, deliberate or accidental. Bobby was a Rangers supporter, admittedly, but not one of the staunch King Billy 1690 brigade. And Archie Blunt had never come across as overtly fervent in his following of the Celtic. It was a total mystery. Out of breath and still dripping wet, he leaped onto the rear platform as the number 61 slowly picked up speed.

'Cunt.' Bobby Souness wheezed at Archie. He looked around the lower deck, briefly considering whether he'd get away with nutting the bastard. Too many witnesses.

'Prick,' hissed Archie as Bobby struggled for breath in front of him.

A grudged handful of copper was passed over, an equally grudged full adult single ripped from Archie's heavy ticket punch machine, and Bobby Souness headed for the top deck. He sat down without looking up. He checked his remaining match. It was still viable despite the soaking. It sparked into life and was deployed into lighting a moist Embassy Regal.

'They things'll kill ye.'

Bobby Souness looked up sharply, his heart sinking to the bottom of a bowel of digested porridge. The voice belonged to Wullie Dunne, the businessman bookie. Bobby Souness owed the man known as The Wigwam – for loans *and* bets. Two hundred pounds and counting. In his current predicament, it might as well have been two million. He wasn't alone in featuring in The Wigwam's book of debtors; virtually every East End male Bobby knew of had a similarly threatened income.

'Of aw the buses, eh Bobby? Almost didnae recognise ye there, son!' The Wigwam was at the other end of the bus, in the front seats the smaller kids normally dragged their stumbling parents to so that they could pretend they were driving.

'Ah was hopin' for a wee word in yer shell-like.' Wullie nodded sideways in the direction of Chib Charnley, his half man, half granite rockface enforcer.

Chib began to move towards Bobby. And with Archie inadvertently blocking the stairwell, Bobby Souness was forced to think fast. Survival instincts kicked in. His eyes darted about. A *dreep* out the back of a moving bus on a busy Tollcross Road had its obvious risks but he'd take them over the ones inside. In one movement he vaulted over two slashed seats like an Olympic hurdler and hit the release lever on the rear emergency window. He landed on the road like Olga Korbut. He still had it: the instinct for self-preservation that had saved him many times as a younger man. Flat feet planted, Bobby rolled with the forward momentum through a rippling stream of shallow dirty water. His bunnet stayed on his head, the fag remained lit and smoking and, as he moved into an upright position, he ran. Sodden but still with the use of his legs.

'Fuck sake,' said Chib. 'That was a bit ae an over-reaction, eh?'

'Never mind, Chib,' said Wullie, from the stationary bus. 'We'll get tae him later. Bigger fish tae fry th'day!'

Archie's novice driver shouted nervously for him to leave it, but Archie couldn't hear. He gave chase. Another fucking bum diving out the alarmed back window of his bus. That made it four in a month, and Archie got a disciplinary every time it happened. Had it been anyone other than that waster Souness, he might've left it. *Well, not this fucking time!*

December 1975

WPC Barbara Sherman looked across the office. Cigar smoke hung in the air, and whisky and Brut 55 fumes combined to make a toxic mix. In the corner, Radio 2 played Bing Crosby, eternally dreaming of a Christmas very unlike the dreary, wet, grey one that the officers of Beat 22 were experiencing. Some of the men had brought turkey legs and round bread rolls back from the canteen. They fooled around with them, pretending to be Chaplin. There was a slackened ambience, as if the shift was celebrating a major operational breakthrough. It wasn't; the inspector had simply relaxed the rules on drinking near the muster room.

Barbara's desk was jammed into a corner, facing away from her colleagues – as if she were a disobedient schoolgirl being publicly punished. Posters of bare-breasted women with false smiles jostled for space with more official papers on the walls in front of her. This was the only seat available to her when she joined the division straight from passing out of basic training at Tulliallan. Her initiation day at Tobago Street three months ago was shared with five others; all male. None of them wanted that desk. And she wasn't given the choice. It was adjacent to the door that led to the toilets. The door didn't close properly. The hinge had been broken during a fight between two young police officers. The smells that emanated from those toilets were truly horrendous – hell came to mind, after the devil had had a heavy night on the sulphur, celebrating a genocide somewhere.

Barbara was certain most of those on duty today were intoxicated. Or still hungover. She could have made this observation any other day of the year; the difference now was the time. It wasn't even 10 a.m. yet. An appeal to let the officers with families have Christmas Day off had, as it always did, fallen on deaf ears. Single female officers like Barbara – who only did the day shifts anyway – had absolutely no chance of being considered for leave. Not that she would've requested it anyway. Christmas always brought a pain and sadness that loneliness only made worse. Better to be here around colleagues, even the drunken, misogynistic ones.

The Strathclyde Police East HQ in Tobago Street was the busiest in the city, and arguably in all of Scotland. So far, Barbara's exposure to this tense new world of wanton criminality had extended no further than three missing pet inquiries, one of which was solved by looking under a bed; a series of reported break-ins at Visionhire and Radio Rentals – crimes which, in the run-up to Christmas, you could set your watch by; and the apparent theft of a Glasgow Corporation bus. The bus in question was soon found, parked on the centre circle of a blaes football pitch up at Dawsholm; the only viable witness, an intoxicated pensioner. It was hardly the life and times of Eliot Ness and the Untouchables. A tiny local radius around the police station was her beat; relatively speaking, it was the safest place in the entire East End.

Despite everything, Barbara was excited to be here. She knew the challenges the position would bring, and already an amused fraternity had made various references to her 'handbag-sized truncheon'. She had campaigned for the Sex Discrimination Act and now that it was law, it seemed to torment male colleagues. In the view of Davy Dodd, E-Division's ebullient sergeant, the Women's Department of the Police was there to do the softer things: dealing with difficult kids, families, and the boring administrative drudgery that the men hated doing. They were there to support the PCs, and to hold the hands of bereaved wives being informed that their husbands had died in a knife fight. The WPCs didn't walk the beat alone, they didn't do night shifts. Because they still had to be home in time to see to the family's dinners, naturally.

Barbara Sherman knew it would be difficult to make a positive impact in such an obdurate environment. She was an outsider;

arguably always had been. Like all new WPCs, she was single. She lived alone, within walking distance of the station. She'd never been pretty; certainly not in comparison to those adorning the walls. The officers already had a nickname for her: The Tank. She was bulky in stature. It could've been worse, she supposed. She consoled herself that if pushed, she could hold her own with most of them in an arm-wrestling contest. On top of all this, they all spoke so fast – words came at her like rapid-fire jabs from Benny Lynch, pummelling her into uncomprehending submission. She'd learned to listen to the tone rather than the content.

'Briefing room, now!' Sergeant Davy Dodd's throaty voice bellowed through the office. Loose ceiling tiles seemed to vibrate, and the dust-covered blinds appeared to shake as if a low-flying jet had just buzzed the building. Davy Dodd resembled an angry bull. He was a man perpetually dismayed at the hand life had dealt him in the form of the fucked-up band of misfits sharing his working environment. He had no neck that was visible. Just a large, square head that rose straight out of a shirt collar struggling with the blotchy girth it was attempting to contain.

'Sherman, move yer fat arse an' get in here!'

The others woke from their slumber, wiped the slobber from their chins and laughed. The Tank would be getting dispatched to the pub when it opened to get a quarter bottle refill for Dodd or sent to find somewhere in the building with enough sugar, tea bags and milk for a round. *Kept in her place.*

'Leave the door!' Davy Dodd was apparently furious. Barbara genuinely didn't know why. He was a volatile man, but when a bollocking from a superior was imminent, she'd usually been able to sense it coming. Not this time though.

'Sir?'

'There's been a complaint, Sherman.'

'About me, sir?'

'Aye, about *you*.' Davy Dodd sat on the edge of his desk, one leg touching the ground, the other dangling, the wooden corner separating them. The position of his lower body was open, like an ape displaying its genitals. But his arms were crossed defensively. Barbara was good at reading people, their body language especially, but her sergeant's was awkward and confused. She took a small pleasure in his obvious discomfort.

'Jamesie Campbell, ye know him?'

'The MP?'

'Aye, *that* Jamesie Campbell.'

'Yes, sir. I know who he is.'

'He claims he asked that a police officer was present last week at a party meetin' his wife was at. Nobody showed. Don Braithwaite out there said he told you tae sort it. That true, Sherman?'

'Eh, no sir. No, it most definitely isn't.'

'Braithwaite!' Davy Dodd's voice roared past Barbara's ears. It was like she was in a wind tunnel. A faint *'He's no' in, sarge. He's just nipped out on a wee message'* drifted back through to them.

'Hmmph.'

Sergeant Dodd was especially annoyed. He too had lost out on the Christmas Day shift pattern draw. He had contemplated a day on the sick, but Inspector Melrose had headed that one off at the pass. Like Davy Dodd, he wanted to see the afternoon Danny Kaye film.

'We'll pick this up later, but Campbell's got a lot comin' up. He's pals wi' the superintendent, an' ah'm gettin' it right square in the baws here because we've let him down. So, never mind Braithwaite, *ah'm* fucken' tellin' ye straight ... when Jamesie Campbell shouts "jump", you say "how high?" Now have ye got that Woman PC Sherman?'

'Yes sarge.'

'You're tae be his *personal* pig, ye hear me?'

'Sir.'

'Now, away an' get me some tea. Dae somethin' fucken useful.'

January 1976

Gail Proctor drove her battered green Mini up the slope. She sat forward in the seat, with her back almost vertical, and her shoulders tense. But it appeared that her surveillance was nearly over. The long black car containing Big Jamesie Campbell had turned in through the gates and up the long, tree-lined road leading to Daldowie Crematorium. She watched her target's car disappear around a bend. She crunched the gears and followed.

Gail pulled into a side space and watched Big Jamesie Campbell get out of his car. He appeared agitated. The pallbearers were waiting, apparently for him. He ambled over and held out his hand to each of them, like a Sicilian don; it was taken awkwardly. Gail made notes. There were four full notebooks in the back seat of her Mini.

'Ye cannae park yer motor there, hen.' The man startled her, approaching her from behind. 'The next cortege'll be comin' up the road in about ten minutes.'

'I'm sorry,' she said. 'I was just, em…'

'Ye'll need tae get a shift oan if yer gaun in. The doors'll be gettin' shut.'

'I will. Thanks.' She pulled out of the space and found another.

She got to the heavy mahogany doors just as they were being closed. Giving the doorman a whispered apology, she moved over to a seat right at the back of the committal hall. Around half the available seats were occupied. Piped accordion music filled the vaulted space. She could see Big Jamesie Campbell – the back of his massive head. He was at the front, with a few people making a point of going to him to offer a hand. Gail wondered if it was a Campbell relative being mourned, such was the obvious deference towards him. She also briefly considered the possibility that the deceased was someone that Big Jamesie Campbell had had murdered. She already knew that he was capable of it. Proving it beyond all doubt was another thing altogether. But she would persist. She owed it to her uncle, if not her deluded mother, living on the other side of the country in a near-constant state of denial.

The minister outlined the quiet life of Fred Calton, cut short as many of his genetic background had been, by heart disease. Fred was fifty-six when he succumbed, Gail learned. 'A man of principle, integrity; a decent, honest, dedicated family man,' said the minister, clearly reading from a prepared text. It seemed to Gail that a life summed up by a man of God who had apparently never met Fred was the ultimate in hypocrisy. How could he possibly know the destination of Fred's soul, yet he offered certainty to a front row of weeping adults who Gail presumed were Fred's immediate family.

Big Jamesie Campbell was invited to say a few words. Gail learned that Fred had been a central part of the Campbell campaign that, in the mid-fifties, saw the then councillor first elected to serve his local community. Campbell said that Fred had espoused the egalitarian qualities they both believed Labour represented. 'Opportunities for all,' said Big Jamesie. True to form, though, Big Jamesie then used the platform for his own ends, turning a family's personal grief into a campaign pitch for his new party. Gail could scarcely believe it when he concluded his valediction by urging those present to sign up and join him in building a new political force; one that would follow the virtuous example of working-class people like Fred Calton. He went so far as to trail an upcoming press conference where all would be revealed.

Big Jamesie Campbell's arrogance dominated the room. His selfishness, a product of a stolen privilege that required no accountability. Gail Proctor left quietly before the final hymn and the minister's empty blessing.

⏻

Gail climbed the cold concrete stairs in complete darkness. Four weeks since being formally notified about it and the landlord still hadn't fixed the tenement's defective lighting. He would be holding out for the clocks going forward, no doubt. Despite having now had a lot of practice opening her door in the dark, she still had to use her free hand to locate the keyhole and guide the key into it. Once inside, the streetlighting made the search for a match more straightforward. Candles lit, she dropped her bag on the bare wooden floor of the front room before dragging the metal tub across the room and sitting it in front of the single-bar fire, which was slowly providing a little more localised illumination. It took half an hour to fill the tiny bath to a useful level. She used the time between kettle boils to read her newest notes, and to summarise them into something that might make sense to someone, someday. To make of these fragments some kind of route map. Currently it had a destination, but no identifiable points on the way – the roads to them hadn't been built yet.

The starting point of her journey, though, was always in her mind: a letter to her mother from her uncle Alec that ended with the sentence: *I might not see you again. Take care of the wee one. I love you. Alec.* Less than a month after the letter was sent, he was dead.

Gail hadn't seen her uncle Alec much when she lived in Edinburgh. She had seen more of him when she'd briefly worked in London, but still only sporadically. They were a distant family. Her dad had abandoned his wife and daughter when she was only two years old. Gail hadn't heard from *him* in twenty-six years. Alec, though, was simply a loner, apparently in love with the solitude that the life of the investigative journalist – of writing and research – required. He had always smelled strongly of alcohol. It was the first thing she recalled when thinking about him. He was also socially awkward and would never meet the adult Gail anywhere other than a library. But for all this she had liked him. And she realised now that she shared many of his traits and binary attitudes. She hoped that she was conducting her quest to uncover the truth about his death with the same spirit and the same determination and drive that he had demonstrated as a journalist. This hope was often the only thing that kept her going.

Gail had struggled with her English literature course at university. She found herself lacking the discipline and academic stamina it required. Nonetheless, she graduated, and, despite Alec's warnings, drifted towards journalism. She picked up a few inconsequential, amateurish commissions, which were published in the Sundays. While the payments barely covered her rent, these jobs gave her a hint of the addictive excitement she thought Alec must have experienced. And now, even though she had a personal agenda driving her, Gail couldn't deny the exhilarating, thrilling rush of pursuing someone like Big Jamesie Campbell; of stumbling upon some new piece of shocking information – information she could use to pave the road she was following. She was still mindful of her inexperience, though. She knew she would have to bide her time until a proper opening presented itself. Big Jamesie Campbell's inappropriately loose tongue earlier that day might just provide one.

Meantime she'd exist frugally in this freezing-cold structure with its damp, peeling wallpaper, temperamental water supply and no lights. She'd taken to cleaning the stairs and the flats of some of the elderly tenants, and this, combined with periodic shifts at the Press Bar in Trongate, provided her with just enough money to survive. She ate like a small bird. She had no television and the lack of lighting meant her bills were small. Her one vice – a taste for Rémy Martin – was accommodated by her boss at the pub; he'd given her a bottle on her last birthday.

Now, she drained the last of this bottle into a small, cracked china teacup, balancing it on top of her typewriter as she eased herself into the lukewarm water of her half-filled bath. Radio 4 played quietly on a pocket transistor radio. The glow from the single bar of the fire made her pale-white skin look healthier. She sipped the last of the cognac and relaxed as the warmth from it coursed through her. She put her preoccupations aside and thought of nicer, more feminine things: the nape of Bardot's neck or the curve of Raquel Welsh's breasts, the dramatic cheekbones of Faye Dunaway. As she did, her right hand slipped into the milky grey water and down between her thighs.

January 1976

This had to be significant. For three consecutive nights, Big Jamesie Campbell had been dropped off at The Balgarth Inn near Provanmill just before midnight. Gail was reduced to observing him from what she considered to be a safe distance, concealed in the undergrowth of a tree belt running along the adjacent railway cutting. Campbell was always dressed in a dinner suit and accompanied by three similarly dressed males. They arrived in the same remarkable black car that had ferried him to Fred Calton's funeral. Gail couldn't see who the other men were – the lights from every lamppost in the street were out. The moon appeared every now and again from behind the fast-moving cloud cover, but the only other useful illumination was from occasional car headlights.

The Balgarth had a deserved reputation as a dangerous den of various iniquities. A cabal of feared Glasgow gangsters had owned it, running it as an unlicensed casino and brothel. No one was entirely sure who owned it now, but it was one of the few buildings in Glasgow's East End that ordinary people crossed the street to avoid walking past. The whole *who the fuck ae you lookin' at?* exchange was not one you wanted to have right outside The Balgarth's frightening lead-lined doors. With the council's East End slum-clearance policy progressing apace, The Balgarth was now the only remaining structure in the street. The tenements it was once part of were gone. Gail imagined the difficult decisions about its future being deferred by local officials who were far too scared to take them.

Tonight, Gail had left her car parked near the railway station, skirted the tracks, then clambered up the embankment and through a hole in the fence, coming out opposite The Balgarth. She'd gambled on Big Jamesie showing up for a third time, and he did. His car appeared an hour later than on the previous two evenings. Countless other vehicles had already deposited suited gentlemen outside the pub. If it had been a business dinner or a boxing event at The Albany in the city, nothing would've been out of place. But these smart men arriving at this bizarre lump of two-storey masonry in this bleak no-man's land looked as out-of-place as Regency diners on an active battlefield.

Gail watched Campbell enter the building. A shaft of light from the front doors, opening to grant him entry. No light spilled from anywhere else; she assumed the windows were boarded over or blacked out. A temporary clearing in the night sky; an ugly, scarred moon shone on Big Jamesie's driver moving the black car closer to the end of the street. It was likely to be a long night.

She was dozing when a commotion woke her. A group of angry men – dressed in the black of controlled aggression, rather than that donned for a refined function – were chasing a staggering, semi-naked man along the street. He had a decent head start but it looked to Gail like he was injured and they would catch him. He slumped onto the bonnet of the car that had delivered Big Jamesie Campbell to the Balgarth. He clambered inside, and it sped off.

The three bouncers briefly began arguing among themselves before stomping back to the building, where two other men had emerged. When they were within striking distance, four set about the smallest of the initial three. A punch took him down whereupon all kicked relentlessly at his head and torso, until he lay motionless in the road. They went inside and a few moments later another, slighter man, wearing a white overall, came out, picked up the unconscious victim awkwardly by his arms and proceeded to drag him inside. The door slammed shut. Quiet blackness returned. It was a strange scene all round, and Gail had twice wiped her eyes watching it unfold, as if unable to believe that it was happening.

⏻

When her uncle Alec was found dead, at first Gail Proctor was confident that Scotland Yard would conduct a thorough investigation. But the post-mortem concluded that his death had occurred after significant blood loss from a self-inflicted knife wound. A substantial intake of aspirin, presumably to combat narrowing arteries, would've contributed to the speed of the death. However, no explanation was offered as to why a generally healthy man with no recorded history of cardiac complaints would slice into his veins outdoors and potentially in full view of a local school. Wasn't this type of painless suicide always undertaken at home, and in a bath? Gail knew the post-mortem was flawed. And when any talk of a more thorough inquiry was hastily suppressed, she knew something was being deliberately hidden.

Big Jamesie Campbell had moved back to Glasgow full-time just before Christmas. His new political initiative was building momentum, and his bulk was being witnessed everywhere – at public appearances at schools, hospitals and bingo halls across the East End. The man of the people, back to steal the ground out from under them. Hypnotising them – taunting her. She had to do something, if only for her own sanity.

⏻

Gail left the cover of the tree belt before Big Jamesie Campbell left The Balgarth. She had more, and dramatic, material to add to her notes, but still no firm idea as to what it all meant. But she was excited and enthused. If her suspicions were correct – if the picture she was slowly making from the pieces she had gathered over these past few months was the real one – this would bring Campbell and his friends down. It would be a delicious irony if Big Jamesie's downfall resulted from his unshakeable belief that he was above the law. Wasn't that how *all* despots ultimately fell?

Big Jamesie Campbell's upcoming press conference offered her a slim chance of getting into the same room as him. Of asking a pointed question or two. Maybe get under his dimpled skin. She'd need a more convincing ID. A regular from The Press Bar could help. He had done before. The hardened hacks in there would do anything for a free slate.

March 1976

For the first time in months, Archie had slept well. He felt confident that four unbroken hours had been achieved. He attributed them to a good evening spent with his dad. Earlier in the week, father and son had settled down in Stanley's sparse new living room to watch their new favourite programme. It was an American cop show. It featured a son and his retired, truck-driving father, living together in a shiny, metal caravan overlooking the Pacific Ocean in California.

'Turn the sound up, Archie son, will ye? An' get us a wee Bakewell fae ben the press.'

'Right da,' Archie had said.

Stanley turned sideways to speak directly to Rocky, the father from the show. And Archie did the same, but to the main character, Jim Rockford. It didn't feel weird to Archie, it felt natural. It calmed his father. They both loved it.

Maybe it's better for you tae accept his new normal ... rather than you always tryin' to pull him back the way into yours. It had taken Archie a long time to fully understand what Cathy, the lovely young woman who looked in on his dad from time to time, had meant by this. But now he realised she was right. Stanley Blunt resembled an elaborate and complex charcoal drawing being erased a few lines at a time. Archie understood the immense value of celebrating the good times. He knew there would be less and less of them.

'Know what's good about this yin?' said Stanley.

'What's that, da?'

'Ah'm sick ae aw they cop shows where the main characters have tae have somethin' wrong wi' them.'

Archie hadn't given this much thought previously but his dad was right. There was Ironside and his wheelchair, Harry-O and his bad back, '...an' Kojak wi' the hair loss!' Archie wasn't sure Stanley's diagnosis of Telly Savalas's baldness as a medical flaw was accurate, but Jim Rockford did indeed seem different. He wasn't a cop, or a detective admittedly, but he was far more identifiable to East End males: a guy in the wrong place at the wrong time, jailed for something he didn't do, and now simply trying to make a better life for himself. Many in Shettleston could surely identify with that.

It had only been a few weeks, but Archie Blunt found himself speaking to Jim Rockford more often, and increasingly when he was alone. He had begun to find comfort in having someone to confide in; someone who understood the isolation that enforced suspension was putting him through. That his companion was a figment of his imagination was irrelevant. It made him feel connected to a part of his dad's existence that had begun to seem increasingly blocked off. Cathy had been right; seeing reality from his dad's skewed perspective had given them both a foothold. That was enough for Archie. He'd deal with the downward slope of Stanley's diminishing capabilities one step at a time.

⏻

Out in the damp, morning air, his initial vibrancy was wearing off. Archie's shoes were letting in. A sole, repaired a few years ago, was working its way loose again. The metal segs that had protected it were gone. His left foot looked like a muddy version of Donald Duck's flapping beak. An hour's saturated plod through the wet open spaces of Tollcross Park then along the local back roads and Archie Blunt finally stood outside The Barrachnie Inn and breathed in its distinctive vapour. It was a stereotypical East End hardman's place, dressed up as if it was preparing to host a shotgun wedding. A fraught Geordie McCartney – Archie's union representative at the Corporation – had summoned him here. Archie wasn't entirely sure why. Neither of them ever drank here. Such a pastime could be life-limiting.

The rain had eased. Rays of sunlight had broken through thick heavy clouds that only ten minutes earlier seemed so low that you could've reached up and touched them. Fucking Glasgow weather; it could change its outlook faster than a pub argument. Archie looked either way along the street. A high level of caution was the default setting when entering places like The Barrachnie alone.

He stepped through the arcane wooden-panelled doors. They swung back and hit him solidly, propelling him into the pub like a faded gunslinger in a comedy Western, the smattering of uninterested drinkers strategically placed extras. They looked up, and then looked away. Archie peered through the grey haze and saw his man. Geordie McCartney was positioned at the other end of the bar, in a dark corner. Even from this distance, he appeared unsteady and anxious. Archie assumed they were here to discuss his misconduct case. Geordie had said they needed a witness to support their case. All Archie's faith had been placed in his friend's judgement.

The cigarette smoke cleared. Geordie had slumped forwards. His forehead was now on the bar.

'Geordie.'

There was no response to Archie's whisper.

Slightly louder: 'Hey, McCartney.'

The bald dome rose up only when Archie prodded the back of it.

'Aye, ah'm up ... wh'izzit?' He had been dozing. Counter as a head-board. McEwan's bar towel as a pillow.

'Fuck sake, mate. Look at the nick ae you. Whit's goin' on?'

'Well Arch, she's went an' done it!' Despite the escaping peripheral drool, Geordie seemed calm.

'Done *what*? Geordie, what's the story?'

'Ah'm fucked, man!' Geordie laughed. Archie was beginning to sense that it was delirium and not alcohol that was responsible for Geordie's diminished senses.

'A couple ae nights ago,' Geordie slurred. 'Teresa.' He giggled, but it was the type of nervy, impromptu laugh of a lunatic on death row, walking to the chamber. 'Kicked us out, an' then shot the craw!' He stood up and yelled, 'Fuck sake!'

'Jesus. Lower yer voice, eh? An' stop makin' a tit ae yerself in here.' Archie suspected that those who frequented The Barrachnie early on a Tuesday morning wouldn't think twice about knee-capping a couple of low-level saps just for the 'crime' of some unwarranted sound pollution.

'He's just a bit upset, y'know what ah mean?' Archie said to those now looking on sternly. 'The budgie's deid. Been wi' him for years. He's devastated ... as ye'se can aw see.'

Archie wrestled his pal back down and onto the bar stool. 'Mate, what happened? Whit the fuck are ye goin' on about?' asked Archie.

'Teresa's left me. Threw ma stuff out in the front garden. Changed the locks, an' buggered off.' Geordie dabbed at his eyes.

Jesus Christ, he's greetin' now!

Geordie threw an arm around Archie's waist. Now Archie felt certain that they'd both be picking their teeth out of the sawdust.

'Aw my own fault,' wailed Geordie. He reached into an inside pocket and pulled out a folded sheet of paper. The words on it had been formed of newspaper letters, cut out and arranged like a ransom note.

WEEKLy PAyMeNT INCReASE NOTiCE
– Now UP TO Twenty POUnDS

'Christ, Geordie ... who wrote this, the fucken Black Panther?'

'It was him, it must've been her man ... that Susie yin!'

'Who the fuck's Susie, pal? Yer no' makin' any sense here, mate.' Archie took the paper. He read the words carefully again, like he was a code-breaker from Bletchley Park. A realisation dawned. Geordie McCartney had been with a woman. Susie. *That* Susie. The coquettish clippie from Dennistoun. The one that always wore her Corporation green shirt unbuttoned and wide open, advertising a pale cleavage, as white and dramatic as an alpine ski run.

'How did ye get this?'

'It was stuck in ma locker at the ... up the depot,' Geordie lied.

'An' did Teresa see it?'

'Eh ... naw. Ah don't think so.' Another lie.

'An' what does it mean by "increase"?'

'There was another note, the first yin,' Geordie admitted. 'Ah just about managed the payments. Tre was none the wiser.'

Large numbers of questions were forming in Archie's mind, but he was struggling to put them in any logical order.

'So... why's Teresa left ye, then?'

'Susie, ah helped her out,' said Geordie, answering a question that Archie hadn't actually asked yet.

'Ae her knickers?'

'Naw ... well, aye ... but she had some money troubles.'

'Jesus Christ, what age are you?'

'Ah've been duped, man!' Geordie wailed, drawing more dark looks. 'When ah got home, Teresa was holdin' a brown envelope.'

'What was in it?'

'Ah don't know. She didnae show me.'

'So...' Archie wasn't sure what to ask next. Geordie filled the gaps.

'Susie's man had been round. Telt her ah'd been pumpin' his missus.'

'Cannae imagine that'd've been a first for him!'

'Hey, enough!'

Archie couldn't believe his friend was jumping to defend the honour of a woman widely acknowledged to have 'comforted' more desperate and delusional men than Johnnie Walker.

'He telt Teresa that ah'd been givin' Susie money for sex. For tae shag her, like!'

'An' did ye?'

'Naw. Well, it might've looked like that tae him, but ah swear, ah just liked the lassie. Thought she liked me tae.'

'So, where've ye been the last two days?'

'Slept in the motor.'

Archie reread the note. He didn't know Susie Mackintosh's husband. Didn't even know she had one. He did know several boys in the Corporation who had been with her though. And that – even accepting the bus-depot bravado – she was regularly the instigator.

Archie knew there was yet more confessing to be done, but looking around he knew it couldn't be done here. 'We need tae get out ae here,' stressed Archie. 'An' now!'

Outside, Archie decided to head back to the comparative cover of the park. He dragged an exhausted Geordie like a ventriloquist with a bear-sized puppet. Archie was out of breath by the time they reached a secluded bench.

'Right, fucken spill, George! What the fuck have you done?'

Geordie looked down. He pulled his shoes in so that the soles touched; a child sitting in the headmaster's office trying to compose a version of the truth that mitigated the worst judgement. He blew out his cheeks.

'Ah was invited out ... a couple ae months back. Ah got asked by a guy, tae stand *in* for a guy. Last minute, like. A union do, by all accounts,' said Geordie, mournfully. 'A few big wigs at the Corporation, know?'

'Aye. Ah suppose.'

'Big Jamesie Campbell, that Labour guy, was gonnae be speakin', settin' out his plans for that new fucken "free party" bollocks. It was a fundraiser. Tre says "Ach just go ... it might help ye get on". So, ah went. Didnae want tae, though. There wis a buffet ... wee square bits ae cheese on cocktail sticks stuck intae a pineapple. Fucken bananas baked in ham, man. It was mental. Free bar, tae.'

'So, what happened?' asked Archie.

Geordie looked left and right. An old couple strolled slowly up the path towards them. The old man tipped his cap. The old couple were fifty feet away before Geordie continued in a lowered voice.

'We're at The Balgarth...'

'Haw, haud on ... The fucken *Balgarth*?' The Barrachnie was bad enough, but The Balgarth, with its 'guns an' gangsters' reputation? That was ratcheting the fear up another notch altogether.

'Well, aye. Didnae fucken know that's where we were headed aforehand, did ah?' Geordie was defensive. *Somethin' big tae hide*, reckoned Archie.

Geordie continued: 'It's well by midnight. There's loads ae pished union guys droolin' ower wee lassies servin' them drink ... an' then a crowd ae these other guys turn up. Telly personalities, some ae them. In cahoots wi' the big man Campbell an' some other politicians. Ah recognised a couple ae them.'

'In The Balgarth? Ye sure?'

'Aye. Nae fear. Ah was three sheets myself, but ah could still see them. They came in, pressed the flesh a bit, an' then headed through these big double doors tae roulette wheels in a back room. It felt a bit like a fucken high-class gentleman's club!'

Archie was struggling to align The Balgarth with an establishment that sounded like it should have been in Mayfair.

'They'd been in there for over an hour, before ah spotted some ae them comin' out an' goin' up the back stairs. Two ae the guys ah was wi' were stocious ... out for the count. So, ah staggers away lookin' for the bogs, an' ah takes the wrong turnin' an' ah'm shufflin' along this corridor when ah hears these weird sounds. *Moanin'* sounds, y'know?'

Archie was enraptured, like he was listening to an X-rated *Jackanory* story.

'Somebody sounds like they're in serious bloody pain, so ah edges this door open a wee bit, an' well ... fuck me!'

'What ... fucken *whit*, Geordie?'

Geordie gulps. 'There's five ae these cunts – the famous yins – haudin' this kid down while another yin is stickin' somethin' up...' Geordie pauses, as if acknowledging it out loud would implicate him in the act. '...Somethin' up the kid's arse!'

'Fuck off!'

'Ah'm bloody tellin' ye, Arch. Ah saw the bastarts doin' it.'

'A boy or a lassie?'

'Eh? Aw ... em, a boy.'

'A wean?'

'Naw, naw ... dunno. Maybe a twenty-year-old. Ginger-haired kid. His skin was aw blue tae.'

'Jesus Christ. You sure? Were ye pished at that point?'

'Aye. But God's honest truth, Archie. Oan the weans lives!'

'Fuck. Did he see ye ... the boy ah mean?"

'Naw, he had a blindfold on.' Geordie wiped the saliva from the corners of his mouth. 'The door creaked, an' the rest ae them aw looked up.' Geordie was teary again.

'But did they clock it was you?'

'Ah dinnae think so.'

'But ye said they looked up.'

'Aye ... but we were aw wearin' masks.'

'Masks? What in the name ae the wee man for?'

'It was a fucken masked ball thing!'

'Wis there any women there then?' Geordie's head slumped further. 'Well?'

'Aye. A few.' Another pause, but Geordie had to say it. It was the very root of his predicament. 'Susie Mackintosh. She was workin' there. Servin' drinks. Long story but ah got a blow-job off her when ah went in.'

'Ach, Jesus Christ ... ye couldnae have just asked for a ticket for yer coat?'

'We were just sittin'. She came over. She didnae recognise me, wi' the mask an' that. But she starts greetin', sayin' how desperate her life is, that her man gives her nothin' an' takes aw her wages off her tae plough intae The Gartocher an' the bookies.' Geordie spat out some phlegm.

'Yer no' a bloody charity, mate.' Archie sighed. 'Can you no' just say it wisnae you? Has he got any proof?'

'He knows about the tattoo.'

Geordie's distinctive *1972 RFC* tattoo was inked onto the right cheek of his ample buttock ... just above Teresa's name.

'Susie's obviously telt him about it.'

'Fuck sake, Geordie.' Archie sighed. He read again the note Geordie had given him earlier.

'Ah mean ... blackmail? Yer a bloody bus driver. Yer *Geordie* McCartney, no' Paul!'

'He sees me as an income-generator, Archie. Disnae give a shite about Teresa. This a payment demand ... or a batterin'.'

'How many times then, big man?' Geordie looked down. Ashamed.

'The Balgarth was the first.'

'And?'

'Ah've shagged her three times since ... naw, four!'

'Christ on a bike!'

'Look, Tre an' me ... it was never like you an' Bet. We had tae get married. No' a great kick-off when ye have tae put the registrar back two months because ae her waters burstin', is it?' Geordie sighed. 'It'll maybe be for the best, mate. There was nae love there, last few years. We were just goin' through the motions, an' that.'

'Aye, glad yer able tae be so rational about it all, eh?' For the not-knowing of what else to do, they both laughed. Geordie was in a corner, but at least he'd regained some composure.

'Hey ... if you live by the willy, you need tae be prepared tae die by the willy.'

'Right-o, Grasshopper,' said Archie. 'You sound like a fucken Carntyne Confucius. He was a baldy bastard, tae!'

'*Que sera*, mate.'

'Did ye tell Blakey?'

'Did ah fuck! Sub-section 4.2: *Nae inter-depot fraternising*. The first note said that if ah paid this cunt a tenner a week, naebody needs tae know anythin'.'

'What about the guys ye went wi', ya balloon! Did they get their baws munched tae?'

'They've never let on. Ah dunno.'

'An' ye've been payin' it ... the money?'

'Aye. Four weeks straight.'

'Christ, Susie an' her man ... they're Bonnie an' fucken Clydebank! Scammin' horny auld bastards like you out ae their superannuation.'

Geordie's eyes widened, as if he hadn't yet considered that a possibility. 'So how come he went tae Teresa?'

'Ah've missed a couple ae payments.'

'Ya daft bastart! Why?'

Geordie paused. He took a deep breath. He had been holding

something else back. Something he didn't want to tell his friend but had now been forced to. 'Cos ah had tae pay Chib Charnley tae show up as a fucken witness at your hearing!'

6

April 1976

It had been four months since *that* New Year's Day shift. Barbara Sherman's police colleagues had held her down, lifted her skirt, pulled down her tights and knickers, and branded her backside with *E-299*; her collar number stamp. 'Just a daft wee Ne'erday prank,' in the words of her commanding officer. 'Let it go, fuck sakes. High spirits,' he had continued. 'The men needin' tae let off some steam after the pressure ae a tough Hogmanay shift.' Platitudes and worn clichés from a sergeant who seemed to base his policing on the new TV series *The Sweeney*.

WPC Barbara Sherman had filed a complaint, against her commanding officer's advice. 'Dinnae go makin' a target ae yerself, hen,' he'd cautioned, his complicity only making her situation worse.

In the weeks that followed, none of the men she'd cited would speak to her. Her daily beat was still limited to the streets around the station HQ. She was paired with the same 'buddy', Don Braithwaite.

Don cared less that she was a woman than he did about her being yet another of the 'Heilan Mafia' – the influx of new cops from the Highlands and Islands. In his view, if she'd been born in a tightly packed Tollcross tenement, like him, she'd know the rules of the game here. But she hadn't been, and she didn't. If Barbara Sherman had grown up in Barra, then the vast open spaces of the Western Isles are where she should have been sent, not straight into the scalding sectarian heat of the former second city of the empire. In some respects, though, he could understand Sherman's desire to escape the quiet of her home. The tedium alone must've been like a five-stretch in the Bar-L, but with fresher, colder air. He just didn't see why it should be his responsibility to show her the local ropes.

Barbara Sherman *did* want to escape, that much was true, but for reasons that Don Braithwaite couldn't have begun to comprehend. Her father, Edward Sherman, was the chaplain on Barra. He had come to the island in 1949 as part of an Ealing Studios production crew shooting the movie, *Whisky Galore!* Edward was a close friend of the film's director, Alexander McKendrick, and having visited the island once previously on clerical duties, was invited to accompany his friend to provide 'spiritual reinforcement' for the Christians in the crew. When filming was complete, Edward surprised everyone by electing to remain. He took on the official responsibility for developing a Presbyterian foothold across the islands. He uprooted his wife and their baby daughter from their London home and moved them to the tiny village of Castlebay on this remote island in the Outer Hebrides with its population of less than a thousand, all of them smelling of liquor and smoke and coal and horses, and speaking a language neither he nor his wife understood.

The island was only six miles wide and eleven miles long; physically bigger than the centre of Glasgow. But if divided equally, each inhabitant could've had a hundred square feet to themselves. All the places where a person might hide were natural, not man-made – the clefts and coves of the eastern edges, and the brochs and Iron Age ruins higher up towards Heaval. Barbara knew them all like the smoother terrain on the back of her hand. Apart from the infrequent summer visitors, the faces – pitted and ravaged – she saw only changed with the passing of their allotted time. So Barbara Sherman grew up knowing everyone in the wild and lonely island community. All the women. All their offspring. The fishermen, the shopkeeper, the doctor, the teacher, the handful of farmers. And she knew Albie Grant, the local policeman.

Albie was the person who had put his comforting arm around her shoulders on Christmas Eve ten years ago as he informed her that her parents were dead. Albie Grant, the white-haired old copper who assured her that it was fate ... 'the Lord's will'; a tragic accident in which a fisherman's truck had ploughed into her dad's car on the dark, single-track dirt road up to Brevig. Albie Grant, the head of a tight-knit community that conspired to shift the blame onto her outsider father and his 'reckless driving'. Albie Grant, brother-in-law of Angus McNeil, the driver of the truck who, by common acknowledgment, had been in the pub all that day – and part of the previous one – because his fishing boat couldn't put to sea in the tempestuous winter North Atlantic swells. Albie Grant, the policeman who covered up a crime that resulted in the deaths of two innocent people and put the wheels in motion for something with much more sinister consequences.

⏻

'Sherman.'

'Yes, Sarge!'

'You're on these, doll.' Davy Dodd handed over a large cardboard box. The corners of it were scuffed and torn, and the edges bulged with the pressure of too many files having been jammed into it.

'Take yer time. Nae rush,' he added.

Barbara heard sniggers coming from behind her. The box had the initials *M* and *P* marked on it in handwritten black marker pen. The box had been in Sergeant Dodd's room for as long as Barbara had been at Tobago Street, and almost certainly far longer. She had tripped over it on her first day, its normal job being to hold his office door open.

'Missing Persons, sir?' She wasn't that green that she didn't appreciate the dead-end connotation of a Missing Persons detail. If someone reported missing wasn't picked up in the first twenty-four hours, the likelihood of a successful outcome dropped in direct proportion to the police interest in the case.

'There a problem wi' that, Sherman? This assignment no' good enough for ye, after yer bloody Jamesie Campbell stint?'

Barbara was aggrieved that having instructed her to respond instantly to any requests from upstairs concerning Big Jamesie Campbell, she was now being castigated by the entire Dodd squad for it being the ultimate in cushy jobs. Ironically, she was fulfilling the only type of task her male colleagues assumed her capable of. WPC Sherman's on-off job was to chaperone the Labour MP's ditsy wife on various trips when he had 'official' business, especially if the venue for it was his Mount Vernon home.

Barbara lugged the heavy box back to her desk. She had to lift it by the base for fear that the bottom would give out.

'Meals on wheels duty, is it now Sherman, ya lucky bitch?'

'Naw, The Tank's just havin' tae sort through aw my fan mail, Des.' Raucous laughter from the assembled plod.

'Haw, Sherman, stick my letter tae Santa in there afore ye go tae the Post Office. Ah'm hopin' for a shag affa yon Anthea Redfern.' Guffaws, farts and belches.

The jokes continued but Barbara Sherman had zoned out from the buffoonery. She despaired at the sheer number of open files in the first box. And another two that accompanied it. All representing the not-knowing that was making someone out there distraught.She flicked through the files – aimlessly at first. But then, beyond a sequence of middle-aged wives claimed as 'lost' by fraught husbands, no doubt unable to switch the cooker on, a different pattern emerged. As she scanned the basic details of each case, Barbara totted up twenty-eight young missing males in a six-month period. It was hard not to conflate these with the current spate of suicides from that same demographic. But as far as she knew, no one in this station had yet made what was now, to her, an obvious link. For some months now, the lifeless bodies of young men of no fixed abode had been washing up on the banks of the Clyde. George Parsonage, the riverman from the Glasgow Humane Society who recovered them, had observed the worrying upward trend in a recent report in the *Scotsman*. He'd talked about the life and mood of the city, and of how the numbers of people attempting to kill themselves escalated in times of war or economic downturn. Having patrolled the steep sides of the dirty, freezing-cold river scyth-ing through the city for almost twenty years, George Parsonage was genuinely stumped as to what was prompting the current spate.

Barbara Sherman was lost in the possibilities that these files offered.

So many stories. So many tragic people feeling like there was only one way out of their various traumas. She hadn't noticed the hours passing. Her shift was nearly up.

She was about to pack up for the day, when, near the back of the second box was a file that rocked her – suddenly and almost physically. A nineteen-year-old man had been reported missing six months earlier by his worried mother, Esther. The boy's name was Lachlan Wylie. His last known address had been in Dowanhill. The first eighteen years of his life had been spent living on Barra.

She lifted the file out of the box and took it home.

7

May 1976

Archie woke suddenly from another night of bizarre, fevered, alcohol-induced dreams. There had been a steady stream of them lately. His dad's dementia had taken a turn for the worst, and with the hearing looming Archie was fearful of the impact unemployment would have on them. And there was Bet, a nocturnal spectre constantly pulling at the unravelling thread of culpability. It had been more than five years, and the subliminal pictures were less frightening now than the ones he used to observe. At times, he felt like his eyelids were held open mechanically. No respite. Forced to watch the painful memories and recollections being filtered through a hallucinatory kaleidoscope. The big double bed still held fears that he knew other, more rational people would find hard to believe. But they weren't him. They didn't carry his guilt. Many times, he wished he'd just deposited the mattress at the dump; gotten himself a single one. But every time his resolve had broken. He just couldn't.

The phone rang. Archie's slick, new second-hand answering machine kicked in after the third bell, like an outclassed fighter's corner throwing in the towel to save their man. He'd traded it for an old bike. It was the size of a small suitcase, and it had taken Archie about three days to set up, but in the turbulent months since he'd been suspended, it had proved its worth. With the proliferation of union reps and Corporation bosses calling to influence him to suit their agendas, it was often better to be out, even when you were in.

'This is Jim Rockford. At the tone, leave your name and message. I'll get back to you. [Beep]*'*

'Archie, old buddy. Buddy? It's Angel! You know they allow you one phone call? Well, this is it!'

Christ Almighty, Angel, thought Archie. He was thoroughly sick and tired of bailing that shifty loser out of gaol. Angel was always getting nicked. Often, it wasn't his fault, but that only made it worse. As a career criminal, he was useless. And what was with that tag? Wandering about the East End of Glasgow answering to the name of Angel was a surefire way to get battered. But, nevertheless, Angel was a mate. He and Archie went way back. Friends since school. Blood brothers. There was nothing Archie wouldn't do for...

The phone rang again. Archie refocused, and staggered out of bed. He ventured gingerly through the warzone of alcohol-related detritus over to where the ringing sound was coming from and, having uncovered it, gently lifted the receiver. It was Geordie McCartney. Agitated.

'Where the fuck have you been? Ah've been tryin' tae get a hold ae you aw last night! Ah've been ringing about every five bastart minutes.'

'Aye ... em, ah dunno. Just up, an' ah kinda zoned out a bit there.' Archie stared at the receiver as if it Scotty had just beamed it down from the *Enterprise* straight into his sweating, calloused hand.

'Deary me, yer a fucken dreamer, you! Ye know that, don't ye?' Geordie's tone had switched. It had transformed into his more professional shop steward's one. 'Are you ready, Arch? Did ye sleep?'

'Naw, no' really,' said Archie.

'Worried about this?'

'Aye, ah suppose. Bad dreams tae, though.'

'Did you take the pills ah gave ye?'

'Naw. They were fucken enormous, Geordie. The size ae hard-boiled eggs!' Geordie laughed at this. 'Ah just tanned the rest ae the booze,' said Archie. 'Didn't stop me thinkin' about her again though.'

'Ah know, bud,' said Geordie, although he really didn't. He had his own preoccupations.

'Anyways, how are *you*? Ye heard fae Tre?'

'Naw. The boys came 'round. She's well done wi' me, accordin' tae them. Cannae say ah blame her.' Geordie was back at his eighty-one-year-old mum's place. Not ideal for either.

'Christ, Geordie, ah'm sorry pal.' Archie felt for his friend, but he needed him to focus. Holding on to his job unfortunately rested on Geordie's performance at the hearing. 'Ye aw set?'

'Well, it'll be what it'll be,' said Geordie. It sounded profound to Archie, like something Shakespeare had composed. Even if it wasn't, it made Archie feel better; as if Geordie McCartney knew what he was doing.

'Try an' sound a bit more enthusiastic, bud, eh? Fuck sake!' said Archie, before laughing to let his friend know he was joking.

'Christ. Aye. Right ... ya cunt, ye!'

Archie laughed again.

'Get somethin' inside ye, an' don't be fucken late!' warned Geordie. 'See ye there.' The flat tone confirmed that the conversation was over. It was just after eight-thirty.

I thought you handled that well, boy. Jim Rockford's calming Californian drawl filled the small front room. It wafted gently around the space and enveloped Archie Blunt like a warm eiderdown.

'Thanks Jim. His friendship's everythin' tae me. Sometimes think this hearin' means more tae him than tae me. Cannae let him down.'

Yeah, that's friendship for ya.

'Other times though, ah think it's too much the one way, this thing wi' Geordie.'

I know what you mean, man. It's the same with me and Angel.

Archie nodded and sighed.

But you've just gotta put that to one side, Arch. Loyalty to a friend is the only thing that matters in our game, y'know.

'Aye, ah suppose you're right, Jim. Totally fucken bang on.' Archie got up sharply and walked towards the kitchenette through a door-frame that had, seconds earlier, been filled by the coolest guy Archie Blunt knew.

He lit the stove with his second to last Swan Vesta. The other went back in the drawer for later. He watched hypnotised as the small brick of lard became formless in the tiny pan, melting into a half-inch deep milky puddle. His mind was suddenly racing like it was flying out the Cheltenham traps and being ridden by Lester Piggott. He should've prepared better. He couldn't afford to lose this job. The financial consequences of such an outcome were beginning to become apparent. Although his suspension had been on full pay, thanks mainly to the bullishness of Geordie McCartney, the agreed limit was three months. For the last four weeks, the only money coming in was from irregular stints at the club, knocking out Beatles tunes to largely uninterested audiences. And he was sharing that income with Geordie, to help deal with the demands from Susie and her man, who had now raised the threat level from the personal (the wife) to the professional (the Corporation). Geordie McCartney was desperately defending the employment position of his close friend, fearing all the while that someone else might shortly be doing the same for him. It was only a matter of time before Archie would be sharing his flat too. Geordie and his ma drove each other crazy. The longer they lived together, the more likely actual bodily harm became. And the odds favoured the feisty old battle-axe in that scenario. Archie looked on the bright side. Last month's tips had bought provisions.

'Right Jim, fuck off an' let me get my tattie scone, fried egg an' a slice ae square.' Archie said this out loud, knowing it would break the spell. Imaginary friends are fine for lonely children being bullied, or dislocated old men in sheltered housing, but for lonely ex-bus conductors? Perhaps not so much.

It was the last of his tiny fridge's meagre contents. With today's judgement looming, this was likely to be the end of the recent spell of decent days. But there surely must be better times ahead. This monastic existence was depressing.

Archie let the hot food slide onto a nearby plate, which still bore the encrusted remnants of a previous meal. The lava-like lard obscured it and temporarily absolved his sloth. He walked gingerly back into the bed-sitting room. The Green Lady was still smiling from her place on the wall. Always smiling. She was his mystical oriental muse; always there for him, always willing. Never judgemental. Always deceptively happy. Just like Bet.

⏻

Archibald Renton Blunt had met and married Elizabeth Ann Ferrie within the first six months of 1961. Back then, she had the lustrous blonde hair of a Marilyn or a Mansfield. He had found her intoxicating from their first meeting as potential jurors on a serious assault trial at the High Court. Elizabeth was selected; Archie was dismissed. He got himself signed off on the sick and waited daily for his new friend at the same spot on the edge of Glasgow Green. Archie Blunt wasn't such a different man back then. Still basically kind, considerate; an optimistic dreamer, but a little better groomed – a dark-haired romantic. Elizabeth was also smitten. At twenty-seven, she was ten years younger than Archie. They were older to marry than most couples but, in the opinion of her strict father, she was still too young for him. The aftermath of Peter Manual, blamed for the murders and rapes of young women all over working-class Glasgow, was taking a long, long time to fade. Young women meeting older men from the East End of the city continued to raise understandable fears for protective fathers.

A not-proven verdict delivered, there was no such ambiguous uncertainty about the couple's future. They were engaged following a festive night out dancing, two months after meeting, and they married in Elizabeth's local church in Pollok.

The only negative remnant of their big day was Archie's new name for her: Betty Fury. She displayed that fury on the day, and often in their ten years of marriage, especially when Archie suggested going for a drink with Geordie. Glaswegian men never ever went out for just one drink. It could be a stopover lasting several shifts. Bet would also disappear for days at a time following what seemed the most inconsequential of arguments with Archie. But his drinking bouts weren't the real problem. He should've seen the signs. She couldn't conceive, and it tortured her.

By the late sixties Bet had calmed down considerably. Beyond the absence of children, there was nothing remarkable about them. And then, one dark, wet, unremarkable afternoon in December 1971, Archie's world fell apart.

'What's wrong wi' you? You're like an auld jakey wi' aw that coughin'. Away an' get some water, for Christ's sake!' Archie wasn't normally this irritable with Bet, but she'd been keeping him up at night for over a fortnight with her rhythmic rasping.

She'd been moaning about feeling tired and lackadaisical, but everybody did that after the clocks went back. He had his own complaints. He had terrible toothache. He was keeping that close to his chest for now in case she coerced him into a traumatic visit to a dentist.

'Aye. Aw'right ... ah hear ye.' Bet cleared her throat and got up to go into the kitchen. She stumbled.

'Jesus, are you steamin'? It's a bit early tae be tannin' the Advocaat, is it no'?'

It was intended as a joke. But Archie caught the look on his wife's face and he immediately knew something more serious than a chesty cough was at work.

'What? Bet, what is it, hen?'

'Ah...' She sobbed. 'Ah've been coughin' up blood...'

Archie knocked over his tea. 'Christ, Bet ... for how long?'

She hesitated. She sniffled. Wet-faced, she looked totally vulnerable. 'About a fortnight. Three weeks, mibbe.'

'Jesus fuck, Betty! Why did ye no' tell me?'

'Archie, ah'm really scared.' Teardrops raced each other down her reddened face, merging at her chin. Archie tutted and hugged her. She was shaking.

'Look, love, everythin's gonnae be fine. We'll get the doctor in an' ... it'll aw be fine. Nothin' tae worry about, eh?'

But Archie was worried, and it transpired, with good reason.

He left her to head down to the shop – the tiny newsagents on Cathcart Road, the one where Betty worked. They could see it from the flat's bay window. He'd only be fifteen minutes, he assured her. He returned with cigarettes and painkillers. He had been gone too long;

nearly an hour, held up by a drunken Bobby fucking Souness arguing with Bet's boss over the increased price being charged for a quarter-bottle of vodka, and then continuing the fight with Archie outside.

When he finally got back, Betty was sprawled on the bathroom floor. His wife was dead. Killed by a rare form of leukaemia; a disease that Archie knew nothing about, and that Bet didn't even know she had.

⏻

As he knew he would, Archie Blunt felt calmer with his stomach lined. He opened the plastic bag. He had taken Geordie McCartney's advice, eventually: *Get a suit, Arch. We're gonnae need tae appeal to the panel. Imagine you're goin' tae court, son.*

It had been more than five years, yet all his clothes were still those bought for him by Betty. This was the first time he'd ever shopped for himself. He had picked up some appropriate items from the stalls at the back of Paddy's Market. Light-grey trousers and matching jacket, beige shirt, dark-blue cardigan and a light-blue tie. He wouldn't normally have been seen dead in such a formal combination. He shuddered. The last time he'd worn a full suit was at the funeral. He wasn't wearing that one again. Yet he couldn't bring himself to throw it away. Bet had picked it out for him from John Collier's in Argyle Street for a dance they had been invited to. They didn't go in the end. She never saw him wearing it, outside of the shop's changing room. He shook his head, and thankfully that thought evaporated. He reckoned that the punters at the club would now have to look twice to recognise him. The glasses were an old pair of Geordie McCartney's that Archie surreptitiously lifted six months ago because his eyesight was failing. He also needed a haircut. He put on a flat bunnet, concealing the embarrassing fact that his long hair was tied up at the back, like a geriatric gypsy operating a waltzer at the Kelvin Hall shows. Geordie's tactic, if all else failed, was to appeal for sympathy on behalf of a suffering man, down on his luck. Archie prayed there was more. He collected the remaining fags from his last packet and picked up a fiver and some loose change; all he had until the next *broo* day.

Don't worry, kid. Big things are right around the corner, I believe in you, boy.

'Thanks Jim,' Archie muttered as he pulled the door behind him and headed for the streets.

8

May 1976

'Comrades ... ah hope it's still OK tae call ye'se comrades...'

Nervous laughter greeted the opening line of Big Jamesie Campbell's address. This was his first time back in the City Chambers since he'd led his controversial breakaway from a Labour Party with which he had become disillusioned.

'It's been a fractious time for evryb'dy in the Labour movement. Most ae ye'se know that ah was close to Mr Wilson. An' although we were always movin' on with the new party, ah was personally dismayed when he resigned.' A pause. Jamesie took a white hankie out of his top jacket pocket and theatrically wiped his glasses – and an eye – before replacing them on the bridge of a bulbous red nose that Rudolph would've envied. Big Jamesie was revelling in this; a *get it right up ye* to those in the controlling Labour Party who had stifled attempts to discuss a Scottish Assembly.

The big man knew it was time to strike. Circumstances were going his way. This press launch had been set up a few weeks earlier, but only three days before John Stonehouse had decided to resign the Labour whip – from his cell in Brixton Prison. It had thrown the new Callaghan cabinet into crisis and the fact that the Labour Party hadn't expelled Stonehouse months earlier brought it widespread public scorn. And Jamesie Campbell's championing of Scottish political autonomy now looked virtuous; he could claim the high ground from a group of incompetent and self-interested dinosaurs. Few knew the real motivations behind the shift.

He concluded with a flourish, explaining what the new Scottish

Free Labour Party would represent. And then he leaned back and pointed, statesmanlike at a journalist, his remaining fingers hooked into his high waistcoat pockets, as if Dickens had created him.

'Aye, Barry.'

'Mr Campbell, is it true that you are investing your own money into the regeneration of the East End of Glasgow?' A plant, no doubt.

'Yes, Barry, an' ah'm very grateful for the *Herald*'s support in gettin' that message out there to the people of Shettleston an' beyond. For too long, they've been handed a rough deal. It's time for them to get a *new* deal!' Jamesie Campbell smirked. He was the new Roosevelt, Attlee and Bevan rolled into one. Nothing surer. A pixie-like face caught his eye. It appeared unconvinced.

'Yes, you there. Front row. What's yer name, hen?'

'Gail Proctor, *Sunday Post.*'

Campbell's PR team had been lazy – they hadn't checked Gail's borrowed credentials closely. She's noticed a few looks from some of the veterans as they all waited in the side chamber, but she had passed unchallenged. She hadn't recognised any of them as Press Bar regulars, so she put their attention down to her look. Androgyny was something of a default setting in Carnaby Street, but here, among the broken teeth, the Brylcreemed quiffs and the pale-grey nicotine skin, she stood out.

'Aye. What's your question?' Campbell thought there was something strangely familiar about her. But he couldn't place it.

'Mr Campbell, do you not feel awkward accepting an honour from Mr Wilson? Doesn't it feel strange to be on his resignation pay-off "lavender list"?'

Big Jamesie shuffled his feet. He'd anticipated a walkover, but he'd just been clipped round the ear. 'Eh, no ... no I don't. Why should I? Ah was happy to serve a Labour Party led by Harold Wilson. An' ah did my share wi' the whips to secure that victory in seventy-four.'

'So why are you splitting the party in Scotland, if you're such an avowed Wilson man?'

'The Prime Minister resigned because the party was movin' away fae its roots. I agree wi' him.' Big Jamesie Campbell nodded to the young journalist to indicate her turn was over. 'Yes, you son.' He pointed away to the back.

'Is it true that you are a Rangers season ticket holder, Mr Campbell.' A collective 'wooooh' went up around the room.

Big Jamesie laughed. 'Naw son. Ah'm a Thistle man. Partick born an' bred.'

'Will you be resigning your Westminster seat, Jamesie?' An older male voice from middle left; this one seemed to Gail like another prepared question, particularly given the speed and numerical assuredness of the answer.

'A total of 13,652 people voted for Big Jamesie Campbell in the last election. That's more than fifty-eight percent of the Glasgow Shettleston electorate. Ah'd call that a positive personal mandate, wouldn't you?'

'Mr Campbell, what's your personal involvement with the plans for the Great Eastern Hotel?' Gail Proctor again.

This time Jamesie Campbell was less composed. He looked around. Most of the other journalists were scribbling, heads down. If it was a loaded question, he wasn't convinced they were aware of it. But how could this skinny wee lassie know anything specific? She looked like she was a cub reporter for the *Jackie* magazine. Short hair ... *One ae they fucken lesbians, nae doubt,* thought Big Jamesie. His ire was rising. People were looking up now. He'd have to answer quickly, and concisely. But what to say? He coughed. Hesitated. Not a good start. He remembered the training: *Breathe slowly, deeply in, deeply out. Look them straight in the eye.*

'When ah was a boy, growing up in Partick, my ma used to tell me how important it was to look out for them that were less fortunate than us. My da worked in the shipyards. We were lucky. The dinner table was always stocked...' Big Jamesie looked up. Puzzled faces stared back. He needed to rein it in, or he'd lose the more important ones. *Focus, Jamesie, focus.* 'My ma volunteered with the Salvation Army an' told me stories ae poor wee weans that were made homeless. No chance in life given tae them. Ah've never forgotten that. Look at yerselves ... *inside* yerselves. Consider aw the things ye take for granted, an' the single most important one ae these is the roof over yer head.' He paused, everyone was now paying attention. Thinking of their headlines. That they might be witnessing something pivotal. Something legendary ... *Jesus, those media tips fae The Circle really* did *work!*

'Ah'm determined tae help rid the Scottish cities ae they youngsters ... ae the *need* for youngsters tae be on the streets ... the dangerous streets ... startin' here, in the greatest city of them aw. Ah want tae help set up hotels for the young homeless. Places that get the strays off the booze an' the drugs an' put a roof over their heads.' He paused again, hoping for some acknowledgement, and it did briefly come, but only from the older ones, the career head-nodders who were more malleable, and therefore of more use to a man like Big Jamesie. He had rescued the situation and delivered a speech Jimmy Reid would've been proud of.

'An' that's the spirit ae Scottish socialism right there. That's what the Scottish Free Labour Party stands for.'

He folded his notebook and, right on cue, supportive applause rang around the ornate room on the first floor of the historic City Chambers. Those bottles of Black Label dispatched with the press invites had worked.

Gail Proctor looked up at Big Jamesie Campbell, bemused. As the ranks of the fourth estate disassembled, Gail watched the politician embrace a policeman who had advanced from the front row. His shiny epaulettes told her he was very senior. Over his shoulder, Big Jamesie Campbell glanced again in Gail's direction. She looked away. Big Jamesie stared on before stepping down from the platform. A sly smile formed. He knew the power of conviction; that it could beguile and entrance and ultimately conceal. This young one, though, she would have to be watched closely. Or maybe even leaned on a bit.

Big Jamesie Campbell moved his twenty-stone bulk slowly down the granite steps. He'd specifically asked for a room on the ground floor. He was sure the local-council bastards had done this on purpose, hoping, no doubt, that he'd slip on the surfaces, specially polished just for him, and break his neck. His shovel-sized right hand gripped the six-inch-wide, profiled wooden balustrade capping. The other arm was linked with an assistant's, steadying him. He was accompanied by four others, carrying his bag and files and papers, and generally clearing a path as he headed towards the front door.

Gail Proctor watched this procession from the upper balcony. There was something odd about this entire event; something that didn't quite add up – even in the context of her personal interest in Campbell.

He reached the bottom of the stairs, then stopped and glanced upwards. She nodded casually. He smiled falsely. She turned away first, walking slowly, a broken shoe forcing an irregular heel click on the terrazzo. She had breached a defence, she was sure of it. This press conference might prove to be the breakthrough she had needed. She had a few more landmarks to place on the map she had spent so long trying to draw. She could finally begin constructing the road to the truth.

Big Jamesie Campbell also turned away, content that he had held their gaze longer. These small battles of will were important, he'd realised. He moved to the door, accidentally bumping into a slighter man who was heading into the City Chambers. The man went down like a toddler being barged by a prop forward from the New Zealand All Blacks. Big Jamesie Campbell managed to keep his anger at this internalised.

'Ah'm sorry, mister,' said the man from the floor, even though he wasn't at fault.

Big Jamesie said nothing. He glowered, the promotional smiles all used up for the day. He stepped between the legs of the man and headed out of the doors without looking back, followed by a pack of photographers, all snapping constantly.

'Jesus Christ! Ignorant bastard.' The man got up, dusted down his crumpled suit jacket and approached the receptionist. 'Ye *see* that there? Was that yon politician guy?'

She didn't reply.

He adjusted his tie. 'Em ... hullo. Ah've got an appointment with the Corporation. Transport Department. Sorry, ah'm a wee bit late.'

'What's your name?' asked the receptionist.

'Eh, aye, it's Archibald Blunt.'

9

May 1976

'Sorry mate. Ah've let you down.'

'Fuck off, Geordie. Naw ye didnae. Aw this was my fault. Ah should-nae have left the bus tae chase that fucken diddy.'

Archie and Geordie walked out of the imposing City Chambers building where representatives of Glasgow Corporation had just delivered their damning verdict on his future employment. In hind-sight, Chib Charnley's absence from the hearing, despite having taken Geordie's advance payment, was unsurprising. But the lack of a witness had made them look naïve and desperate. Geordie was embarrassed. They shuffled across the road and found a bench on the edge of George Square, in the welcome shade of the Cenotaph, Glasgow's principal memorial to its fallen sons. Geordie peeled back the tinfoil wrapped around a sandwich his ma had reluctantly prepared for him.

Archie took no joy in in the realisation that the Corporation's offi-cials would soon be moving on too, as part of the whole consolidation of local services into the newly formed Strathclyde Regional Council. In fact, after delivering their decision, it had been revealed to Archie and Geordie that this determination would be the last one laid down by the Corporation disciplinary panel before it was disbanded.

So change was afoot at the Corporation, and it was evident that the beneficiaries of the restructuring wouldn't be those on Glasgow's Transport services' front line. Archie Blunt – and Geordie McCartney too, in time – might simply be part of the wider collateral damage.

'C'mon. Let's go an' get fucken pished,' said Geordie.

'Naw, it's fine, pal. You need tae get back tae the depot. Christ, last thing ah want is you gettin' yer cards tae. You need tae keep yer own head down just now.'

Geordie sighed. 'Aye.'

'Might get ye in there later,' said Archie.

Geordie dropped part of his sandwich at his feet. Within seconds, there were more pigeons around them than either of them could count.

'D'ye think these birds ever go anywhere else?' said Archie.

'What, as opposed tae just hangin' around the square aw their lives?'

'Aye.'

'Christ, man ... ah've never really thought that much about that.'

'Aye. Suppose no'. Ah mean if, they're happy ... an' there's a constant supply ae bread an' stuff, then why venture further than the edges ae George Square?'

'That's their *bit*. Where they're familiar wi',' Geordie mused. 'They're maybe shitin' it to go further ... in case they cannae find the way back.'

'Aye. That must be it, Johnny Morris.'

'Fuck sake, dinnae give me that, ya tube. Ah wis just tryin' tae humour ye! They're fucken pigeons, for fuck sake. They eat an' they shite on folk, an' most ae them hobble about cos their feet are aw fucked fae gettin' them jammed in places that they shouldnae be in.' Geordie laughed. He nudged Archie. 'For fuck's sake mate, if yer gonnae pick a metaphor for yer life, dinnae pick a stupid doo fae Glesga.'

'Is that a wee Robin?' Archie pointed across the square.

'Naw ... that's just a sparra wi' a chest wound.'

Archie laughed too. He stood up. 'Look, ah'll see ye later,' he said.

'Ye'll be fine, mate. Yer only one decision away fae a totally different life, remember that.'

'Holy fuck, Geordie. You get that message out ae a Christmas cracker or somethin'?'

They laughed again. They stood. They shook manly hands. An embrace was only for funerals and a bad loss on the horses.

'Ye gonnae be aw'right?'

'Aye. Ah'm away tae see ma da.'

They parted, intending to head in different directions, although

Geordie McCartney waited until his friend had disappeared out of the vast civic space commonly known as Glasgow's living room.

⏻

It was a five-mile walk back to Shettleston from the city centre. It was generally flat, but the weather was still stiflingly hot. The city hadn't experienced rainfall for more than forty days. He slipped off the new jacket then undid the new tie and dropped it in a bin. And he walked. He walked towards the Royal Infirmary, where he'd had to identify his ma's body after her heart attack. Archie had been at work when it happened. By the time he'd got back to the Parkhead depot, she was dead. His gaffer, Blakey – normally an arsehole of the highest order, just like the character from the TV sitcom he was nicknamed after – was surprisingly tender when telling him the news, displaying a level of compassion few of the men in his charge suspected he possessed.

Archie then walked past the Provan's Lordship; the first house in Glasgow, evidence of the medieval origins of the dear green place. Onto John Knox Street, named, many were convinced, as a constant reminder to the Catholics of their overthrow by the Presbyterians. He strolled down the slight incline towards the vast, dirty-grey stone bulk of the former Great Eastern Hotel, where many of Glasgow's scourged found temporary shelter. Archie glanced up at the summit of the Necropolis. It was one of his favourite places in the city; a peaceful, tranquil place of contemplation, glowing in the blistering midday sunshine. Birds were still singing, an ice-cream van's horn sounded. A song played from a transistor radio: 'Silly Love Songs' by Wings. A sonic frippery for young hearts, running free. It sounded close by; a young couple lying on a tartan blanket just over the high wall, perhaps. Hiding from the rest of the city. Imagining they were somewhere else. It was hard to be downcast for too long.

He started towards the gates but spotted a restless pack of free-roaming Alsatians fighting over a large bone. *Some poor cunt's arm, probably.* He smiled ruefully, veering away from the Necropolis, fearing that his own bones might become the next target for the hungrier dogs at the back. He headed instead towards the comparative safety of Duke Street, where he weighed his options. Rather than wait on an overdue bus and face the inevitable interrogation from a former colleague: *How's it goin', Archie? Ye still drawin' the wage, Archie? When's the disciplinary hearin', Archie?* Archie Blunt continued his way on foot, head down. Although his dad wouldn't be expecting a visit, Archie wanted to see him.

The street bustled with activity. Women and washing hung out of the windows high above the street. Boisterous kids, who should've been in school, threw balls at the kerbs between *peep-peeping* traffic. A sudden trail of buses eventually overtook him, taunting him. He bumped into a few old acquaintances asking after his father, and life for the majority progressed unperturbed.

After a short detour to Tennyson Drive, he rejoined the route. At the traffic lights in Duke Street he passed Coia's café, where he took his dad in the early days of his illness. It always seemed to anchor the old man. Something about being amid the tenement blocks again, as opposed to the new, soulless brick structures that were gradually replacing them. Archie made the final turn. The sheltered housing was totally out of character with the East End. Archie thought it resembled a slice of Battenberg cake; different colours of beige brick and pastel-pink painted blockwork. The complex looked like a toddler had designed it. Substantial, muscular Victorian buildings, which had stood for a hundred years, were being bulldozed daily to be replaced by these characterless lumps with their tiny windows, their flat roofs and their incongruous, overgrown front gardens.

As he approached, Archie walked slowly. His da wouldn't care about him being late. Might not even recognise him anyway. Archie thought it might even be better if today was one of those days.

⏻

'Aw'*right* son?' Stanley's greeting was a mix of happiness at seeing his son and surprise because he hadn't expected to 'What are you doin' here? Wait, was ah meant tae know ye were comin'? Did ah invite ye round?'

'It's OK, da. Ah'm fine. Just thought ah'd nip in on the way past.'

Relieved, Stanley stepped to one side and Archie walked into the tiny hall. It was brutally hot inside the small flat. Eggs could've been fried on the bonnets of cars and the softened tarmac was pockmarked by newly made footsteps, yet the flat's heating timer hadn't been adjusted to compensate. Before closing the front door, Stanley looked out, and up and down the street, as if checking Archie wasn't being followed.

'Nice tae see ye,' said Stanley. This was one of the good days, Archie discovered.

'Aye.' Archie removed his jacket. 'Da, ye need tae open the windows or somethin'.'

'Ah'm worried ah forget tae shut them, an' the wee yobs that hang about the shops break in.'

'Ah'll shut them before ah go. Where's the thermostat thing?'

'Ah cannae remember, son. It's fine … ah like it warm.'

'Warm's one thing, but it's like the bloody Costa Brava in here. There's a flamin' heatwave goin' on outside. Ye've nae need tae have the heatin' on.'

'Whit's that ye've got there?' asked Stanley, trying to change the subject.

'Ah brought some records … just picked 'em up fae the house. Thought we could maybe listen tae them, if ye like,' said Archie.

He headed to the kitchen to put the kettle on, then watched as Stanley flicked through the LPs. He seemed to remember all of them. The Everly Brothers, Nat King Cole, Buddy Holly, Bing Crosby … and Old Blue Eyes. It was like seeing a group of long-lost friends being reunited.

'Did ye bring somethin' tae play them on?' asked Stanley.

'Naw, sorry.'

'Ach, never mind … we'll just imagine what they sound like, eh?' Archie could tell his father was gently mocking him. It was a good sign. Stanley had a wicked sense of humour and one of Archie's initial fears was that it would be lost forever.

'An' everybody thinks *ah'm* the one without a full bag ae marbles tae.'

'Aye, sorry da. Ah'll bring it next time. Just had a load on ma mind, y'know?'

'Just as well ah've got a record player then, eh?'

God bless Carol. She'd brought hers over last week. Stanley recovered it from a cupboard that, two weeks previously, he'd been convinced Archie's mum was living in. He plugged it in, lifted the lid, removed a disc from its sleeve and placed it on the turntable before lifting the arm across to the second song of the LP – all with the care of a palaeontologist dusting down a priceless fossil.

'The summer wind came blowin' in from across the sea...' There were fewer things in life as emotionally calming as Sinatra's distinctive voice. It should be an NHS-prescribed alternative to Valium, both men agreed.

'Right then, let's hear it. S'up wi' ye?' Stanley's paternal instincts had sensed his son was troubled. He sat down in his old armchair, the one thing that had travelled the across the East End with him, and indicated with a casual sweep of a wrinkled left hand that Archie should sit too. Archie sat, sighed deeply and looked down as if he was about to cry.

'Christ sake, son ... what's happened? Tell me!' Stanley was mentally assessing who might've died, and whether he'd even remember who they were once told.

'Ah lost ma job, da. Ah'm sorry.' Archie was less worried for himself than he was concerned about the effect it would have on the man who got him employed at the Corporation in the first place. He'd already decided to tell his father only if it was clear the information would mean something to him. It wouldn't have been fair on the old man otherwise.

'Jesus, Archie ... it's just a job, son. An' ah don't mean any disrespect here, but it's a bloody bus conductor, yer no' exactly a brain surgeon.'

Archie thought this harsh, but he knew his dad didn't mean it to sound that way. He decided to believe that his dad was suggesting that a better door was opening, and that they shouldn't focus on the one that had just closed.

'So what ye got planned then?' The question took Archie by surprise. Did his dad mean for the afternoon? For the remainder of the week? For the rest of his life?

'Ah dunno, da. Might try an' get away for a bit?'

'A bit of what?' It was a genuine question.

'A bit ae a break fae here, ah suppose. Ah couldnae do anythin' while the hearin' was comin' up.'

'Have ye got money?'

'Naw.'

'No' be gettin' very far then, will ye?'

'Ah'm thinkin' ae applyin' tae go on *Sale of the Century*,' Archie joked.

'Aye, good move, son. The one thing Shettleston folk cannae live without is a bloody speed boat.' Archie laughed.

The LP finished. The old man got up. 'Look son, the job ... dinnae worry about it. Ye'll get another yin, wait an' see if ye don't,' he said.

Stanley walked through to the kitchen, ostensibly to get the biscuits. But mainly to hide his disappointment from his son. A fifty-two-year-old, recently dismissed by Glasgow City Corporation for misconduct wasn't getting another job any time soon. Not a proper one, at least. Both men knew it, but career optimists couldn't afford to dwell on negativity for too long.

'Aye, da. Yer probably right.'

'Ye've still got yer turns at The Barnabas?' called Stanley from the other room.

'True.'

'So, that's good, naw?'

'Aye. It is, da. Decent punters at the club. Good tips an' that.'

'Ye should dae a tape ae yer songs. Send it tae thon Heady Hendricks fella.'

Archie laughed at the thought.

'The shite that's on that show week after week...'

Archie stopped laughing.

'...Dancin' dugs, daft magicians, ugly wee brats shoved up on stage by their desperate ma's an' da's.'

Archie got up and followed his father's voice.

'...Ye'd surely stand a better shot than aw ae them, eh?'

Archie was standing in the kitchen doorway. His dad was down on his knees, the lowest kitchen drawer fully opened in front of him, its contents scattered all around.

'Da, what are ye lookin' for?'

'Ah don't know, son. Ah cannae remember.'

⏻

Archie left his dad's place after making him supper. It was almost 9 p.m. but Stanley's escalating disorientation had affected his lifelong rhythms. He no longer had his tea at four in the afternoon like most people his age. They had shared a tin of spam and Archie had peeled some potatoes for chips. Afterwards, he'd waited until the oil in the pan had cooled then flushed it down the toilet, just in case. It had indeed been a good day for them. Stanley had been coherent, funny and content. Archie had been persuaded that losing the job on the buses could turn out to be the pivotal incident his life had been waiting for. There was scant evidence to support his theory, but he wrapped himself in it, nonetheless.

He turned at the bottom of the street and waved, his dad – still visible in the clear midsummer's night – reciprocating from the tiny ground floor window. Archie was off to The Marquis, for a pint before last orders – to celebrate becoming newly free of the shackles of paid employment, and to dream once more of exciting possibilities.

TWO

That Was The Week That Was

10

July 1976

In the months following Big Jamesie Campbell's week-long Balgarth sojourn, he had returned only sporadically. There was no real pattern to his visits. Gail's nightly observations offered little clarity. So, she'd taken the bull by the horns and approached the driver of a car who she'd witnessed dropping off a woman each evening for a fortnight.

'Aye, ma missus works in there,' he'd said. 'If yer after a shift, ah'll get her tae ask.' He'd swiftly followed this with: 'You scratch ma back, an ah'll dae yours, ye know what ah mean?'

She'd toyed with the notion of having sex with this repulsive character; she certainly couldn't pay him what he was requesting for the introduction, which had been his first suggestion. Gail sensed that neither he nor his wife would have any clout with the owners. Something about him persuaded her that he wouldn't even make the request.

The euphoria of the press conference had faded fast. Cul-de-sacs were all that remained. Faked requests for an interview went unanswered by Campbell's office. Even an attempt to identify the police chief she'd seen warmly congratulating Big Jamesie led only to some detailed questions about her and why she was asking. It looked as though she may have ruffled some feathers. But that was all. Her roadmap still led nowhere.

It had been her original ambition during her time at Edinburgh University to write fiction. So, with no progress in her investigation, Gail decided to refocus her attention on the draft of the novel she was writing. During the lighter nights, her typewriter tapped away until darkness descended. Shifting her preoccupations to something imaginary for a moment, and away from the sinister reality she was sure she was close to uncovering, gave her some unexpected relief.

One morning, Mrs Hubbard from upstairs rapped on the floor; usually a sign that she'd fallen or dropped something important that she couldn't reach. But on this occasion, it was merely to ask if Gail might pick up her pension for her. Her daughter was on holiday and she didn't feel up to venturing out in the intense Glaswegian heat. Gail was happy to do so, as Mrs Hubbard always paid her for such messages. Gail was embarrassed at taking payment, but the kind old woman insisted, perhaps sensing how much the young, emaciated woman needed the extra revenue.

The traffic seemed unusually heavy given it was Glasgow Fair Fortnight. Gail had to wait several minutes before anyone would let her out into the traffic. Finally, she pulled out, gears crunching awkwardly. She was running out of typing paper and had decided to head over to the south side of the river, to a small place that sold it more cheaply than anywhere else. Since Mrs Hubbard was paying for her trip, she wouldn't lose anything on the longer journey. Plus, she could do with a change in scenery.

The traffic thinned out as the Mini climbed the Cathkin Braes en route towards the lovely country roads surrounding Eaglesham. Higher above the city, the air really was clearer. She wondered why she didn't venture out here more often. It was a lovely drive, and the car's radio still worked, although the broken window-winder was a pain during this exceptional spell of weather.

She accelerated over the humps in the road, feeling that excitement in the pit of her stomach as the wheels almost left the tarmac. Gail imagined a different life; one full of friends retained from university, or even school. A steady job that offered enough money to live comfortably. To go out socialising and not suffer the paralysing anxiety of meeting new people. Had genetics made her the joyless person she now was? If so, it was unfair she'd taken after her dead uncle. Perhaps the addiction that had gripped her these past two years – the obsession with discovering why he'd died, and revealing the wider picture his death was part of – was just a way of not facing who she really was. A convenient life-raft where otherwise there would be none. But with so little movement in her investigation, and the novel now progressing well, maybe she should make *that* her purpose.

A car flashed full-beam lights in her rear-view mirror. It took her by surprise, even in this strong sunlight. She slowed, assuming the driver might be alerting her to a problem with her defective exhaust pipe. For the last fortnight, she'd resorted to tying it up with part of a washing line to prevent it dragging on the road.

She pulled in to the edge of the narrow road, intending to let the helpful driver pass, before getting out to inspect the rear of her car. But the driver of the other car also stopped. Gail looked in the mirror. Although perhaps thirty yards behind her she could see it was a man. He wore black sunglasses and had short black hair. She waited for him to get out to see if he could assist her. But he sat there, motionless, with the engine still running. Gail opened her door carefully, mindful that a car coming over the hill in the other direction wouldn't have much time to adjust. She looked down at her exhaust. It was as it had been when she left. She looked up. The driver put on the full beam again and held her in it. Despite the sunshine, the brightness of the lights alarmed her. This man wasn't alerting her to a fault on her car.

She was suddenly frightened. She got back inside the car, turned the key, and trying to pull away, stalled the engine. Watching the mirror constantly, she saw the man kept his lights trained on her, but didn't advance. Her hands and feet working in uncoordinated panic, Gail eventually made the hesitant Mini move forwards. The car behind her moved forwards too. She was shaking now. Visions of her uncle out for a morning walk across the heath. Being followed on foot by a man, or men, just like this one. How naïve had she been to have assumed all those pointed questions about Big Jamesie Campbell would go unnoticed.

She accelerated, hoping that her knowledge of the twists and turns of this narrow road was better than her pursuer's. She took a corner at nearly seventy miles per hour. The Mini's engine spluttered loudly, like a Corporation bus. And still he kept close behind her. Twenty yards between them now. Lights still on full beam, blinding her when she glanced up.

The heat haze made the road ahead disappear at the crests of the hills. Gail was crying. Trying to grip the wheel and wipe away the tears. Ten yards now. Five. She could see his face. He was smiling broadly. The Mini couldn't go any faster. Steam was coming from the bonnet. She was going to die. A coach was approaching on the other side of the road. A distance away but she would almost certainly hit it at this speed. She looked up and saw the driver behind her pulling back.

She watched him, and in watching him, failed to see the sharp bend just beyond the hidden dip in the road.

11

August 1976 – Friday

'Yer late.'

'Eh?'

'Fucken late, ya prick! Yer meant tae be here at half eight.'

'Ye sure? The Wigw— ... erm, Wullie said nine would dae just fine.' Archie Blunt looked at his new watch. He'd picked it up at the Barras market. New stock, just in fae Switzerland, he'd been informed. Its digital numbers were hard to decipher in the blazing sunlight. But he was sure it read 08:53.

'Naw, he fucken didnae. He widnae have telt me tae get up an' get in this early for yer inducation, wid he?'

'Indu-*cation*?'

'Ach, the fucken ... the showin' ye where everythin' is. The motor, an' that. Don't fuck me aboot, son. Ah'll rattle yer jaw!' Chib Charnley was growing more annoyed by the minute. He would gladly have given Archie a good dull jab, especially after all that carry-on with the bus. The enquiry might've been weeks ago, but, like the elephant, whose muscular bulk he resembled, Chib Charnley never forgot appointments. Archie had requested reimbursement of the payment Geordie had made to Chib to turn up to the Corporation hearing. But that had been like poking a wasps' nest with a stick. Chib's furious post-match conviction that Geordie was a total fuckwit who had given him the wrong date, had Archie doubting his shop steward's account.

'Just tae be clear,' Chib said now, 'ah widnae have gie'd ye this job, but the boss said ye were the only man for it.'

'Look Chib, ah'm sorry, pal. Ah wis, em ... Wullie said it wis a slow week, an' that kickin' off at nine wis gonnae be fine. Honest, he did.' Archie tried sounding placatory. He didn't want to be getting off on the wrong foot.

'Well, it's anythin' *but* quiet.' Chib stood up, huge in his black suit. He lifted his brass-handled stick above his head. Archie flinched, but Chib was just using it to point.

'The motor's round the back. The big black yin wi' the DUNNE 2 reggie.'

'Aye ... righto, Chib. Ah'll be back in a minute then.'

The car that had been sleeping underneath an unusual, camouflaged tarpaulin blanket was, when unveiled, hugely impressive. There were no identifying marks or insignia of any kind. It had blacked-out rear and side windows, and a thick pane of internal glass, so the driver and the distinguished occupant wouldn't share the same airspace. Archie knelt and looked at himself in a hub cap's polished convex reflection. An angry gargoyle stared back. He opened the wide, heavy passenger door. He assumed the weight indicated concealed armour-plating. That was comforting. There was substantial space inside. Just behind the driver's seat, a built-in compartment concealed several bottles of malt whisky and six cut crystal glasses. A side door to the same compartment slid back to reveal cigars longer than sticks of Edinburgh rock. This was a vehicle built for some serious pleasure, thought Archie. His new employment was to drive it. He flicked a switch. Radio 2. Pre-set. *'Mama Mia, Mama Mia, Mama Mia let me go ... Be-el-zebub has a devil put aside for me...'*

'Aw, Jesus fucken Christ.' Archie sighed. That bloody song! Number one for months about a year ago, and it was still everywhere. Archie hated it. He could've done better, he was certain. If only someone would give him the chance to prove it. Archie fiddled with the knobs. 10CC's breathy, dreamy 'I'm Not in Love' came on. Much better. Archie relaxed into the driver's seat as the quadrophonic sound lapped around him. He shuffled his arse cheeks, creating a profile in the velour until a more threatening but less progressive sound cut through the music:

'Haw, fucken daydream believer?' A darker, deeper voice. 'Want yer first day tae be yer last? Ye've got a job tae dae. The hire flew in late last night. It's a pick-up at eleven … so get the fucken tin flute, an' get a fucken shift on.'

Archie stiffened, like the devil himself had commanded attention.

⏻

Archie emerged, a few minutes later, suited and laundered, from the tiny toilet next to the office. 'Whit dae ye think, then?' He looked up at his new employer; at the tee-pee shaped space left on the large, flat forehead by the exuberant centre parting that had spawned his nickname all those years ago.

'Ah think you should be at the fucken Central by now, know whit ah mean?' Wullie Wigwam was agitated. Archie had no idea what was causing it; fortunately, in this instance it didn't seem to be him.

'Is this the job, boss?' said Archie.

'Aye … ah'm the boss, that's right,' Wullie Wigwam replied, not quite hearing the question properly. 'Mind ae that an' ye'll dae aw'right here.'

The Wigwam had lit up an Embassy Regal. It sat awkwardly between third finger and fourth, allowing him to dexterously pick at a nostril with his forefinger while drawing on it. It was an impressive sight. With his other hand, he'd written some details on a sheet of lined paper. He'd followed that by gulping a mug of tea and inhaling a Tunnocks Tea Cake. It had all been done so quickly and mechanically that Archie wasn't exactly sure how he'd managed it all with only two hands. Regardless, the process seemed to have calmed the Dunne Driving head honcho down a little.

'Big important client. This is the one we talked about, the one that ah hired ye specifically for,' he began. 'Up to see some mates, an' dain' a bit ae business tae, so he is. Needs a driver tae move him about the city. Naebody can know he's here though, right?' Wullie tapped his nose and winked. 'Remember our motto…'

'Done driving,' proclaimed Archie proudly.

'Naw, ya fucken moron. That's the name ae the company. It's "discretion guaranteed".'

'Aye. Sorry boss. Discretion. *Guaranteed*. Nae worries. Ah'll no' let ye down.'

'Don't,' squeaked Chib, '...or ah'll be lettin' *you* down ... an open-cast mineshaft.'

'Ye've tae pick him up at eleven at the Central Hotel. He's here tae the end ae the week, an' you're his driver. Take the cunt wherever he wants tae go, but fucken stay wi' him, right? Make sure there's nae trouble, know what ah mean?'

Like a plastic dog on a dashboard Archie nodded vigorously, but, since Wullie didn't elaborate on what type of trouble might be anticipated, Archie actually didn't know what he meant.

'An' another thing.'

Archie looked up sharply.

'He's a big noise in showbusiness. Very big in fact, so don't go aw fucken Vegas an' glassy-eyed ower him. Yer there tae dae the job we talked aboot, no' tae get bastart autographs, right?'

'Right, boss.'

But Archie's fickle and impressionable heart was already leaping higher than a Russian pole vaulter. Showbusiness; the business that there's no business like. And his client was *the* biggest, according to The Wigwam. The biggest ... Aye, that's exactly what he'd said, wasn't it? The *capo di tutti capi*. Fucken hell, thought Archie, his imagination racing and swelling. What if it was Sinatra? Archie had read that his Hoboken hero was currently in the UK. It had to be him. His dad had been right. His heart was thudding. Ole Blue Eyes gave massive tips; it was a well-known fact. Plus, Archie was a decent singer in his own right. They'd have that in common. Just five minutes in his company, and Archie would be able to demonstrate he was different from other starstruck sycophants encountering their idols.

Three weeks ago, the night after his dad had restored and reinforced his confidence, Archie had come second in the club's summer talent night. Archie sang 'All the Young Dudes' first, followed by a more obscure Kenny Rogers song. Many said he was the best act of the night. But a young guy from Springboig with long hair and a flashy keyboard won. He had written his own song, the showy bastard. Another so near, yet so far brush with fame for Archie. But getting sacked from the buses, picking up a pity job from The Wigwam, and now driving Frank Sinatra around town on his first day … well, that was all surely written in the stars. There was a Hollywood movie screening in his brain; *A Star Is Born*. Archie Blunt, talented but down-and-out Weegie hobo, discovered by the Chairman of the Board and whisked off to become the newest member of the Rat Pack. He'd be screwing cocktail waitresses four at a time before the turn of the year. He was an unrequited dreamer, he acknowledged that, but what were dreams for, if not pursuing? He'd be risking going off The Wigwam's script a wee bit, but the whole thing seemed so straightforward that he was sure he could cope with some personal latitude.

⏻

Archie parked the car in a basement delivery space under the Central Hotel. It was the only one big enough to take the vehicle's length without blocking anyone else in. The labyrinthine vaults under the Victorian station concourse of which the hotel was a part and where he was now parked had once been a makeshift morgue. The broken repatriated bodies of many of Scotland's young First World War dead had lain there until their relatives, mainly the women, dragged them above ground and onto various improvised wooden hearses. The place reeked of morbidity, and despite the amount of British Rail staff milling around its dark corners, it still felt threatening. The heat blistered the roads above ground, but down here it was strangely cold. Archie Blunt normally dismissed such things, but the tales that it was haunted by the spirits of those who'd perished in the Somme suddenly seemed plausible. Breathing heavily, he headed up the fire-exit stairs towards the third floor, and room 392; the number written on the piece of paper given to him by The Wigwam. His instructions would come a day at a time. There was a specific plan, but Archie Blunt hadn't been trusted with the full details of it.

The Central Hotel was a massive structure. It was one of the most famous buildings in the city. A point of orientation for many arriving in Glasgow for the first time via the public railway station it enveloped. Archie's skin bristled as he walked along the faded Victorian corridors. This was his first time inside the hotel. As he'd anticipated, the room numbers increased the further they were from the dramatic main staircase, which looked like it had been salvaged from the *Titanic*. The corridor must have been close to the length of Hampden Park. Looking along its heavily patterned floor and flock-wallpapered walls was akin to peering into a massive kaleidoscope. Archie was dizzy by the time he reached the last four doors. He brushed it off as anticipatory nerves. He looked again at the paper in his hand:

11 o'clock. Room 392. Central Hotel. 4 days. Don't fuck it up.

He looked at his watch: 08:53

'Fuck sake! Piece ae Swiss shite.' He shook his wrist, then looked hopefully at the face. 08: 3. The '5' had vanished. He sighed deeply. He'd purchased three of them from Ally Devlin at the market, and all three were likely to be about as much use as a chocolate fireguard. Archie leaned in to listen at the room's door. He briefly sensed someone moving sharply some way down the corridor behind him but when he turned no one was there. He listened again. There were sounds but they weren't clear. Then, the sound of a woman giggling. He could hold back no longer. He lightly knocked on the door.

'Yeah, what do ya want?' A gruff, mid-Atlantic accent. Not at all redolent of the Sultan of Swoon, but nevertheless, strangely recognisable.

'Eh, ah'm yer driver, Mr Sina— ... em, sir.' Archie paused. It might not be the 'New York, New York' superstar. Reality stepped in and gripped his shoulders, shaking them. Neither Wullie Wigwam nor Chib Charnley had said it was. His beating heart beat a little bit slower.

'Just a minute, man,' the voice said. The door opened just wide enough for Archie to see the surprisingly dishevelled, unshaven form of Hank 'Heady' Hendricks looking back at him.

'You my driver, boy?'

Archie nodded and nervously whispered, 'Discretion, em ... guaranteed.'

'Give us a few minutes then son, will ya?'

12

August 1976 – Friday

Hank Hendricks was the pre-eminent light entertainment star in the British television firmament. He had been for nearly twenty years. He had created an original and fast-moving talent show for radio in the late fifties called *The Heady Heights*, successfully transferring it to BBC television as the swinging-sixties obsession with pop music mushroomed. A bidding war between the broadcasting companies, skilfully plotted and manipulated by Hendricks, resulted in the show moving to the commercial ITV network. It was now a staple of Saturday night television, and 'Heady' – as he was now affectionately and universally known – was its executive producer and presenter.

Heady Hendricks was 'represented' by a brash Canadian known as Daryl W. Seberg. It was the stuff of legend that Seberg was an alias used by Heady Hendricks when negotiating his contracts. Heady had allegedly been witnessed by an industry insider answering the phone as Heady, responding that the subject of the call was something his associate would deal with, pausing, then continuing the call in a totally different voice ... as Daryl W. Seberg. He reinforced this complex fabrication by ensuring Daryl's severe agoraphobia was widely acknowledged. The Seberg Agency had one client and did not prospect for others. Daryl did all the tough negotiating; Heady – the talent – signed the deals. So Heady Hendricks had no agent and managed all his own contracts and legal affairs. This eccentric autonomy made him one of the richest and most powerful personalities in Britain. Even though he had no apparent influence over the programme's guest judging panel, or the famous studio-applause rating mechanism, the clap-o-meter, when he uttered his catchphrase 'My word, I think you're heading for the Heady Heights', no one ignored it.

In the early seventies the show had suffered a marked dip in ratings. Acts were felt to be either too insipid, too dull, or frankly too talentless. They were either cardigan-clad country-and-western crooners reclining in rocking chairs, or magicians sawing beaming, large-breasted female assistants in half. Additionally, damaging rumours of Heady's voracious sexual appetite began to surface. A friendship with the newspaper magnate Robert Maxwell guaranteed tabloid media protection but only to a certain level. The star's shining public profile made him a target of those wanting to see his polish tarnished. Heady Hendricks' response was to get out of the big city spotlight to take the show on the road. He would fly his panel of judges around the country in his small Cessna 172. With their help, Heady handpicked the contestants personally. These new auditions had given the show a more regional flavour, resulting in its renaissance. Earlier in the year the show had made a victorious return to the London Palladium, as a segment on the Royal Variety Performance, with four previous series winners on stage in front of the Queen. And with Heady himself presenting the whole extravaganza, he was back on the very top of the showbiz pile. Rumours of a different kind now circulated – an honorary knighthood, perhaps – helped by his highly publicised donations to various homeless charities.

Archie Blunt was hyperventilating as he took in his charge's identity. The *only* person equivalent to Sinatra in his fantasies was Heady Hendricks. He hadn't dared imagine that it could possibly be him – The Dreammaker – in room 392. Yet, it was. And Archie Blunt was to be his Glaswegian chaperone.

Fifteen minutes after that first tentative knock on his hotel-room door, Heady Hendricks was on the other side of it, ready to take on the world. The dragged-through-a-hedge backwards look had disappeared and in its place was the very definition of showbiz sheen. His skin seemed several shades darker to Archie than it had only minutes earlier. Now it was the colour of teak. He wore a fawn three-piece suit with a large-collared shirt open at the neck. It revealed a large coruscating disc of silver, nestled comfortably into a nest of dark hair, like an alien spacecraft that had landed in a dense forest clearing. Shiny black hair was slicked back from a widow's peak, giving Heady the air of a seductively tanned Ray Reardon. A pencil-thin black moustache hinted at charismatic menace. His flattened boxer's nose made him look like a bank robber sheathed in American tan. Unlike many in the showbiz firmament, Heady Hendricks looked like he could handle himself in a pub brawl. The knuckle ridges and callouses on his thick-fingered hands, which could've built ships on the Clyde, hinted that he might've started a few fistfights as well. Heady Hendricks looked like a million dollars ... and he smelled like he had just bathed in Hai Karate. This was surely Archie's big chance.

'Right kid, let's hit the road. Whaddaya say?' Heady's earlier course dialect had morphed into the smooth mid-American twang that Max Bygraves and Des O'Connor employed, despite being from Rotherhithe and Stepney, respectively.

They wasted little time in the corridor back towards the lifts, Heady striding, Archie gambolling. Archie was still praying no one he knew would see them and take this most special of all moments away from him. He pressed the lift button.

'You look a bit anxious, son. Don't be. I don't bite, ya know.'

Archie laughed into his sleeve like a village idiot freshly released from the stocks.

Heady smiled, endeared. His teeth dazzled Archie. His own full-face, toothless Joe Jordan smile remained hidden for now. The lift arrived and they stepped inside. Archie slid the heavy iron grille across and pressed the 'B'. The old Victorian lift shuddered slowly into life. But just as the doors had almost closed, a green golf brolly darted through the narrow gap. They parted, and the grille grated back loudly. A small, squat frame with close-set beady eyes stepped in stealthily. There was no apology proffered and no obvious recognition of the celebrity within. Archie was astonished.

A moment after the lift started moving, Beady Eyes pressed the emergency halt switch. The car shuddered. It was between floors. He turned to face Heady Hendricks. He looked angry, and dangerous. Probably not after an autograph, then, thought Archie. Heady remained calm. Beady Eyes withdrew briefly, temporarily overcome by a different smell. Nerves had gotten the better of Archie. He had farted. It resembled malodorous feet. Heady gagged.

'Ya fucken dirty cunt, ye,' yelled Beady Eyes, at Heady though, not Archie. 'Where's Mag'ret, ma bastart missus, eh?'

'Aw Christ,' said Archie, louder than he had meant to.

'Calm down, sir. I really … really don't know whatcha talking about.' Heady remained steady, but Archie noticed the star's left hand twitching.

Beady Eyes began screaming, forehead thrusting forwards until it just about touched Heady's perfectly moisturised chin. 'Ah'll fucken chib ye, ya Yank bastart! Her sister said she came here wi' you last night. Now, where the fuck is she, eh?' Beady Eyes raised his other arm suddenly. There was a shiny blade at the end of it. A brolly and a knife; a confusing combination, unless you were Steed from *The Avengers*, which this gadgie most certainly wasn't.

Heady Hendricks gasped. He stepped back. Archie Blunt brought his elbow across instinctively to protect himself, and caught the small, squat bulk right on the temple. Beady Eyes went down, rotating as he did, like Foreman in the eighth round. Shaking, Archie dived for the lift buttons.

Heady Hendricks beat him to it. 'Not down, buddy. *Up*.' He pressed '5'. 'Don't want the doors opening in the foyer and the world asking awkward questions, ya see?' Heady winked.

The Glaswegian was impressed by the star's equanimity. Maybe this wasn't his first time. Archie's rattled brain pondered this possibility like a monkey presented with a thousand-piece jigsaw puzzle. What had just happened?

They got out on the fifth floor, stepping carefully over the unconscious assailant. As Heady had anticipated, there was no one around. He searched for the closest fire exit.

'This way, young man.' Heady winked a sparkling eye. It had been a long time since anyone had referred to Archie as young. He'd reached the age when, if he fell over in the street, no one laughed. Heady's potent odour wafted around Archie, enveloping him like a blanket. It smelt to him like the very elixir of life itself. He resolved to get himself some.

'Sure ... erm, Mr Hendricks.' It was the first time since arriving at the hotel that Archie had addressed his hire directly. He wasn't quite sure what else to call him.

'Son, ya just saved my life. From now on, and forever more, it's "Heady" to you. I'm in your debt, my fine man.'

Son, ya just saved my life replayed in Archie's head like a stuck record for the rest of the morning. He knew the truth, but it made him feel fantastic nonetheless.

Archie was instructed to drive Heady Hendricks up to a posh hotel overlooking Loch Lomond, where he was due to be having lunch with a female BBC Scotland producer. *Hush Hush* he had reminded Archie. *Of course, Heady*, Archie had assured him, tapping his nose melodramatically.

⏻

Archie Blunt sat on the bonnet of the car he now regarded as his. From inside it, a song effortlessly toasted the day he was having: *'Sky rockets in flight, afternoon delight'*. He had no idea what it was about but, looking out over the awesome panoramic beauty that stretched in front of him, it was the perfect soundtrack to Archie's vibe.

Scotland was such a beautiful country. Archie visualised driving across it in the leisurely fashion that only real wealth permits. Just him, these wheels and his dad in the back. Great songs like this one blasting out of the motor's speakers. No one to answer to. No depot shift clock to punch. Those wee remote, twisting B-roads and single-lane dirt tracks. Tractors pulling over, to wave him past. The heather. The gorse. Magnificent stags and hefty, hairy Highland cows. He opened the map and folded it back. Idiomatic place names: Drumnadrochit,

Drumochter, Rest and Be Thankful. Imagine someone resting, and being thankful in Shettleston? Not a fucking chance!

Yes, such a fucking beautiful country. His dad had never got the chance to see more of it. That saddened him and inspired him to consider it differently, in equal measure. Archie Blunt wasn't sure if he had ever felt more alive. Confidence flooded through his veins.

On their return to the city from the edge of the Trossachs, a well-oiled Heady sat up front, next to Archie Blunt. There was no glass screen separating them now. They were brothers in arms. Archie had sunk a couple of single malts while waiting and now saw his chance.

'Heady, ah've got this idea for a gameshow.' Archie paused. Testing the ground, to see if it could take his weight. He had anticipated *yeah, you and five million others, son*, but instead he heard, 'Shoot buddy. I'm all ears.'

Archie Blunt swallowed hard. 'Well ... Heady, ah've been thinkin' a lot about a show like this one. Everyb'dy loves telly stars, right?'

'You betcha,' confirmed Heady, before burping.

Archie took a deep breath. 'It'll be called *Celebrity Arseholes*...'

Heady spluttered, then laughed loudly, unsure if Archie was serious.

'There would be a few sportin' challenges in a format a bit like ... em...'

'*Superstars*?' ventured Heady.

'Yeah, exactly. *Superstars*, but wi' real showbiz stars. Bona-fide celeb-rities, y'know?'

Heady laughed again. 'I think I do, son,' Heady confirmed.

Archie pressed on. 'But in this version, the first challenge would be a classic hundred-metre sprint.'

'OK, that might work,' said Heady, encouragingly.

'Each celebrity contestant would have a stick ae dynamite stuck up their arses wi' a different length fuse ... dependin' on the agreed handicaps.'

Heady's face creased.

'Hattie Jacques would get an extra few seconds over Twiggy, an' that. It's got tae be fair, like, y'know?'

Heady seemed to be visualising such a race.

Archie's enthusiasm rose. 'The fuse would burn for about ten tae twenty seconds, an' it'd be lit on the 'B' ae the starter gun's 'Bang'.'

Heady was convulsing with laughter now. Archie had hit on an instant ratings-winner.

'If the stars make it tae the finish line, a big bucket ae water'll provide the means tae put out the fuse...'

Heady Hendricks snorted a bubble out of his nose.

'...an' offer progress tae the next round for them that have put in the proper trainin'.'

Heady regained some composure. He acknowledged that many agents would think this a viable proposition for their more fame-hungry clients, and he mused that some stars already on the slide would seriously consider its profile-raising opportunities as risks worth taking. But, he reasoned, the world maybe wasn't ready to see much-loved public figures like Larry Grayson, Freddie Starr or Mike Yarwood demean themselves purely for viewing figures. No, it was just too ludicrous.

Encouraged by Heady's hand, which now rested on his knee, Archie briefly lifted his gaze away from the road, turning to address the UK's biggest star squarely. 'Heady, look me straight in the eye an' tell me ye wouldnae cancel aw yer plans tae watch a programme like that?'

Heady Hendricks nodded, and tears ran down his leathery cheeks.

⏻

Archie Blunt dropped Heady Hendricks off under the elaborate Gordon Street *porte-cochere* of the Central Hotel. A sweating busboy dashed to open the door for the star. Heady slipped Archie a rare fifty-pound note, doing so smoothly, as if it had slid down the inside of his jacket sleeve and found its way into Archie's palm as part of a warm handshake.

'Boy, I haven't had as much fun in ages.' Heady walked away then paused after a few steps. He turned and leaned into the passenger-side window, dropping his head slightly to maintain eye contact. There was a definite glint, Archie noticed. He pondered whether all television personalities had it. Was *that* what marked them out from the proles?

'Pick me up here tonight at ten. We'll head out. Have some high jinks.'

'Aye, sure thing, Heady.'

The start ae a beautiful friendship, Archie was certain. He had broken the ice.

13

August 1976 – Saturday

'Ye know how ye said ah could ask ye anythin' ... after the, y'know ... the wee bam wi' the blade?' This wasn't sounding as polished as it had when Archie rehearsed it in front of his tiny, cracked bathroom mirror.

'I'm not sure I actually meant *anything*, Archie,' said Heady, brushing a dusting of dandruff flakes from the left shoulder of Archie's black jacket.

'Well ... it's, em ... a big personal favour that ah wanted tae ask, y'know?' Archie was making an unqualified arse of this, his big chance. He should've waited until they were in the car, but his excitement had got the better of him and he was now blurting it out incoherently as they strode through reception, Heady waving and air-kissing complete fucking strangers all the way to the revolving door. Archie had hoped to press his afternoon advantage, but Heady said nothing. Heady Hendricks the performer was back. No more sitting up in the front seat with the driver, it appeared. He sprung deftly into the back through the door Archie opened for him.

Archie sighed. He felt deflated. He started up the car and rolled down his window. He extended an arm with flat palm down as if he was transporting royalty and pulled carefully out into Gordon Street as the light, and the seemingly relentless heat, slowly diminished. It took another ten minutes for him to pick up the thread again. Archie flicked a dashboard switch. The glass screen that had separated them like a desperate bank customer from an impatient teller disappeared into the bulkhead slot behind Archie's seat.

'So ... like ah wis sayin' just back there...'

'Hmmm.'

Archie wondered if Heady was feigning lack of interest because he knew what was coming. Archie decided to come straight out with it. 'Can ah get an audition at the King's oan Friday? Ah'm a fucken great singer an' ah can play the piano, the moothie, an' ah write ma ain songs ... an'—'

'Sorry buddy. Let me stop you right there. We're done with the singer-songwriters for this series of shows,' said Heady politely, but firmly, and in a manner that refused further discussion. He now regretted having told the driver about the local auditions on the way back from Loch Lomond.

Archie was devastated. And Heady knew it. Despite himself, he felt bad. It wasn't a feeling he was accustomed to. This man had saved him from an irate, knife-wielding Glaswegian husband; the least rational kind there was, in Heady's experience. Heady decided to let his driver down more gently. He felt he owed him that, at least.

'It's just that the audiences at home don't want any more Val Doonicans, they want another Little Jimmy Osmond or a teenage Showaddywaddy. It's not my opinion, but we're a slave to the ratings, you understand. The viewers are always right, son.'

Archie Blunt didn't respond. Heady was sure the chauffeur's shoulders had slumped by a few inches. Heady was experiencing new sensations. Christ, what the fuck was this – guilt? The star exhaled dramatically. He tried to throw Archie a bone.

'Now ... if you had a young gang of fit kids ... boys, I mean, with a bit of swagger, then it might be different. Just might, mind you. They'd still have to be able to sing.'

Heady Hendricks relaxed and sat back in the seat. He drained the large Macallan he'd just poured himself and considered the exchange over. But were those shoulders now being held higher? He looked again at the back of Archie's head, at the slightly askew chauffeur's cap that rested on it, unaware of the beaming smile that was bursting out of Archie's face.

An embryonic notion was subdividing into multiple cells in Archie's head, all seemingly capable of sustaining the life Archie Blunt now had in mind for them. He knew he'd be running the risk of a severe battering from Chib Charnley, or worse from The Wigwam, but such a deviation from the prescribed instructions would be worth the gamble.

⏻

'Can ah get a picture of ye ... an' ah couple ae autographs for the boys at the club?' Having confirmed the audition offer and verified that the date of it was now firmly fixed in Heady's mind, Archie played to the star's ego.

'Em, course you can. Just not here, OK. Later, son. All the pictures you like back at the hotel, right?'

The car had pulled up on a quiet road in Mount Vernon, as instructed by Heady Hendricks, who seemed to know these suburban Glaswegian streets better than his driver for the evening. Heady studied his watch, holding it close to his ear and tapping its face. Archie offered to flick the lights on in the back to let him see it clearly but Heady sharply closed that down. He appeared unusually anxious.

And then, just as suddenly, the unruffled Heady was back, polished and completely in control. 'Let's go. About a hundred yards up on the left. The one with the big gates, got it?'

'Yes, Mr Hendricks.' Archie deployed formality once more. He figured deference would assist his ambitions.

'There. The big house at the top of the hill,' said Heady. 'Wait for the gates, then drive on up. We're just picking up a pal.'

'OK. Ye got a big night on?'

'Hmm. Somethin' like that.'

Archie judged he should stay silent. Once again, his rear-view mirror contained an image of a surprisingly edgy and apprehensive man. Further small talk would be pointless.

The gates opened electronically, giving Archie a fright. He had no idea such a device even existed. Old castles had drawbridges, admittedly, but the thought of someone flicking a switch instead of three hundred serfs winding a wooden wheel boggled his mind. *How the other half fucken live.* The car crawled slowly through the leafy margins of this substantial Mount Vernon residence. As they rolled between the verdant trees and up a long gravel driveway, the house seemed to expand exponentially. Archie gulped at its scale. It was the sort of house that Errol Flynn would've held decadent Hollywood orgies in. A light was on in every window. The electric bills must've been more than Kenny Dalglish earned in a year. It looked totally out of place in this normally grim, grey, Glaswegian context. He couldn't even imagine who would live in such a place, and he hadn't been told.

Archie stopped the car, taking care not to graze it against the edge of a circular stone fountain that propelled coloured streams of water upwards in a choreographed dance. They waited. Archie watched for movement from the heavy wooden doors that could've belonged to Count Dracula. He was transfixed by the thick metal rings threaded through lions' mouths.

'Wait here.' Heady Hendricks opened the car door and jumped out.

Archie watched a door open. An animated conversation took place with someone on the other side of it. Archie couldn't see who it was, and he didn't want to be so obvious as to lean over and stare. But it did appear that they were discussing him. Eventually, Heady's compatriot came out. He was a big man, tall and bulky, dressed in dinner suit and with a cummerbund so substantial it could've been tailored from a hammock. As they approached the car, and the uplighters of the fountain crossed the faces, Archie recognised the man. It was Big Jamesie Campbell, the former Labour politician and newly self-appointed social guardian of the city's poor and destitute. The ignorant man who had barged into Archie on the day he lost his job.

Archie Blunt was stunned to learn that their destination was The Balgarth Inn. He learned nothing else, as, at the insistence of the new passenger, the glass partition was kept raised. But his mind was racing. Could these be the very same personalities that Geordie McCartney had witnessed at The Balgarth during his dark night of the soul? Was that just a coincidence? Either way, it did lend his friend's story a credence Archie had hitherto been struggling to find.

It appeared that Heady Hendricks was guest of honour at this very late-evening soiree at The Balgarth. The new leader of the Scottish Free Labour Party ushered one of the most famous and well-loved showbiz entertainers in the country through those fearful doors, and – even more strangely – on the way in they both shook the hands of the two bruising doormen, and then hugged them.

Archie anticipated a long night ahead, having been specifically instructed by Heady to wait in a concealed parking bay and not out in the street. He had located the car's cooling system, although he'd yet to figure out how it functioned. Wearing the black suit in this oppressive heat was playing havoc with his personal hygiene. Despite official drought warnings having been in place for the last fortnight, he was being forced to wash his oxters twice a day.

Half an hour passed. Half an hour of Johnny Cash live at Folsom Prison, on eight-track, with fucking amazing sound quality. The first thing Archie would buy in his future showbiz life would be a motor with an eight-track sound system.

By the fourth listen, though, his boredom threshold had been breached. He got out of the driver's seat, jumped in the back, and slowly reached for the door housing the spirits. He briefly considered that such a vehicle might have hidden cameras, but then dismissed the idea – something so ludicrous would only feature on *Tomorrow's World*.

More time passed. He had rolled the windows down to allow some fresh air in, and some less than fresh personal air out. He reclined. Stars blinked brightly in the velvet sky framed by the edges of a fur-lined sun roof.

A sound startled him. Over the road to his right, a tree shivered and a bush shook. It didn't seem to do so naturally. There was no breeze. Archie was disorientated. He wiped his eyes, struggling to keep them open.

A full bladder woke him. He had fallen asleep. He'd been having a surreal dream wherein he had been publicly unmasked as the Boston Strangler, but despite this, had still been elected by a landslide as the new leader of the Liberal Party. He shook his head, got out of the car and slowly stretched arms and legs, like a bear emerging from hibernation.

'Ach, for fuck sake!' he whispered. In taking cover for a piss at the rear of the building, Archie had stepped in something big and soft. The rising stench confirmed his fears. In the far distance, a dog barked; a chain reaction that set others off, presumably the countless stray ones that roamed the East End like it was an urban safari park.

Having wiped his foot against the kerbstone, he came around the side of The Balgarth to see movement ahead, beside his car. He remained in the shadows cast by its gable, like an anxious mugger waiting for an easy mark. Someone was bent over, peering in through the windows. It was a woman. She turned when she heard Archie's footsteps on the gravel.

'Archie Blunt?' This startled Archie. From around forty feet away, the woman was only a silhouette in the darkness, her outline distinguished by the distant sodium glow from the other end of the street.

'Who wants tae know?'

'Well, if yer gonnae be like that, ah'll just go back intae the Big House!'

Archie was flummoxed. It wasn't Susie Mackintosh. This one had a voice like the rusty boiler on the *Vital Spark*.

'Sorry, but dae ah know you, hen?' he said.

'Your American pal off the telly sent me out here tae gie ye a blow-job. Free gratis.'

Jesus Christ! Archie panicked. Wasn't this exactly how Geordie McCartney had been snared? Archie couldn't contend with another blackmail payment on top of the one he was still helping Geordie deal with. The Wigwam hadn't stipulated the length of his driving contract. He might still be on probation. Then again, Heady Hendricks had offered him an audition if he could get a young group together, hadn't he? Maybe this was a test? If he declined the gift, the offer might be rescinded. It was a dilemma. His opinion swung back. He'd examined the car like a forensics expert poring over a crime scene. If there were cameras, he'd surely have found them by now. Plus, it was Hank 'Heady' Hendricks for God's sake! Who wouldn't trust the very bones of their children – if they had any – with such a universally loved man?

'Christ, pal, hurry up, eh? Let me in the back, an' get a move on wi' it, eh? Time's money, by the way.' She sniffed the air.

'Look, ah'm really sorry ... ah stood in a shite just there. It was pitch-black an' ah couldnae see where ah wis goin'.' The world's worst chat-up line, but Archie figured an explanation was required otherwise the woman might suspect he had shat himself.

A few moments later, Archie was watching the woman's head bouncing up and down as she sucked furiously at his cock. His trousers and his pants were at his ankles and they were preventing his legs from opening as widely as he'd wanted. He thought of touching her bleached-blonde hair, running his fingers through the black roots of it as she worked away. He decided against it. He thought instead of those wee plastic long-necked bird things he'd bought a few years ago at the seaside. You dipped their beaks in a glass of water and – with the counter-balance of a ball of red liquid at their arse – they continuously bobbed up and down as if taking a drink. He tried to think of the scientific explanation for this ... of the quantum mecha— ... of Mecca Bingo ... of Mary Whitehouse. *Shitehouse*. Mary getting fucked. By a bird. By Big Bird. Off *Sesame Street*. By ...... bye. Bye Bye Birdy .... by .... aaaaahhhh ... FUUUUCK! He opened his eyes. Briefly thought he saw someone staring in through the windscreen. Wiped them sharply. Opened them again. No one there. His over-stretched imagination.

Archie mumbled an apology. He started to tell her how long it had been, the sudden guilt making him feel that he had just cheated on his dead wife. The woman lifted her head sharply. It made little difference to her, she was on a fixed rate. The timid light from the car's drinks cabinet illuminated her glistening face.

'Fuck is this ... a hearse or somethin'?'

'Naw. At least ah dinnae think so.' Archie poured her a whisky from the decanter. He felt he should.

'Just a quick yin, then,' she said. 'Better head back in. Ah'll be gettin' ma jotters.' She drained the glass in one gulp, said thanks in response to Archie saying it first, and got out. Archie watched her sashay back towards The Balgarth.

'Fucken show business.' Archie reclined, zipped himself up and laughed loudly. The sky was undoubtedly the limit.

14

August 1976 - Monday

'Right, whit's the score, Parker? Lady Penelope still happy?'

'Day off. Ah've tae pick him up tomorrow. Nae idea where we're goin' though. He says it's a secret, although tae be fair, he says *everythin's* a fucken secret.'

'When did ye get back last night?'

'About five in the mornin'. He was pished an' ah had tae help him get in tae the back. He never said anythin' at aw oan the way back tae the hotel. Ah think he was out cold.'

Wullie Wigwam acknowledged the overtime. He also appreciated Archie's unquestioning acceptance of an additional passenger, even though he wasn't strictly required to make the return journey to Big Jamesie Campbell's Mount Vernon home. The driver assured Wullie that he was aware the Dunne Driving company motto extended to everyone that stepped over the running boards. To Archie himself, however, that understanding cut both ways. He didn't feel that Wullie Wigwam needed to know about the Havanas left in the car by Big Jamesie Campbell, nor the free blow job. That was a gift, an obligement. Like the multi-pack cartons of fags and the forty-ouncers The Wigwam brought back from his regular trips to Benidorm, it didn't need to be declared.

'Any tips?'

'Nup. None,' said Archie, determinedly. He'd decided to hand over the first fifty Heady had given him, rather than keep it. Wullie Wigwam would no doubt find out about it anyway, and besides, Archie was enjoying the cachet of being a chauffeur to the stars.

Wullie disappeared into the small room at the end of the portacabin.

He came back out five minutes later. He was holding a faded photograph and a wad of cash held together by elastic bands. The image on the still-glossy paper was of Bobby Souness's young son. A name – Joseph – had been scrawled in blue biro on the back.

'Archie, there's a wee job on the Southside that ah want ye tae dae. Extra bunce in it for ye.'

'Aye, Boss. Anythin' ye say, Wullie.' Archie knew he had to keep his options open. He was already beginning to suspect that celebrities had very selective short-term memories when it suited them. So there was a possibility that the auditions might go badly. It wouldn't harm to have this to fall back on. Chib Charnley was an arsehole, but Wullie Dunne was a decent sort ... on the evidence to date at least.

Archie headed over the Clyde via the Kingston Bridge. It had been there for nearly six years now, but this was only the second time he'd crossed it. He remembered watching them constructing it. He'd come down to Anderson in the late sixties, when he was on regular late shifts, just to watch its steady but impressive progress. But, despite having seen its formidable structural skeleton, he still didn't trust it. He expected it to fall crashing into the murky brown river under the substantial weight of the tens of thousands of vehicles that now crossed it daily. Additionally, Archie considered it to be the Huns' bridge; built purely to accommodate the vociferous council cohorts who dragged their knuckles to Ibrox once a fortnight. They already had a new tunnel under the Clyde, he reasoned, *and* a fucking underground system. Nothing like that was offered to the East End, which – in Archie's opinion – was more deserving and in more need.

The traffic was slow. The temperature gauge was recording twenty-six degrees. The heatwave had lasted more than a month. Archie was boiling. His earlier exuberance had evaporated in the haze. His overheated brain was calculating the odds of finding a young vocal-harmony group capable of passing an audition for a national television show in only three days' time. It wasn't looking good.

The car had moved only fifty yards in the last twenty minutes; the road ahead blocked by broken-down vehicles, steam bursting from old, overworked engines. He'd passed the first ten minutes in a rational debate with Jim Rockford about the best groups on which to model his new puppets. Jim – clearly hearing 'Last Train to Clarksville' playing on the car radio – reckoned The Monkees. A good shout, thought Archie, but that would rely on them being about to play their own instruments, which might be a step too far given the time constraints. Jim left, and Archie drifted into a frustrated daydream. And as he did so, the car he was driving ran into the back of a bus.

'Fuck sake, by the way!' The conductor was rightly perplexed. Then, 'Archie, is that you? Archie *Blunt* – rhymes wi' cunt?'

Archie burst out of the car. 'Eddie *Foley* ... rhymes wi' toley?'

The former colleagues embraced and then simultaneously remembered they were men; Glaswegian ones. They jumped back until two feet of manly Glaswegian air was between them.

'Fuck me, you've landed on yer feet,' said Eddie, examining the big black car.

Archie was also examining it, but for other reasons.

'Ah saw that, so ah did. He ran right intae the back ae ye ... aw deliberate like.' Both men turned sharply. A pensioner stood on the rear platform, writing in a notepad like he was Dixon of Dock Green.

'Fuck off ya nosy auld prick, or ah'll charge ye full fare.'

Good old Eddie, thought Archie Blunt. *A man ye don't meet every day*.

They both reviewed the damage. A big dent in the rear panel of the bus; a broken number plate and a scuffed front bumper on the big black motor. It could've been much worse, Archie figured. Eddie caught up rapidly with Archie's recent story, then realised they were holding up not only the bus, but the mounting queue of traffic all the way down Paisley Road West. They said their goodbyes with promises to meet up for a drink in a week or two. The bus pulled away. Eddie wouldn't even report it. The busybody pensioner would get a free *hurl*. And even Archie now began to perceive this as some form of positive karmic sign. A plasterer-rough idea that had been fermenting during the nocturnal hours was now maturing into a creative visionary concept.

That kid Sledge Strachan was working at Mad Max's body shop. Archie knew that much. He would take the car in and casually offer the boy and his mates a deal. He'd been looking for a way in, and the car and its busted number plate was it. Sledge Strachan was a big, spiky gadgie and approaching him out of the blue to ask him to enter a singing competition could still result in a double date with *Accident*, and her scarier big sister *Emergency*. That was a task for later though. First, he had to head over to Pollokshaws, to hunt for the missing Souness lad.

Archie Blunt parked the car near to the stained concrete of the Pollok Shopping Centre. The cut letters O, P and P were missing from the middle word, replaced by a spray-painted A, G and G.

The car immediately drew a crowd of gallus delinquents.

'Cool motor. Watch it for ten bob, mister?'

'Ah'll give ye a quid,' said Archie, fully rehearsed in the way of the young bam.

Bemused looks were returned. Archie took the note out of his pocket. The tallest of the five foremost kids leaned forwards to take it from him. Archie pulled it back. He tore the note in half. There was a gasp from the smallest child. Archie looked down at him. He couldn't have been more than eight years old.

Archie handed their leader half of the pound note. 'Ye'll get the other bit if ah get back an' there's nae scratches. Deal?'

'Fucken good is that tae us? Ye've ripped it up!' said the tall boy, on the verge of rage.

'Tape it back th'gither then. Shops'll still take it,' said Archie calmly.

As he walked away towards the school he heard: 'Aye, but the fucken sellytape'll be more than the note itself. Arsehole!'

Archie laughed. He briefly wondered why these kids weren't in the school he was heading for and then remembered the infrequency of his own school attendance. He was in no position to judge.

He stood at the school gates. The playground was a mass of unimpeded movement. Swarms of wee people running wildly in different directions, like clockwork toys set free on springs that had been overwound. Kids as aeroplanes. Kids as boxers. Kids as playground footballers, thirty-a-side, with an Irn-Bru can for a ball. Archie Blunt had little chance of identifying wee Joseph Souness among this throng.

'Lookin' for someb'dy, bud?'

Archie turned to face a wiry, hard-looking youth who was staring directly at him. A new gang of variously aged kids stood behind him. Back-up; essential in every confrontational Glaswegian exchange.

'Ah'm trying tae find a kid, goes by the name ae Souness.' Archie wasn't hopeful that they'd give him up even if they knew the boy.

'Naebody about here wi' that name, like. Whit's he done?'

'Nothin'. He's been doggin' it an' ah just need a wee word.' Archie knew he didn't look like a *dogger man*, but he was hoping this crew would buy it anyway.

'Ye sure ye're no' just an auld poofter?' The other kids laughed.

Archie faced it up. 'What's your name, son?'

'Think ah'll gonnae fucken tell *you*? Beat it!' The boy hadn't blinked once.

'Too feart?'

'Feart fae *you*? A fucken kiddy-fiddlin' nonce? Gie's peace.' The boy looked around at his subordinates, then back at Archie. Bluster took over, as Archie suspected it would.

Archie turned away from them without responding. He headed for the car. The kids laughed. A stick hurtled past his head. After about fifty feet, he turned to look back. Most of the gang had become distracted by the ice-cream van at the school gates, but one of them was slowly following him. Archie stopped. The kid momentarily stopped too. Then he continued slowly in Archie's direction. About ten yards remained between them.

The kid looked around. Satisfied no one else could hear, he spoke: 'Ah used tae be called Souness.'

Archie took the crumpled photo out of his pocket. The hair was longer, a bit darker and he was now wearing National Health Service glasses, like Joe 90. But it was him. Archie was sure of it.

'Are you lookin' for ma da?' said the kid, softly and sadly.

'Yeah ... maybe, son.'

There was a pause, and then on the verge of tears, the kid said: 'So am ah, mister.'

Poor wee cunt, thought Archie. He's got Bobby Souness for a dad, and he's been shipped out to the deep Southside, like a worn sofa in a midnight flit. Archie felt certain that some bampot would find wee Joseph Souness, or whatever his name was now, and he would be used to force his father to repay his mounting debts. But Archie decided that bampot wasn't going to be him. Souness Senior was climbing steadily to the top of The Wigwam's most-wanted chart. Soon, he'd be number one. Archie had no cares for Bobby Souness, far from it; but threatening what was left of his family was a step too far, in his opinion. He wanted no part of that. Archie checked that no one was looking, then gave the kid a pound note to himself and told him not to worry about anything. To work hard and stick in at school.

Archie got back to the car. Another five kids had joined the first five. They guarded all sides of it.

'Gie's the poun' then, mister!' one demanded.

'Will ah fuck,' said Archie. 'Look at the front ae it … it's aw dented, son.'

'Haw, fuck off. That wis' aw'ready there when ye drove up, ya big cheatin' bastart, ye,' another spluttered.

Archie laughed. He handed over the other half of the note and then scrambled a handful of change, watching as they swooped on it like vultures.

He smiled, seeing them fight over the money in the big mirror, as the car pulled away, heading for the comfortingly familiar landscape of the East End, and Mad Max's Body Shop.

⏻

'So … fancy it then?'

'Singing? In front ae folk? Oan a stage?'

'Aye.'

'Whit aboot ah just gie you a boot in the baws?'

'Eh?' The flip in the direction of the exchange caught Archie Blunt off guard.

'Are you rippin' the pish, big man?' said Sledge Strachan, calmly and without looking up from inspecting the front of the damaged car.

'Naw. It's a talent contest thing, gen up,' replied Archie.

'Whit's in it for you then?' asked Sledge.

'Well, ah'd guide you, like ... a manager, like, y'know?'

'Like Stein or Waddell?'

'Eh ... aye, sorta.'

'What yin?'

'Stein. *Definitely* Stein.'

There was a long pause. Archie wasn't sure he'd scored with this last response or whether he'd just blootered it miles over the bar from six feet out.

'Ah'll have a word wi' Max. See if ah can get ye the day off for it?'

This was a direct hit. The young man looked up, wiped a running nose on an oil-stained sleeve and pursed big chapped lips. 'Make it the rest ae the week.'

'Well ... ah can ask. Maybe ah can offer him a favour. A wee bit ae mutual back scratchin'.' Archie was drifting into territory he had no control over. Quite how permitting an apprentice mechanic a few days off could result in a reciprocated favour from Archie was far from clear. But Archie was moving in elevated circles and that was greasing the cogs of his imagination.

'Aye. Aw'right then.' Sledge valued time away from this hell on earth more than anything else. He was just about to turn seventeen and had worked here since expulsion from St Kentigern's more than a year before. 'What dae ah have tae sing? If it's some fucken soppy bollocks, ah'm no doin' it.' Sledge seemed quite firm about this. Archie would have to tread carefully.

'Well, ye'se might dae a Showwaddywad—'

'Haud oan ... "ye'se"? Who's the "ye'se"?' Sledge stood up.

He was over six foot; unusually tall for teenage boys from this part of the world. A future centre half, or a potential goalkeeper, maybe. Shettleston teenagers were invariably small and emaciated. They also looked like they had just gone three rounds with the school nit nurse, losing by a bruising knockout. Sledge bucked that trend. His hair was dark and wavy. His frame was wiry, admittedly, but he looked older than his years. He had a darkness to his skin that indicated a more continental lineage. And although Archie felt awkward looking at him in such a manner, he was undoubtedly a good-looking kid. Just what Heady Hendricks seemed to prefer. He also had a foot-long wrench in his hand. Archie took a big step backwards, out of the swing zone.

'Ah need a group. Five ae ye'se. Ah was thinkin' that you could maybe rope in that crowd you hang about wi'.'

Archie had a good ear for a voice that could hold a tune. He could hear it anywhere. There had been times – in the Jungle at Parkhead – when a cultured voice close to him had risen from the generally abusive throng of supporters. If you could recognise talent in that heaving, drunken context, you could do it anywhere. Archie had heard Sledge Strachan and his mates a few weeks earlier at the start of July. They were engaged in taunting a passing Orange Walk, singing *'you're gonna get your fucken heads kicked in'* repeatedly from the safety of a second-floor Bridgeton tenement window. Archie had been caught coming out of the bookies on the ground floor, and – as convention dictated – had been made to wait for more than twenty minutes by the police before he could even cross the road. Nothing, it seemed, ever got in the way of the Walk. To Archie, the five voices above him sounded like a foul-mouthed celestial choir of angels with pasty faces. He could hear the potential. He could identify the harmony. When Heady had indicated the shift towards young male-vocal harmony groups that *The Heady Heights* was taking, these voices were the first thing Archie had thought of. He simply had to work out the safest way to broach it with them.

'How ah'm ah meant tae persuade the rest. They'll aw think it's for fucken poofs.'

'They'll listen tae you son, you're their leader,' said Archie hopefully, opening his wallet. Another lightbulb illuminated over Archie's head. 'What about a harder number then? Somethin' by The Faces, or The Stones?' Archie didn't think Sledge would know the back catalogue of these groups. The suggestion was more to do with *him* seeming relevant and on the ball as a potential impresario.

'Aye. Mibbe. Ah prefer the Sensational Alex Harvey Band though … or The Stooges.'

Archie could detect his developing interest. If the young man was musically informed, so much the better.

'Is there money in it?' asked Sledge, staring at the wallet.

'Aye,' replied Archie, although there wasn't.

'How much?' asked Sledge.

'A hundred … maybe more if ye'se win,' Archie lied.

'Whit's the cut ae the dosh?' asked Sledge.

'Sixty/forty tae me,' said Archie.

'Seventy-five/twenty-five us,' replied Sledge immediately.

'Fuck sake!' Archie drew air in sharply through his remaining teeth, as if recovering from a straight-armed dig at his solar plexus. 'Aye … aw'right. Daylight fucken robbery, mind you.' Archie quickly reminded himself that seventy-five percent of fuck all was still fuck all. 'Fine then. Ye drive a hard bargain here, son … but aye, fine, ah suppose.'

'Will there be burds there?' asked Sledge.

'Aye, loads,' replied Archie, although he knew there wouldn't be.

A dirty hand with fresh spit on it was offered. Archie shook it. A small price worth paying. It would wash off.

Archie Blunt was exhilarated when he finally drove away from Mad Max's place. The car's number plate had been fixed, although it had cost him twenty simply to keep it quiet from The Wigwam. And another fifty to seal the deal to secure Sledge's release. But at least now he had a plan. He was a contender. Opportunity was still knocking stubbornly at his door. The drive back was a celebratory one, Jim Rockford reclining, cowboy-boot clad feet up on the dashboard.

What did ah tell ya, Arch? The sky's the limit for us now, man!

15

August 1976 – Tuesday

'Archie, come over and meet my main man, Vince.'

Archie wasn't quite sure what to do next, so he extended a hand and bowed, as if the man he was being introduced to was next in line for the throne. Vince Hillcock *was* showbiz royalty after all. Younger and smaller in real life than Archie expected him to be, Vince flashed a smile so bright it almost gave Archie a glare headache. Archie looked at the dripping gold around Vince's wrist. He was part of the establishment and he had almost single-handedly created a vocation: the celebrity publicist. He now represented Heady Hendricks, and strangely enough, Big Jamesie Campbell.

They sat down at a table in the Blue Lagoon Cafe. It was dark, smoke-filled and very noisy. The cafe was right in the centre of the covered piece of Argyle Street known widely as Heilanman's Umbrella, after the influx of Highlanders who had come down to Glasgow to work as navvies on the new station and its rapidly growing tentacles. The reverberating sound of trains passing only a few feet overhead, and the vehicles stopping and starting right outside made it difficult to hear anything that was said. When Archie nervously blurted out that he was a singer and had just written an original song called 'Sammy and the Radio Man', he was subsequently relieved that the two men hadn't heard him. Vince Hillcock's introduction into the most bizarre week of Archie's life so far was another indication that his future was destined to change. But he'd have to learn to bide his time, to wait for the appropriate opening.

'Archie's my driver. He's the best in the business, Vince. You're up here all the time. You should hire him for all your Scottish initiatives.'

'Does he know the landscape well, then?'

'He surely does. Had me up at the Loch of Lomond just past. Smoothest ride ever.' Heady winked. Vince Hillcock brayed. Archie wasn't sure what was going on.

'I love the fucking Jocks, me,' said Vince. 'And it's my favourite of all of our colonies.'

Archie sniggered, then realised the brash young Londoner wasn't joking.

'Archie here wants to get into the business.' Heady patted Archie on the shoulder.

'What business is that then?' asked Vince. He may have been feigning interest. Either that or he was just indulging his client. *No matter*, thought Archie.

'The inter-*tainment* yin,' said Archie Blunt proudly.

'Jesus Christ, bud, who doesn't?' sighed Vince.

'I love the way he says that, don't you Vince?' Heady laughed. 'Like it was an Italian football team he was talking about. Say it again.'

'What? Inter-*tainment*?' Archie said.

The two men laughed loudly. Archie immediately felt foolish.

'Good man. Well played there,' said Vince.

Archie couldn't see why it was so funny. He repeated the words over and over in his head. *Nope, still about as funny as a tent peg up the bellend.*

'Archie here manoeuvred me out of a potentially difficult and embarrassing lady situation th'other night.'

'You mean a difficult *husband* situation?' It was Vince's turn to wink. He did so. Twice. He looked straight at Archie and leaned forwards on his elbows. 'That right? You that good, m'friend?' said Vince. He lit three cigarettes and then passed one to each man, keeping the first for himself.

'Ah'm good, aye. Anywhere ye want tae go … *Discretion guaranteed*, by the way.' Archie tapped his nose, anticipating a laugh. None came his way though.

Instead, Vince Hillcock's jocular manner vanished like snow off a hot metal roof. 'Does he know?'

Heady shot Archie a strange look. Archie acted quickly. He took out a card and handed it to Vince while maintaining eye contact.

'Jimmy Johnstone?'

Archie had given Vince Hillcock a prized football card. He quickly took it back and replaced it with another.

'*Dunne Driving: Discretion Guaranteed.*' Vince read, looking relieved; Heady looked even more so.

Archie had defused a potentially suspect device without fully understanding why it had been so threatening. He decided it wise to focus exclusively on the tattie scone and beans that the waitress had brought him. He sat back, hoping to offer the impression to his hosts that he was now keeping his head firmly down, and that the motto of his employer would be his bond, regardless of what he subsequently overheard. He drowned the food in HP sauce and turned his seat to the side to press the point home.

The ensuing and almost whispered discussion between the two other men revealed Vince Hillcock to be unlike his tabloid-newspaper persona. His vibrant, effervescent charm had disappeared. Archie caught murmured accusations about the apparently scurrilous behaviour of top stars like Jimmy Savile and Gary Glitter that couldn't possibly be true. A roster of other famous and well-loved personalities was also mentioned – it was evident that Heady knew all of them. There were also multiple references to something called The Circle.

Archie concluded that Vince was a prick; a view confirmed when he used a twenty-pound note to wipe away a food stain from the table. Having done this, he tore the note in half. If it was clearly a deliberate act, intended to irritate Archie and the young waitress; and it worked.

But Archie also detected an emerging air of tension between the two men. Both were careful not to talk in direct terms. They seemed to be referring to a series of events in the third person and using the future tense; it was bizarre. Archie had no clue how to decipher it. He zoned out. His mind ambled back to yesterday afternoon, and more promising preoccupations.

⏻

'Hey ... Earth to Blunt, come in Blunt, your country needs you.' Heady's good-natured tone dragged Archie back into the present. 'You're a real dreamer, son. No mistaking.'

'Aye, Mr Hendricks. Sorry about that.' Archie looked around the cafe. Vince Hillcock had gone but perhaps just to the tiny downstairs toilet. 'Talkin' ae dreams, you know how ye said about the boy groups ... for the auditions an' that?'

'Hmm.'

'Well ... ah've got one.' It was a big statement; a revelatory moment for Archie. He had picked the right time. No one around, just two showbiz colleagues ... *friends*.

Seconds passed. Became minutes. No response. Heady's beak was deeply immersed in the racing pages of the *Daily Record*.

Fucken celebrities, thought Archie; so immersed in their own insulated worlds of arse-kissing bullshit and self-indulgent hedonism, they couldn't lend a helping hand to a punter who was simply trying to secure a foothold on the same ladder. Archie felt like he was traversing a minefield; a wrong step and the alternative future he and Jim Rockford had carefully constructed could be blown to smithereens.

Archie Blunt breathed in deeply. 'So ... any chance, Heady ... er, Mr Hendricks?'

Stony-faced.

Archie knew it was time for the ace card. Perhaps the only one he had left to play. 'After all, ah *did* save yer life ... remember?'

Heady looked up sharply, his face a mask of solemn impenetrability. He was harder to read than the shipping forecast. It was a bust or a flush.

'Yes. I suppose so. Alright.'

Ding, ding, ding ... fucken jackpot! Archie Blunt's heart leapt.

'But we're totally clear after this, you understand me?' Heady's irritation was evident. He'd been called on for a favour and he didn't like it.

But Archie didn't care. He was in. This was his chance. All he had to do now was make sure the Bash Street Kids didn't fuck it up.

16

August 1976 – Wednesday

It was the best day any of the men could remember. Those with deep-rooted addictions chose not to recall much anyway, but they were all agreed that this was a very special day at the Great Eastern. The residents partook wholeheartedly in the free drink and food provided as if they were commemorating the end of Prohibition. In fact they were marking the new Scottish Free Labour Party leader's visit to this famous haven for the homeless and destitute; Big Jamesie Campbell was in the Great Eastern to announce his vision of a new future for the building.

Bobby Souness was warier than his colleagues, though. Bobby was a new resident, still coming to terms with the tumultuous events that had brought him to this point in his life. He took Big Jamesie Campbell's socialist proclamations with a big pinch of salt. In his experience, few such initiatives were truly altruistic. Everyone was playing an angle, especially those in positions of power.

Bobby took the drink that was offered, but a look down the corridor as the party arrived made him shudder. Through the phalanx of dignitaries, he glimpsed Wullie Dunne, bringing up the rear of the Campbell entourage. Wullie Dunne was the nouveau riche of Glaswegian businessmen. He had muscle and could control and organise it to his own ends. And Bobby Souness was here, in this freezing stone-clad Victorian penury, as a direct result of The Wigwam's temper. Newspaper and television cameras were circling like vultures. Lights and trailing cables performed an uncoordinated dance around the feet of the volunteers, tripping up staff and visitors alike. Big Jamesie Campbell, his manatee bulk central to the whole event, seemed to revel in the chaos and celebration going on around him.

In addition to ensuring that the bookie didn't see him, Bobby Souness also studiously avoided the cameras; no one knew that he was even here, and he'd prefer it to stay that way for a while.

The flesh around Campbell was now being pressed. It seemed clear, though, that water was being trod. A very special guest was on the way, and he was currently running half an hour late.

The Great Eastern had been constructed in 1849 as the Duke Street Cotton Mill, but at the dawn of the twentieth century the imposing structure, stained industry-black, had been converted into a shelter for homeless men. Latterly, however, concerns had been widely expressed over the integrity of the mill's original construction. The building had been built using a very early example of mass concrete and, following an investigation into a recent fire, fears had grown that the shell might be prone to progressive collapse. A mystery still surrounded the fire itself. It was apparently started by a tormented young resident, whose dead body had subsequently been discovered floating on the surface of the Clyde. The building was briefly and controversially closed. But now, riding in from the East End on his white charger, was Big Jamesie Campbell. The future was immediately bright. The resilience of this – and other decrepit parts of the formerly industrial east of the city – were being salvaged by a consortium of moneyed men.

'Hullo folks,' boomed the man of the hour.

From his narrow viewpoint at the back of the pack of the unwashed, Bobby Souness could see a flurry of activity on the pavement outside. Through a gap in the net curtain, Bobby saw a man in a black suit and a cap who he vaguely recognised. Out of context he couldn't quite place him though. The man opened the rear door of a stunning black car, and another recognisable man, equally shorn of normal context, stepped out. It was the television star, Heady Hendricks. Bobby might not have had regular access to a television in the last decade, but he'd slept rough under enough copies of the *News of the World* in that time. Another man with an artificial skin tone also stepped out of the car. He must have had a recent haircut though, as the brown stopped about half an inch from the hairline. 'What a fucken diddy,' Bobby muttered.

'Just a few wee words from a shy and humble man before everybody can get back tae the free booze an' the scran,' began Big Jamesie.

The men of the Great Eastern Hotel cheered, as if cue cards had been raised.

Big Jamesie reaffirmed his commitment to this great city, concluding with: 'We're gonnae rid the Glasgow streets ae the stain ae homelessness for once an' for all! An' now...' he turned and urged his guest, who had now officially arrived, forwards '...ah'd like tae introduce a man who, em, needs nae introduction.' Heady Hendricks winced. 'He's a good friend ae mine, *and* of our great city. Please welcome Mr Hank "Heady" Hendricks!'

Cheers and applause broke out instantly. There were a few 'fucksake's and 'is that really him?'s and even a 'wunner how much wedge he's got in his pockets'. Big Jamesie allowed them all to be heard. His indulgence, the extent of the coup he'd carried off, made clear to the watching media.

'A few words fae this great, humble man in a minute, but first ... ah'd just like tae acknowledge that this magnificent institution has been lookin' after unfortunates like yersels for nigh' on a century.' Campbell turned to face the cameras, pointing back at the gathering guests. 'Ah've seen men urinatin' on these poor sods that've, through no fault ae their own, slipped intae the doldrums. We're a carin' city an' that reputation has slipped with the last administration...'

A chorus of boos rang out, as if Big Jamesie was delivering this from the stage of the Pavilion in the middle of panto season. He paused, allowing it to make its point and then settle.

'But under Big Jamesie's direction, that's all about tae change. Who knows what's just around the corner for any ae us, eh? You'se aw go where ye go purely by the grace of God.'

This confused the men, and Big Jamesie knew the words hadn't come out clearly. Like he was *blaming* God, rather than purely reflecting on the impersonal nature of fate. He glanced over at Vince Hillcock, standing portside of Heady. He'd make sure that got edited out of any later broadcast clips.

The politician refocused. 'The working-class men ae Glasgow, down on their luck an' destitute for reasons that are their own personal business, need this great hotel. Ah'm goin' tae make sure it's here for them, for another century!'

Camera bulbs flashed, and applause rang out. Bobby Souness looked around nervously. Wullie Dunne had apparently left, possibly as keen to maintain anonymity as Bobby, although clearly for different reasons.

'An' now, Heady Hendricks…'

'Thank you, Big Jamesie. I'm delighted to be here today, and I mean that most sincerely, fellas!' More bulbs flashed at the precise moment Heady launched that million-dollar intercontinental ballistic smile towards them. 'Many don't know this, but I was once on my uppers too … just like you all.'

It seemed impossible to conceive. This well-to-do gentleman, with his yellow tailored suit, his beige-and-maroon spats, his flowery cravat and a fat Havana cigar the size of one of Fanny Cradock's rolling pins.

'Although I was born in Montreal, my daddy, Hector, came from this very city. He sailed to Canada on an Allan Line steamship in 1911. He worked his passage as a boilerman.' Heady Hendricks, the showman. He knew how to pace and deliver a line. Big Jamesie looked on enviously as Heady paused professionally. 'I was only thirteen when my dear daddy was knifed to death in a brawl on the docks. It was over an unpaid gambling debt … amounting to the princely sum of four dollars.'

There were gasps at this revelation. Bobby Souness glanced down at his bandaged hands. Was this a coincidence, or, given The Wigwam's appearance, something more pointed?

Heady pulled out a patterned handkerchief from an inside pocket with the sleight of hand of Houdini. He dabbed an eye with it. 'I had to leave home at fourteen and find work to support my momma and my five brothers. I joined a travelling show, a circus … but many's the time I was on my own. Sleeping rough, eating scraps out of bins in back alleys, seeking companionship anywhere I could find it.'

Bobby Souness had heard enough. He edged backwards, aiming to disappear completely into the shadows.

Someone saw though. His withdrawal had been noticed.

'I'm honoured to have been asked to lend my name and personal support to this wonderful venture led by my close friend, Big Jamesie Campbell.'

Heady leaned behind the dignitaries. A board was passed to him. He turned it over and held it up. Flashbulbs again. The board illustrated a painting of a building; like the one they were standing in but with clean, light-grey stone rather than its current black. Colourful curtains had been painted into the windows. Happy, young carefree people 'boardwalked' the frontage. And exotic-looking cars populated the foreground. More like Chicago than Glasgow.

'I'm truly delighted to unveil...' Heady paused '...The Heady Heights Hotel!'

Arms full of pale ale cans and a large Scotch pie, Bobby Souness retreated to his tiny cell on the third floor. He heard the others bursting into song to rejoice their good fortune to have been homeless and here on this great day. Bobby lay back on the bed. The tiny window, bars on the outside to stop those who felt they had fallen to their lowest ebb from opening the window and deliberately falling even further. The brick wall of the adjoining building only six feet away, meaning the fluorescent strip light had to be on constantly. An incarceration of the mind. He thought of his wife, long gone and better off without him. Of young Joseph. Of how he'd fucked up their lives as certainly as he'd fucked up his own. And he thought of Wullie Dunne. Wullie fucking Wigwam, the architect of all his pain. The self-centred, thieving cunt who had virtually committed him to this life sentence as surely as if he'd been a High Court Judge. Bobby Souness wept as he weighed the only option now open to him.

A voice from beyond the open door dislocated his sorrow. 'Souness! Well, well, well. Almost didnae recognise ye. Cannae say ah'm surprised at this turn ae events.'

Archie had spotted Bobby slinking out the back of the big room and, satisfied Heady was settled, he'd followed the sly waster. He'd waited a very long time to tell Souness what he thought of him. To be doing it here, with circumstances that allowed him to really rub it in, to make him suffer ... well that was just too good an opportunity to miss.

'Christ! What dae *you* want, eh? Ah thought that was you ... in that fucken bingo-caller's gear ... at some cunt's bufty-end, just like always.'

'Still a wise-arse, eh Souness?'

'What the fuck are you talkin' about, pal? Look, if yer here tae stick the knife in, then fucken fire ahead. Water off a duck's back tae me, now.'

Archie looked at the squalor surrounding the defeated Bobby Souness. His hands heavily bandaged, a faint brownish-red stain in the same place on each. Archie wasn't a bad man. Why couldn't he forgive Bobby Souness? Deep down, Archie knew only too well that Bet's death wasn't Souness's fault. But the man was a convenient outlet for the corrosive guilt Archie felt over not being at her side when the last breath left her body. The whole thing had been so sudden and shocking that fixating on Souness and his peripheral involvement had been a way of coping, of remaining sane.

Archie was normally relaxed and laconic – by day, a day-dreaming optimist but at night, his subconscious tortured him, like a cat playing with a captured, stricken mouse. And Bobby Souness was present at these games – a lift-car attendant on Archie's descent through the circles of Hell. More than five years of this now – of Archie inventing his own alternative reality with Jim Rockford, of indulging in dreams of escape, of a life somewhere else, doing *anything* else. A few minutes in the company of his old nemesis, though, and Archie Blunt felt nothing but pity – for himself and for Bobby too.

Uninvited, he sat on the edge of the thin mattress. 'Happened to yer hands, then?'

'What the fuck dae you care?'

'Looks painful.'

'Aye, well. Gettin' yer thumbs hacked off wi' a butcher knife isnae exactly a night up the Locarno, eh?'

Archie was shocked, but perhaps not surprised. Those who knew Bobby Souness knew about his walks on the wild side. Booze, drugs, the bookies; he was an addict, without the means to support his habits.

'Who did that tae ye?'

'A big boy. He did it … an' then he fucken ran away!' Bobby Souness smirked. 'What is it tae you, eh? Why aw the fucken questions, Blunt?'

'Look, ah just didnae expect tae find you in here.' Archie sighed, as if he had just tracked down a long-lost relative. He was finding these complex and contradictory feelings confusing. 'Ye've got a wee laddie, haven't ye?'

Bobby Souness jumped up and lurched towards Archie. Archie put up defensive hands.

'What's happened tae him? Are you workin' for that Wigwam cunt?' Swear tae God, if anythin's happened tae my boy, ah'll fucken kill ye!' Bobby stood, shaking and leaning in like an old lightweight, hands bandaged and waiting for the gloves. One last comeback bout. But there was little fight left in him. His forced breathing betrayed his anxiety. He was a shell of his former self, only going through the motions of East End swagger. It was pitiful.

He sat down again, exhausted. He couldn't back up his threats. And he was now aware of his unwitting and peripheral part in the saddest moment of Archie Blunt's life. For Bobby, it explained a lot about Archie's attitude towards him these past few years.

Bobby gestured towards the cans. He had taken them, but he couldn't open them. Archie lifted the ring-pulls back for both and they drank. Not to anything or to anyone. And not really with each other, just reflecting. Separately remembering tormented times past and trying to make sense of a bewildering present.

17

August 1976 – Wednesday

'We'll go into House of Fraser again, hen? I think I liked the purse I saw in there best.'

Maude Campbell was a woman Barbara Sherman would now gladly strangle and serve time for. Five hours in her company meant a visit to virtually every department store in the city centre. Barbara was at her wits' end. Chaperoning this vacuous shell around town weekly was testing her loyalty to the job to the absolute limit.

That loyalty had been sorely tested in another way, too. Three months had now passed since she had made a request to travel back to Barra on official police business to reinterview Lachlan Wylie's mum. She had been denied, and aggressively so by Davy Dodd – as if she was directly challenging his judgement. He'd left her in no doubt: 'That fucken kid's down in London, fingering some pin-striped banker's arsehole for a ha'penny bag ae skag ... ah'm bloody tellin' ye! Now just leave that yin, Sherman. That case is dead, just like your time in here'll be if ye raise it wi' me again. Got it?'

She'd been handed those boxes full of potential crimes, but instructed to do no more than sort them into alphabetical order. No one seemed interested in the people who lay within.

A week after her sergeant refused her request, and six months since he had initially been reported missing, Lachlan Wylie's missing persons' file had been removed from the box. It had been removed because Lachlan Wylie's body had been found. It had been recovered by George Parsonage.

Barbara was in plain clothes on this interminable detail. It was yet another slap in the face. The uniform mattered. It was still remarkable to see WPCs on the beat. She liked that. But here, suffocating in perfumed aromas, the ludicrously expensive cashmere and the silk and the Egyptian cottons, she was merely a ghastly woman's assistant. Ordinary people working the tills wouldn't know the truth of the situation. She yearned to yell out. Laden down with branded hold-alls containing crocodile-skin bags, she struggled back to the car. Maude Campbell waited for the door to be opened for her, and then she slid in as if mounting a horse side-saddle. Barbara shut it behind her. She would return to the station, demanding to know how long this farce was going to continue. It wasn't real policing; nowhere close to it. She knew deep down that circumstances about some of those missing persons cases hadn't been properly investigated. She acknowledged the Barra boy preoccupied her more than the others, and perhaps that had been a failing. But she didn't recognise the family name. And *that* was notable and suspicious.

The car pulled out of the multi-storey car park. Barbara indicated left and nervously nosed out until someone – a woman – left a gap for her. Horns peeped aggressively. She ignored them, and moving up the gears with a crunch, headed for the Campbell family home.

⏻

Archie Blunt manoeuvred slowly up the hill, suspicious about a small green car that seemed to be following them. But as he reached the summit, it disappeared from his wing mirror. Perhaps the strange conversation he'd been involved in earlier that day had made him imagine odd things. After all, these had been the weirdest few days of his life.

The gates opened, and he accelerated through them, careful not to hit any of the low stone blocks that lined Big Jamesie Campbell's Mount Vernon driveway. There were three passengers in the back; all well oiled and with the joyful abandon of the day's celebrations potentially just beginning. The screen between front and back was open by perhaps quarter of an inch. The passengers hadn't noticed. They talked warmly about a *very good friend of theirs*, repeating the phrase regularly.

They referred to him as an investor; someone who might gain access to the founders. It all meant nothing to Archie; he listened only to hear mention of the auditions. There was none.

Archie heard laughter over his left shoulder. It was the type of laughter heard on *The Wheeltappers & Shunters Social Club*; gruff, manly and loud. Not the natural sound of close pals having a laugh in the pub, more the demonstration of bloated ego and alpha-male tendencies. Humour used simultaneously as a weapon of attack and defence.

Archie stopped the car and his cocked ear pricked up as the engine noise shut down. He heard, in a hushed, Scottish accent: 'It's aw fine. We're untouchable. Fucken public would never believe it, anyway, the daft cunts.'

More laughs, and then, in a different accent: 'Well, in any case, there's nothing Vince's people can't bury.'

Archie found it difficult to concentrate. He was still processing the new information Bobby Souness had given him, which was making Archie reconsider his attitude to The Wigwam and his brawny henchman, Chib Charnley. Were they really capable of ... mutilation ... and more...?

Vince Hillcock got out first, helping Heady Hendricks and then coming back to assist their host. All half-cut; not so much that it affected their progress, but lips had been loosened and speech patterns were undeniably slurred. They had stayed far longer at the Great Eastern than had been anticipated. Once the press corps left, more alcohol had been found and consumed. Private, individual visits to certain inhabitants' rooms were undertaken. Big Jamesie Campbell knew all the nooks and crannies of the Great Eastern Hotel.

The vast doors unlocked, the three went inside. Once again, Archie was asked to remain where he was. It was two days to the auditions. He could have done with the time to rehearse the boys, but abandoning his post now might put the kibosh on the whole thing. Especially now that The Wigwam's 'sleeping partner' status had been revealed to him.

In the small, cell-like room at the Great Eastern, Archie had heard the whole tale from Bobby Souness. Bobby actually didn't owe The

Wigwam the substantial funds of Shettleston folklore. Bobby had been driving odd night shifts for The Wigwam, but not the upper-crust talent that Archie was now working for. Bobby claimed he had been instructed to pick up homeless men from the city streets. Young men – exclusively. He offered them a hot meal. A few quid in their pockets. A bed for the night.

A bed in the Great Eastern.

18

August 1976 – Wednesday

'You a driver tae, love?'

Archie Blunt had been sitting on the low circular wall surrounding the fountain, reflecting on Bobby Souness's barely believable story when another car drew in. The headlights had blinded him. A young woman got out. She helped an older woman to the front doors, and then returned to the car for a further two journeys' worth of shopping bags. Archie wandered over and offered to help carry them in. He was nosy. Keen to see what lay behind those intimidating barricades.

'I'm not a driver, no.' Barbara's response was forceful.

'Aw'right, hen. Nae need tae take my head off. Just askin'.'

Barbara sighed. 'Look, it's been a long day. I'm sorry. Just not in the mood.'

'Let me help ye anyways.' Archie lifted the bags that Barbara couldn't.

She had lost the will to say no. 'Thanks,' she said. 'I'm sorry about snapping.'

'Don't sweat it, hen,' he said. 'If she's anythin' like her man...'

'You know her then?'

'Naw. Bumped into her earlier in the week. She disnae seem the full shillin'.' Archie's eyes wandered as his forefinger circled his template.

Barbara's mood lightened. 'Aye, well. You could say that,' she agreed.

'Ah'm Archie,' said Archie offering a hand. 'Archie Blunt. Ah'm a driver for a couple ae guys that are pals wi' Mr Campbell.'

Barbara took his hand. And the cigarette he had offered her with the other one. 'Ah shouldn't really ... but...'

'Ach away. Have a fag. Ye look like ye need one,' Archie said. 'Plus, that must be you off duty now?'

'What do you mean by that?' Barbara's guard went up again. She been told not to let anyone know she was in the force while on 'Maude' detail.

'Eh ... ah just meant yer woman's in for the night. You'll be clockin' off, naw?' Archie had little experience of casual chat with single women – he'd noticed she wasn't wearing any rings – especially ones much younger than him. So much for being nice. She seemed tense. The fag would calm her. A whisky too, maybe. Archie reached into the back and opened the cabinet.

'A wee dram?' he offered. Barbara melted. She laughed.

'No. I don't ... but thanks.'

'Dinnae drink? Sure? Ye a wee Free, or somethin'?'

'Sorry?'

'One ae Pastor Jack's mob?' He laughed. He was only kidding and told her so. Even the mad, minority religions had the right to ply their trade in Glasgow's East End.

'You were right,' she said. 'I am on duty.'

Archie's heart rate raced like Nijinsky winning the Derby as he looked at the card the young woman presented to him.

Barbara shouldn't have done it, but days of pounding the fashion floors had built up. 'It's fine. Don't panic ... but can I see your licence?' It was her turn to laugh.

Archie's in return sounded like Elmer Fudd being strangled.

'Relax, Archie ... and thanks again. I mean it.' She drew on the cigarette and leaned back on the black car.

'Jeez. What for?' asked Archie. He wasn't sure what to say.

'It's been a really rotten day.'

⏻

Archie was staring up at the diamond sky, trying to place Orion's Belt and The Plough. Dreaming ... his default night-time setting. He was wondering why Bobby Souness hadn't gone to the cops. But few in the

East End trusted them. The assault on – or removal of – his thumbs, did seem a cut above the usual batterings that occurred when the pubs spilled out. But that might have given the police more reason to ignore any complaint. If it looked like the work of the organised gangster, the cops rarely stepped in, unless it was part of a bigger initiative, or if a *Sunday Mail* exposé was in the offing.

'Archie?'

The voice rocked him. Not because he didn't recognise it; he just didn't expect it. 'Hey ... Archie, is it?' It was Vince Hillcock. A greasy head peeking out from behind a door leaf. Given his stance, Archie wondered if he was naked. 'We're gonna be a while yet, fella. Important business. Just rest up in the back, son.' Vince was drunk. It perhaps explained his less aggressive demeanour.

The door closed. *Fucken selfish cunts.* Archie wondered why he hadn't simply been dismissed. Given a time to return. But such people of power and influence thought little for those in their charge. Especially the famed champagne socialist himself, Big Jamesie Campbell. Archie was starving. He'd been waiting outside for four hours already. It was dark, and now he would probably be waiting at least that time again.

Two more hours passed. Radio Luxembourg kept him company, David Essex offering stardom and giving him another song idea for the boys. Now he needed a shite. It had been a long, long day. A piss against the car was one thing but hunkering down in the driveway would've been much harder to explain if caught. He'd need to take his chances. Pray that the front door was unlocked.

It was. Archie stepped inside the circular entrance hall. A curving white staircase floated away from him, like they were inside a massive, hollowed-out Walnut Whip. The decor was big, bold and brash, with flowery velvet flock wallpaper so rich in colour and texture that it was giving Archie a headache. Archie touched it. The wallpaper's flock was thicker than the pile on his own carpet.

Archie wandered further into the house, looking for a toilet. He could see or hear no one. Perhaps the 'staff' and Maude had all gone to bed.

Opening a door, he found himself in the kitchen. He instantly decided to just help himself, and his annoyance at the thoughtless situation Heady and Vince had left him in gave way to gratitude. He wouldn't have slept in any case – he had rehearsals with Sledge and the boys in the morning – and with free access to a larder stocked with the best produce Scotland had to offer, the positives now outweighed the negatives. A freezer that could have stored several bodies was overflowing with frozen meat. A door adjacent to it led to a small wine cellar, which was, by some distance, bigger than Archie's kitchen. There was a cooker and hob combination that could have serviced a modest restaurant. And a rack of shiny utensils that Sweeney Todd would've coveted. In the end, Archie settled for a roast-beef sandwich. It saved trying to work out what all the dials on the hob were for. The bread was the softest Archie had ever eaten. His normal starchy fare – the bleached-white pan loaf – could last almost a fortnight if wrapped up properly. But *this* stuff? This must be what they serve at your first full breakfast in heaven.

Archie returned to the roast-beef joint four times. He had three bottles of Strongbow. He'd still be fine to drive, but he now desperately needed to find a toilet again. The house was so disorientating he couldn't locate the one he'd used initially. What the fuck did they expect? For him to sit tight for eight fucking hours without food, drink or access to a lavvy?

He edged cautiously out of the kitchen. As he went down the corridor he caught himself in a mirror. He smiled, realising he was on tiptoes. The house was silent. He gently eased open another set of double doors. It was the snooker room. Big Jamesie, Heady, Vince and another man were in there. All spark-out and snoring. The fourth man was lying face down on a rug with a tiger's head still attached to it. His arms cuddled the head. The tiger looked blankly at Archie. If it could've spoken, Archie felt sure it would've pleaded to him for salvation from these vulgar, rat-arsed cunts. Vapour trails of white powder covered a glass table, a tightly rolled one-hundred note adjacent. For such slaves to the pretty green, they didn't half treat it disrespectfully.

An LP was still spinning, the needle going blunt on its run-off grooves. *Top of The Pops: 1975.* Archie had a copy at home.

His gaze fell on a manila folder left on the baize. The words *Great Eastern Hotel Plans – Private & Confidential* were written across it. *FOR THE CIRCLE'S EYES ONLY* was written on a separate note, held in place by an elastic band around the folder.

Archie was intrigued and, given the Souness story, magnetised. He was in the Glaswegian Blofeld's lair and he didn't know what the fuck he was doing.

He lifted the folder and gingerly removed the band. Inside was an envelope. He was moving slowly and mechanically like a bomb-disposal expert on the 'long walk' in the Ardoyne. If the tiger's eyes were hidden cameras, he'd be totally fucked when these sleeping conspirators woke. He open the envelope and quietly and quickly scanned documents and photographs.

Fuck me sideways.

Souness had been right.

19

August 1976 – Thursday

Tennyson Drive was deserted. Archie Blunt had been peering out through his net curtains for almost five hours, trying to rid his mind of frightening thoughts.

His knees were now aching, and the tension building up inside his shaking muscles had exhausted him. He moved away from the window and slumped into a worn armchair that he knew to be older than him. It was Betty's favourite chair. The only thing he had left that was hers.

His head was spinning. The envelope he had taken from inside the confidential file hours earlier was lying on the low glass table just a few feet from his trembling left hand. He wished he hadn't seen the contents, but he couldn't unsee them. He had had an out-of-body experience in Big Jamesie Campbell's sumptuous snooker room.

Since dropping an inebriated Heady Hendricks back at the Central Hotel as dawn broke, Archie had been building in his mind the basis for a legal defence that he was certain he'd need after his theft of this inflammatory material. Stress resulting from the combined pressure of losing his job and the resultant intoxication of potential stardust was just too much for an impressionable man still grieving the loss of his wife. That would be his argument. Flushed with the rich meat and the free booze, he had also thought about the bargaining value the pictures in the folder carried with them. But he was just an out-of-work Glaswegian bum; he didn't know how to bargain. Or with whom. And now the anxiety of holding this unsought knowledge outweighed any advantage he could see.

Wanna go fishin'?

'Eh?' Archie looked up, shaken from the dwam.

Jim Rockford was a tall man, but one who carried his height and weight with the grace of an athlete. His face was angular and would have been as stoic as the city itself were it not for the impish grin that seemed to be a permanent feature. In many ways, Jim Rockford was more Glaswegian than Californian.

Let's go catch some fish, man.

'Jesus, Jim, there's nae fish about here!' Archie was in shock. He watched Jim Rockford lean over and pick up the envelope.

That's what I mean, Bob. Let's get outta the city. I'll set it up with Rocky. He's always got the cabin all stocked with food and booze. Geez, man, we could really have us a hoot.

'Ah cannae leave, Jim. Not now, fuck sake!' said Archie, his strangulated vocals wavering. 'Ah can't go!'

Whatta you got here that's so important you can't go fishin' with your buddy? I ain't been a good enough friend or somethin'?

'Come on, Jim, don't get personal. Ah'm fucked here!'

'That who I think it is? Archie watched the Californian ex-con take the photographs out of the envelope.

'Well, if it's who *ah* think it is, then aye.'

Jim Rockford dropped the pictures back on the table and left Archie's small Tennyson Drive living room. Archie watched him open the door to the veranda and go outside with a lit Marlboro.

Archie was sweating. *This fucken heat!* His brain was steaming. He looked at the pictures again. The craving for escape into an alcoholic haze intensified. But, still … the rehearsals. They represented a lifeline. Maybe the photos *could* be an insurance policy. Jim Rockford must know a few opportunistic tunes, and how to play them on the blackmail banjo.

Archie got up and went to wash his face, shave and estimate the weight of the bags under his eyes. Almost as big as the sacks that Bazooka Joe, the rag and bone man, carried out of the close entry just last week. Betty's clothes. Finally gone. A new job, a new future. A new *him*. He needed to pull himself together. He had a sort of a plan and despite – or possibly because of – these late-breaking revelations, he had to focus.

He hid the pictures.

Jim Rockford winked. *That's ma boy!*

Archie pulled up his jacket lapels. More now than ever, he needed to fade into the background. He was indeed going fishing, just not the relaxing kind that Jim Rockford had in mind.

Before he could reach the front door, the letter box rapped. Not the gentle knock of a kindly old neighbour, round to borrow sugar. No, this was a determined rap. Police *or* thieves. The former would have been a blessing.

'Whit's the Hampden roar, then?' Door ajar, Wullie Wigwam's greeting was suspiciously warm.

Archie panicked. His nerves already as taut as piano wire, the Souness story put a totally different spin on the bookie's involvement with Heady and Campbell. Did he know about the envelope already?

'No' gonnae ask us in then?' said Wullie.

'Aye ... aye, sorry. Ah was just goin' out, y'know?'

'Wi' the tin flute on?'

'Ach, ah've no' had time tae take it off, like.'

'Where's the motor, Archie?' This question had a bit of edge. Like Olivier, drill in hand, asking it of Dustin Hoffman.

'Ye didnae bring it back, son.' Wullie smiled. It unnerved Archie. 'We were gettin' worried about ye.' This was spoken slowly. A thin façade of concern.

Archie looked anywhere other than straight in Wullie's eye. Not a good idea. Attack was the best form of defence, unless you were the Scotland football team at Wembley.

'Ah'm no' happy,' said Archie, edging onto the front foot.

'Well, let's see,' said Wullie. 'Just which one ae the seven dwarves *are* ye, then?'

Chib Charnley guffawed. Archie hadn't even seen him skulking in the darkness of the stairwell.

Wullie pushed past Archie. 'Nice place ye've got here!' he said sarcastically. 'So, what's up wi' ye?' he asked, sitting down in Betty's armchair. The edge had gone. He seemed happy enough to Archie, but not enough to allow for the chauffeur's blood pressure to return to a normal pre-Heady state.

'Ah'm just knackered. Mr Hendricks had us out aw night ... an' most ae the day leadin' up tae it.'

'So?' said the Wigwam.

Archie saw him glance briefly at the brown envelope on the table in front of him. If that was the real purpose of their visit, there wouldn't be anything Archie could do to stop The Wigwam opening it.

'Ah told ye, the job was tae do anythin' he asked. Discretion guaranteed, remember?'

'Aye. Sorry.' Archie felt his pale cheeks flush. Betrayed by Weegie physiology.

'Are ye no' enjoyin' aw the perks?' asked Wullie.

Archie looked confused. Wullie glanced at Chib. Chib made a fist and then made a motion towards his open mouth that let Archie understand they knew about the free blow-job.

'Archie, focus son,' said Wullie, snapping his fingers. 'Ah need the motor for a few hours. Where the fuck is it?'

Archie was sure his pounding heart could be seen rippling his shirt. He breathed laboriously. Archie explained that he'd left the car parked in a dark, rarely used back-lane recess with a secure gate. If those on the breadline saw it parked in the middle of Tennyson Drive, every flat in the street would get done over in search of the evident windfall that had caused it to be there.

Archie's current employers left, taking the keys, but enquiring nothing about an envelope with contents that could bring down a government.

⏻

Archie headed for Bridgeton Cross, two hours later than originally intended. He'd ditched the suit and was back in the beige flared slacks.

He strode towards the large storage unit he'd rented for a few hours, crossing his fingers that the boys would be there waiting for him. They were; *six* of them.

'Fucken hell, mister,' said one. 'Been here for hours!'

'Aye, sorry, son. A few wee messages tae fix.'

'D'ye bring some ginger?' another asked hopefully.

Fortunately, he had. He'd anticipated well. Their collective ire doused by American cream soda, Archie unlocked the unit and let them all in. The heat inside it rushed out and slapped them all squarely in the face. The campaign was also now hitting him heavily in the wallet. Archie was getting pummelled from all sides. Getting the car fixed, securing Sledge's day release and the hire of the rehearsal unit had cost him almost a hundred in total. And he needed outfits for them, although Bazooka Joe would help limit that damage. The pay-off from the Corporation had all but gone. Only his superannuation remained until The Wigwam squared him up. As Archie looked optimistically at his new charges, he shuddered at the sudden realisation of the mountain that they would have to climb.

Against the corrugated backdrop, they stood in a row. Sniggering and carrying on. *Like weans, because they* are *weans!* Archie shook his head. If they sang like they looked, he would be more royally fucked than a pissed-up British princess at a Caribbean hideaway. Archie pulled up the only available seat and straddled it, his arms folded on its metal-framed back. He scanned the six, left to right. Despite the lack of introductions, he could've picked all of them out of a police line-up – a not unfamiliar experience for them, he speculated – but none as well as Sledge Strachan, and the others only by nickname.

There was Burkie, a quiet and diminutive sixteen-year-old, blond-haired kid with glasses. Not as cute as the Milky Bar Kid but there was some early-teen pant-wetting potential there, Archie felt. Next to him was the slightly shorter Smudge, a ginger-haired seventeen-year-old, and *an ugly wee bastart*. Despite his age, he looked like a constipated Chic Murray. There was no avoiding the fact that if he couldn't sing like David Cassidy, he was out before he was in. Sledge was next, the tallest, loudest and best looking. The next two – Rich and Dobber – were identical twins; a quirk Archie was convinced would come in handy.

These were the five who so melodically had encouraged an entire *diddley-dee* flute band to *get it right fucken up them*. The last in the line was the nineteen-year-old Manky Marvin Mountjoy. He hadn't been invited by Archie, but he knew him as one of the many sons of Borstal Barry Mountjoy – a bona fide headcase who'd acquired his moniker because he'd burned the borstal he'd been raised in to the ground.

'There can only be five ae ye'se in the band,' said Archie eventually.

'Why no' six, eh?'

'Was it The Jackson *Six*? Naw, so stop bein' awkward.'

'Marvin's comin' wi' us. He came up wi' the name,' countered Sledge.

'Eh? Whit name?' Archie was blindsided. '*Ah've* got ye'se a name.'

'We're ... the Fuckwits!' Sledge announced proudly.

'Aye, well, there's nae denyin' that.' Archie sighed. 'Ye cannae have a name like that, Jesus Christ. Ye'll no' get on the telly or the trannie wi' the word "fuck" in yer name.'

'Satan's Bagpipes!' screamed Manky Marvin.

'Right, you ... fucken out!' Archie pointed to the door. The young Mountjoy was most definitely his father's son.

'Naw.' Sledge stepped forwards. 'That wis his second choice.'

'Fuck me!' Archie threw his arms up in exasperation. 'Ye cannae have *any* swears in the name, right? An' the public aren't gonnae phone in an' vote for anythin' belongin' tae the Devil.' He sighed again, louder this time, so they would sense the tone. 'Ah'd thought ae either The Hopefuls, or mibbe Sweet Soul ... but spelt differently.' He wrote the words *Suite Sole* on a piece of card and held it up for them to see. 'Like a play oan words, naw?'

They looked flummoxed and then uninterested. Dobber sneezed, Rich picked his nose and Marvin sloped further to the left. Archie interpreted that as recognition that Marvin's input – and interest – had come to an end.

'He still gets a fucken cut though ... an' he comes wi' us, right?' Sledge knew the name wasn't a deal-breaker. He just wanted to mess with Archie's head.

'Aye. Christ Almighty! Can we get on? The thing's tomorrow!'

Archie plugged his large new portable cassette player into the wall socket. He brought out a tape. Manky Marvin had never seen one before and looked astonished when sound started coming out of it. Archie made a mental note to keep one eye fixed on it. He was certain Marvin would already be three steps ahead in terms of anticipating who he'd sell it to, once stolen.

The three songs on the tape were known by most of those now lined up to sing them. Only Dobber claimed not to have heard them before. He explained that since he was deaf in his left ear following a battering from his drunken da when he was eight, he didn't bother with the radio or *Top of the Pops*.

First up was Showaddywaddy's 'Three Steps to Heaven', quickly ruled out by the twins because 'they cunts aw wear brothel creepers!' Next was 'Sugar Baby Love', by the Rubettes. Generally liked by all but disregarded because none of them were willing to attempt the high notes at the end. Finally, they all settled on 'Hot Love', by T. Rex, mainly because Archie's Shadows-influenced dance steps were easy to master. And Sledge persuaded Archie that they could play it live, with instruments. Just like a proper group. The song was a couple of years old, but it had been a massive smash hit, and everybody knew it immediately the opening groove kicked in.

It took around four hours – and at times it felt like herding cats in the brutal heatwave – but by the end of it, Archie believed they had a slim shot of success. For the most part, they *could* sing; and broadly in tune. And unbelievably they did possess a degree of rhythm. He was sick to the back teeth of the song by the time he left to source some stage clothes for his charges, and although he could've cooked eggs in his sweat-sodden Y-fronts, Archie Blunt had been able to consign the stolen photographs to the periphery. For now, he had a vibrant sparkle in his eye that could've warned ships away from the rocks of the Western Isles on the stormiest of nights. These five degenerates, now known collectively as The High Five, might just be his passport out of the dangerous East End and into the London high life.

20

August 1976 – Friday

Archie had a big day ahead. He was armed with knowledge but hoped it wouldn't need to be revealed. Not yet anyway. He prepared by heading back to the Blue Lagoon. A big urban cave of literal and metaphorical cover. Somewhere to simultaneously think straight and dream big technicolour dreams.

A massive plate of square slice, tattie scone, beans and egg, three cups of tea – with an aggregate score of twelve sugars and two Embassy Regal later, he was sorted. He left a pound tip; important to start living the lifestyle appropriately, he figured. When he picked up the car, it had a parking ticket under the front wiper. He dropped it swiftly in the nearest bin. *The Wigwam's fucken problem.* Then he went to collect Heady Hendricks. It was 9 a.m. The High Five would be rehearsing all morning back at the Cross, before turning up at the King's Theatre for the *Heady Heights* auditions around 3 p.m. He'd arranged for them to go on last. The impact slot, as Archie perceived it.

Heady Hendricks acknowledged his driver with a cursory 'good morning'. No dancing arm waving freely as it had on previous days. A far terser manner was at work. Archie looked for clues that might implicate his recent criminality. None were forthcoming. The short journey northwards on a polluted Bath Street and then west to the slightly cleaner atmosphere around the King's Theatre was conducted in silence. Archie was glad about this. Now that he had secured the audition for Sledge's malevolent mob of miscreants, he considered a more professional demeanour was necessary. Plus, he may still have to put a darker plot in play, one that had fomented in the infernal heat of the metal storage unit. Pleasantries would only make that harder.

Archie parked the car near the scene dock in the lane behind the old Victorian building. He'd been to this theatre with his dad as a member of the audience many times. In fact, his dreams of making it big in the business of show had been born in this very building, as he'd watched the parochial brilliance of Stanley Baxter and Rikki Fulton during the mid-sixties. They'd grown in stature before his eyes under the coruscating search of the arc lights. He'd witnessed them hold an entire audience of legendarily hard-to-please punters rapt with a comic story about common people like them, and with heartbreaking renditions of songs so familiar, Archie now considered them as family members. He'd also seen many artistes flounder, the stage swallowing them whole under the cruel heckling of the demanding Glaswegian crowd. He'd even watched one well-known comedian deliberately faint, just to be dragged off stage early. All of it intoxicated him and made him uncontrollably giddy. And now here he was, carrying the bags and suits of the greatest UK light entertainer of them all through the famous stage door. Archie Blunt couldn't have been happier if he'd suddenly started shitting money. The previous day's anxiety now consigned to the dark recesses. Ludicrous optimism was back in the driving seat.

He followed Heady Hendricks across the boards as the star headed to his dressing room. Although there was no formal TV recording being made, the auditions were being filmed for later, more detailed analysis back at Teddington Lock. Nonetheless, Heady had a polished and manicured façade, and everything connected to *The Heady Heights* relied on it. Even though not directly appearing on camera, make-up and wardrobe – and his dark, lustrous toupee – were *de rigueur*. But Heady Hendricks also had an ulterior motive for filming the auditions. He had hit on the notion of airing a filmed section of the worst auditions during the show's festive finale, although he was keeping that idea within a tightly closed production circle for the time being. His fans might take the view that it would be cruel to laugh at the extreme poverty of people's performances, although *he* found it hilarious, and potentially more entertaining than the broadcast programmes of the last three seasons.

'Are you coming?' shouted Heady from stage left.

Archie had stopped in the middle of the proscenium, transfixed by the theatre's volume. He saw roses being thrown from the balcony, the Queen and the Duke of Edinburgh leading the calls of 'encore', and his dear old dad crying in the front row. A tear welled and grew, then burst into a sprint down his cheek.

'This reminds me ae the Empire, Jim. We went there loads ae times, me an' him. The Empire started doin' its own pantomimes in the thirties. Ma wasn't that fussed about all that palaver, so he took me instead.'

That's a cool memory.

'He loved the place ... the whole atmosphere ae it. The smells, the cigar smoke an' the orange peel. Ah can recall it all that clearly, y' know? My da was never a hard-drinkin' man. He drove the trams, watched the Celtic, an' went tae the music hall as often as he could afford. It was unusual for a working-class fella round our bit, ah suppose.'

You sound like ya loved it as much as yer dad.

'Aye, ah did, Jim. We even went tae see Laurel and Hardy there twice. The two ae them wore kilts. The audiences went daft. They even had tae bring in polis on horses tae control the crowds.' Archie laughed as he gazed into a happier past. 'Ah've definitely inherited a love ae aw that fae him ... the stage, the lights, the great performances we saw back then,' said Archie. 'My God, the turns that were on ... Frankie Vaughan, Bob Hope, Judy Garland. Sinatra! My da was greetin' when The Empire finally shut!' Archie sighed. 'It's a bloody office block now. An' a pawn shop down at the street level. Still, eh?'

'Archie, who are you talking to?' yelled Heady, impatiently. 'I don't have time to spare. I said you'd get an opportunity later today. Now please ... get a bloody move on!'

Eight acts appeared in the theatre that morning. Their quality was decidedly mixed. From the ridiculous Abie the Baby – a fat sixty-year-old man in an oversized nappy, singing 'My Boy Lollipop' – to the relatively sublime Jay Boothby, a Cumbrian wedding singer who belted out a great version of 'Delilah'. In between them, the range was uniformly mediocre. As lunchtime passed, only Boothby was a realistic candidate to progress to the English shows, although the big baby was guaranteed a starring role in the outtakes. However, the young Englishman left in such a state of high excitement he didn't properly record his details. Heady's production assistant was sure 'Jay Boothby' was a stage name. Jay had nervously admitted he'd be fired if his employers had found out he'd abandoned his truck to go to a singing audition. Consequently, Heady Hendricks' mood was darker than a blackout during the three-day week. Heady stormed to the rear of the stalls. He paused at the row Archie was sitting in and turned towards him.

'These kids you're bringing better not be wasting my fucking time, son.'

'They won't be Heady, trust me. Ah really think they're just what you're lookin' for.'

No other words passed between the two men. Heady Hendricks pulled on his jacket and went out into the foyer. Once again, Archie was relieved. The tension he was now feeling could have transmitted itself to an agitated Heady and he might have pulled the plug on the whole day. Archie was already hoping that the next few acts weren't totally dire. Not great either, just promising enough that Heady saw the benefit in seeing out the schedule.

Heady Hendricks retook his place in the second row of the stalls, along with his two female coproducers. Also present were Bogart Bridlington, Heady's musical director, and notably, Vince Hillcock who had returned with Heady.

A succession of overexcited but forgettable panto-style acts were rejected. Archie was surprised to hear the publicist take the lead in voicing criticism, which, in Archie's opinion, was unduly harsh. Despite this, the would-be impresario was certain that The High Five would surely be an improvement. Archie – now watching from stage left – observed a yawning Heady gradually losing interest in the proceedings. The lowest point came immediately before yet another break for tea. A male children's entertainer appeared from behind a table with an orange oven glove on his right hand. Two black buttons had been taped to the garment, which was then introduced as the *real* Sooty. Heady had had enough.

Archie disappeared. He hunted the backstage corridors for a pay phone. He had a number – Sledge had given him it – and he dialled it, desperately hoping someone would pick up, receiving the message that his group of young amateur singers from Glasgow's East End were getting their stage call.

Archie re-entered the hall to the sound of applause. Heady Hendricks was now in a good mood. A fourteen-year-old girl from Rothesay with an unpronounceable surname had just blown his – and everyone else's – socks off with a fantastic rendition of 'These Boots Are Made for Walking'. Vince Hillcock was perplexed by the tiny teenager stalking the stage like a scaled-down panther in shiny black, thigh-high leather boots, black leather hot pants and a yellow sequinned bra. The girl's mother was side stage, apparently having no issue with the older men present leering at her daughter. The green light flashed for Heady Hendricks. The little girl was a star in the making, and her scintillating performance made the show's *real* talent forget about Jay Boothby. Her performance also affirmed that this whole trip north of Hadrian's Wall had been worthwhile. Beyond the peripheral attractions of Glasgow's nocturnal underbelly, his judgement had again been proven correct. There were pearls among the regional swine. And even the worst of that swill would make good television. Heady Hendricks was a legend; a broadcasting innovator. He already knew it; many more would soon accept it as incontestable fact.

Sixteen other acts came and went. Heady's imagination was still turning over the possibilities presented by the precocious little Amy. Vince Hillcock had been dismissed, to go and quickly write up a contract. Heady sized up Amy's family; backward islanders who wouldn't be difficult to deal with. Only Archie Blunt's lot were left before they all called it a day.

Archie met the six young men who bore his hopes – and the ill-fitting clothes he'd procured for them – outside the old theatre half an hour after he'd made the desperate call. They were carrying instruments. All stolen. It was fully apparent what role Manky Marvin had fulfilled. None of them had been in such a building before. They were giggling excitedly. Archie initially thought this was a good sign. It quickly dawned that they were living up to at least *one* part of their name. The sweetly pungent smell betrayed the real nature of their morning rehearsals.

'Ach, for Christ's sake. Ye couldnae have stayed off the Bob Hope for one fucken day?' Archie Blunt felt demoralised. The opportunity was perfect. Heady's mood was high; but unfortunately, so were The High Five.

He herded the noisy, truculent teenagers inside and gathered them together at the lighting rig, left of the stage.

'Anythin' tae eat in here? Ah'm fucken starvin', said one.

'Aye, me tae,' echoed another.

'Me anaw.'

Archie sought out some of the left-over sandwiches offered to the crew earlier. He watched the six inhale them. He hoped this would calm them down a bit. It seemed a forlorn hope.

'Fucken put that down an' concentrate.' Archie shouted louder than he intended, mainly at Manky Marvin, who was attempting to conceal a two-foot-long saw down the flared left leg of his white suit trousers.

'Archie?' A deep voice, stage front. 'Archie Blunt? We're ready for you now. Let's go.'

'Fuck me,' whispered Archie. 'Right, this is it. Time for heroes.' Archie breathed out heavily. 'Ye'se aw ready?'

'Piece ae total piss, man,' said Sledge. 'Take a fucken break fae yerself, ya balloon, eh?' Archie was struck by The High Five leader's sudden composure. 'We've done this before,' Sledge continued.

For the next ten minutes, Archie Blunt couldn't believe what he was watching. They plugged in, no sound check offered or requested. And The High Five were brilliant. Well, at least in comparison to what Archie anticipated when he met them outside, thirty minutes earlier. They moved in perfect sync, like they had been drilled by James Brown at the Harlem Apollo. Admittedly, it appeared as if they were wearing their fathers' suits, but at least these all looked like they had once belonged to the same father. Sledge took lead vocal duties and centre stage. Burkie stood left of him, Smudge stood right. Guitar and bass respectively. Rich and Dobber bookended the line, with a single drum each. How had they worked this out between themselves, thought Archie, and what did Sledge mean by *we've done this before*?

Right at this moment, Archie didn't care about such details. When the High Five stopped, there was sporadic applause from a few King's Theatre stagehands, setting up for the Friday evening show. With Vince Hillcock and one of Heady's young female colleagues gone, only Heady and two others were left. They didn't applaud. Heady simply shouted 'thanks' and got up to go backstage. The other two judges wrote notes on a clipboard. Archie, who'd watched from the stalls, was convinced Heady couldn't say no. Wee Amy from the islands was the undisputed star of the day, but with Jay Boothby slipping rapidly from memory, The High Five were surely in the silver-medal position. And they were firmly in the target demographic previously stated by the show's presenter and star. They'd be heading to the televised shows in London, Archie was certain of it.

Thankfully, the judges had left by the time the boys went back to their stupid horseplay. Sledge kicked Rich up the arse, and then pulled down Smudge's baggy trousers. Burkie pushed Dobber into the orchestra pit, and most worryingly, Manky Marvin was nowhere to be seen. Archie stood up. The stiff envelope that was inside his shirt had been digging into his nipples. It might not be needed anymore.

He headed backstage confident of the verdict but nonetheless nervous about hearing it delivered.

He stood at the green-room door. The dressing rooms were just beyond them. He composed himself, praying calmly that The High Five had made it, and that he wouldn't have to show Hank 'Heady' Hendricks photos of the star being taken from behind by a coloured woman with massive tits, wearing a dildo the sheer size of which made Archie gag. Or other photos featuring a senior cabinet minister in Her Majesty's Government being whipped by a young naked man as Heady, Big Jamesie Campbell and three other famous celebrities looked on, masturbating. And he really hoped he'd didn't have to indicate that he knew of the plans to turn the Great Eastern Hotel into a private high-class gentleman's club, where celebrities, politicians and sportsmen would abuse and exploit young homeless men with impunity, protected from prosecution by a senior member of the Strathclyde police.

The door opened. He peeked around the corner. It was Manky Marvin. The door closed behind him.

'Fuck sake, you,' hissed Archie, as he passed. 'What have you done?' Marvin handed him a piece of paper. It was a standard letter, which Heady Hendricks had signed.

'Calm it, Archie. The boys really wanted this … so ah went in an' wanked the daft auld cunt off! Just tae make sure, like, you know?'

Archie was speechless.

Marvin patted him on the back. 'Plus, ah wanted tae get away. The cops are after me for settin' the dole office on fire.' Marvin laughed. 'Relax, ya prick … we're off tae the London!'

THREE

Obscurity Knocks!

21

September 1976

Bobby Souness had seen a desperate, young ginger-haired man run away up the street in the darkness, escaping from The Balgarth Inn. Heading towards the big black car containing Souness, he collapsed onto its bonnet. Three frightening figures emerged out of the gloom, moving at pace towards them. The boy was terrified. His skin had a strange bluish tinge. He looked like a hypothermia sufferer wandering through the Highlands in winter. He was naked apart from a towel wrapped around his lower half. Blood seeped through it. Bobby pulled him into the back. Apart from a long, curving graze in his left side, he didn't seem to have any other visible injuries. Eyes wide, pleading. Mouth open, but soundless. The three men pursuing the boy were only a few feet from the car. Bobby Souness accelerated and turned the car left at the street end.

When they reached the Royal Infirmary, the boy was unconscious. Souness had dropped him on the path outside A&E at 3 a.m. Laid him out on the tarmac. Arms outstretched, feet crossed, towel still draped like a nappy. It looked like he'd just been brought down from the cross. Panicking, Bobby then drove the car to the Dunne Driving compound and abandoned it. He posted the keys.

Within days, he got himself a different job; a waiter on the Southside. He was nearer to his boy. But only weeks after this, Bobby Souness had been tracked down. He had had his thumbs removed. And had been given a beating. Not as punishment for his mountain of unpaid gambling debt. No. The digits had been hacked off because of what he had witnessed that night in the darkness outside The Balgarth. He'd been saved from being beaten to death by a passing copper on a night-shift beat, who'd interrupted the assailant, thinking it was nothing more sinister than a run-of-the-mill scrap.

The assault on his hands had been almost three months ago now. He'd been here, in the Great Eastern, amid those too anaesthetised by daily life to care about who *they* were, never mind him, or to even remember the name Bobby Souness, should anyone be asking about him. There was a safe anonymity to be found in the apathy of addiction.

The day Archie had appeared in his room, Souness had told him that he knew the word was still out. He'd kept his mouth shut, but he remained terrified that the thumb sanction wouldn't be enough, that those responsible would fear he'd speak out about what he'd seen. Souness was a wanted man.

Bobby Souness had vacated a job. Archie Blunt had taken it. It was this dawning realisation that had drawn Archie back to see Bobby Souness in the Great Eastern for a second time. The more he mulled it over, the more it persuaded him that there was a bigger story. One that might be relevant to Archie's own personal safety. If The Wigwam had taken Bobby's thumbs for an act of Samaritan selflessness, what would he take for the theft of the pictures? As he sat fidgeting in the Dunne Driving waiting room, Archie gulped and crossed his legs.

'Right, whit's the script?' Chib said, irritated.

Archie knew he'd have to answer these questions twice. First, to Chib, the pit bull, and then to Wullie. The boss saved him the trouble.

'Is that Archie Blunt out there?' The Wigwam's voice reverberated around the portable office.

'Aye,' chirruped Chib, like an obedient overfed budgie.

'Tell him his tea's oot!'

Chib drew an imaginary line across his throat. Archie gulped, got up, brushed his work suit down and strolled into the long room as con-fidently as his tremulous knees allowed. When he got there, he saw two cups; one on either side of the table. The palpitations slowed. Wullie was on the phone. He put a finger to his lips. Archie took that as a sign to sit down, which he did. He took in the paraphernalia strewn around The Wigwam's office. He had never really looked closely at it all before; never had to look for clues. Photographs of Wullie pressing the flesh with various sports stars, mostly football players from both sides of the Old Firm; but there was also one taken with the golfer Tony Jacklin and another with Diana Dors. And over his left shoulder, partially hidden by a metal-headed sledgehammer, there was a more recent one taken with Big Jamesie Campbell.

Whatever – and whoever – the subject of the phone call was, Wullie Wigwam hadn't spoken while Archie was in the room. The phone clicked back on its receiver.

'Did you get sorted out last week?'

'Eh, aye. Thanks, boss.'

'There was a wee bit extra in there. Hope ye noticed.'

'Ah did, aye. Much appreciated.' Archie's recent hire involved getting four senior management executives through an angry picket line forming outside of the John Brown's shipyards. Although he agreed with the principles of the strike, he'd broken the picket on instruction. He didn't want to put himself in The Wigwam's spotlight because of something as redundant in Shettleston as principled integrity. The High Five were scheduled to be on the final shows of *The Heady Heights* in late November. Archie needed the wages to keep coming until then, regardless of how objectionable the means of earning them were.

Weeks had passed since the night he'd stolen the photographs, and still nothing had been mentioned. It was important for Archie to try and keep calm. To project monotonous normality.

'Right, what is it? Why ye here?'

'Boss, can ah get a few days off this week? Ah need tae sort out arrangements wi' the boys.'

'Chib,' Wullie yelled through the open door. Chib ambled in. 'Ye got the driver rota there?'

Chib nodded and left.

'Ah should be on a cut ae the winnings, ye know that, don't ye?' said Wullie.

'Ah'm no' sure there's a cash prize, Wullie,' said Archie.

'Ye did secure this gig on my time, though.'

'Ah know. An' ah've apologised for that. We're aw really grateful.'

'Fuck sake, Archie, ah'm rowin' yer tail, son.' The Wigwam smiled broadly. Archie wondered if sharks smiled similarly before devouring a doe-eyed sea lion.

'Quiet week, boss,' said Chib.

'Chib says it's aw'right, then it's aw'right.' Wullie smiled again, tea-stained dentures showing this time. 'Three days, then back here on Thursday, right?'

'Thanks boss,' said Archie. 'By the way, any luck wi' the Souness boy?' It was like an involuntary spasm. Had just come out. Unprompted and apropos of absolutely nothing.

'Eh?' It had taken The Wigwam by surprise too.

It was difficult for Archie to back down now. Why hadn't he kept his fucking mouth shut? A time and a place, and this was neither. The incriminating material stolen from the files was concealed and it was beginning to look like no recriminations were being directed his way via the Dunne Driving organisation. Also, the only prior discussion about Souness's boy was a month ago. He'd told his employer that a potential sighting of the boy at a school on the Southside was a false alarm. The Wigwam hadn't seemed too fussed by this. Eventually, the poor wee boy would be found but, with Lady Luck kissing his dice, Archie would be in London by that time, and leading a high life well away from these dangerously myopic bampots. And now he'd just scored an own goal.

'What's wi' aw the Souness questions?' Chib now, from behind Archie's head.

While Chib may have asked the question; Archie directed his response to Wullie. 'Ah don't know anythin', Wullie, really ah don't. Ah was just enquirin',' Archie lied.

Wullie breathed in, regarding Archie intently. It felt like the thoughts in Archie's head were appearing above it for everyone to read, like he was a character in *The Broons* cartoon strip. The prolonged silence was killing him. A bead of sweat formed on his top lip. Wullie stared at him, not blinking, for what felt like five full minutes.

'Well, ears tae the ground, eh? He needs found, an' quick.'

'Aye. Right, Wullie.' Archie felt like he was teetering at the edge of a hundred-foot drop and had compounded the danger by closing his eyes and standing on one leg. Time to go.

He left, unaware of The Wigwam's instructive nod to his right-hand man.

⏻

Rehearsals were going well. The boys seemed to enjoy them. Manky Marvin had procured some more instruments, and, to Archie's shock, they all picked up rhythm and melody amazingly quickly.

He had their dates. The confirmation letter clarified the position regarding minors. None of those appearing were yet eighteen so he needed to ensure parental permissions were all in order. There was only one outstanding. Although technically, since it was for the twins, it was two. A sad and disheartening ambivalence had greeted his requests for the rest. Once payment had been ruled out, the parents had lost interest. None of the boys were in school. Only Sledge and Burkie had a job of any description. Smudge had an upcoming court date, but it was likely to be in the New Year. His father didn't care if he went to London or not. They had no television, so it seemed pointless for Archie to explain the concept of the show. A depressing scattering of vodka bottles indicated where his interest really lay. No wonder so many youngsters ended up on the streets.

Rich and Dobber lived in the Red Road flats – the brutalist point blocks up near Barmulloch. The family had been rehoused from the Tollcross tenements after complaints about their father's behaviour. Living on the twenty-seventh floor of Glasgow's tallest structures didn't calm him down, though. It isolated and insulated him from other people. Fed his anxieties. Prompted the voices in his head to torment him further. Previously, people had only seen – or experienced – the violence. Hadn't understood the mental torment behind it. Dobber experienced it most. He was most like his dad. It was a relief to the boy when his tortured father jumped from the balcony.

Archie had to climb the stairs. The lifts were out. Yellow tape criss-crossed the steel doors. The smell of urine was overpowering. The utopian dream of a steel-framed Manhattan skyline freeing up the Glaswegian landscape below for its community failed on the most pragmatic of levels. *The pricks that designed them didnae have tae live in them*, Archie was informed by a postman, setting off on the same intimidating ascent to the summit as him. If there hadn't been two band members involved, Archie might've ducked this and gone as a four-piece. It hadn't done The Four Tops any harm.

Out of breath, and about forty-five minutes after starting the climb, Archie had reached the door. His calf muscles were on fire. He knocked. He had paper and a pencil in case no one was home. Jim Rockford's idea.

'Hullo.' An old woman's voice.

'Aye, hullo yerself, missus,' replied Archie. The letterbox had been pushed back. Archie bent automatically to speak through its gap. 'Ah'm here about the boys.'

'Whit yins?'

'Eh … Richie an'…' He hesitated. He didn't know Dobber's real name. Seemed a bit off using a nickname when the boy wasn't an adult and then ostensibly asking if they were coming out to play. 'The twins.'

'Ach, what've they done now? Ah'm gettin' too auld for this shite, son.'

It seemed unlikely. But Archie asked it anyway. 'Are you their ma? Or is she in just now?'

'Ah'm their granny. She's no' here. Don't know where she is.'

'Ah right.' Those stairs, Jesus. 'Should ah come back later … when she's in?'

'She'll no' be in.'

'Ah … OK.' Archie's back was becoming as painful as his knees. 'Listen, ah need tae speak tae somebody about the boys.'

'Are ye polis? Ah cannae afford any more fines, so dae whit ye like this time.'

'Naw, naw … they've no' done anythin' wrong. It's a good thing,' said Archie.

'Ah've got a big dug in here, y'know!'

This poor old woman was obviously living in constant fear of the door being chapped. This high up in the air, and with lifts regularly broken, Archie couldn't imagine that it happened often. The sound of a chain. The door edged open no more than an inch.

Archie directed his attention towards the new gap. 'Ah'm sorry. Ah need their ma or da's permission tae take them down tae London in a couple ae months' time.'

'Are you fae the army?'

Archie now visualised a three-piece. No twins involved; the male Three Degrees. That might go down well at the Royal Variety Performance. Charles was a big fan, after all.

Suddenly, the door opened. 'Their da's dead. He jumped off the balcony. Their ma couldnae cope. She left them wi' me.' A wizened old woman stood in front of him. There wasn't going to be an easy explanation.

'The boys are part ae a singin' group. Ah'm their manager. We got through tae the London shows ae *The Heady Heights*. Ah just need permission for them tae go.' He was almost pleading now. Pleading not to have to climb back to the top of this concrete and steel Meccano set.

'*The Heady Heights*? Get awa' wi' ye. Yer pullin' my leg, son. That's my favourite programme.'

Archie laughed. The old woman didn't crack a light.

'We're on in November. Ye'll see yer boys on telly.'

She seemed to be calculating this. 'Wait there.'

He did. She didn't seem to have a dog. But it might've been sleeping. She came back. Handed him paper. He looked at it. A list of messages:

— *Three tins of beans*
— *A pan loaf*
— *A pack of Old Holborn*
— *Rizla papers*
— *A* People's Friend
— *A bottle of Vat 69*

— *Some Aspirin*

'Get these for us, then.'

Archie took the list. It'd mean having to come back, and it was clear this opportunistic old druid wasn't proffering any payment. But, if it was one-off, and if it secured the release of Rich and Dobber, Archie reckoned it was worth wearing away a little bit more cartilage.

When he reached ground level it was almost dark. He hobbled away, knees and hamstrings now burning too.

When he was almost out of sight, a small car's engine started up. Moving at this pace, Archie Blunt wouldn't be difficult to follow.

22

October 1976

'Aw'right, it's me,' Archie shouted into the flat.

There was no response. Had they gone out? He'd warned them not to, and, since the curtains didn't close fully, to stay clear of the windows. Jim Rockford had prompted that instruction. Archie wouldn't have thought of it on his own. He didn't think that there would be hired Jackals up trees, looking through crosshairs for movement inside a council flat in the East End of Glasgow, but you couldn't be certain. He'd just told them there were some right nosy bastards in Tennyson Drive.

'Ah got us chips!'

'Who ye talkin' tae, dopey?'

Archie almost had a heart attack on the spot. He turned. Chib Charnley was behind him. He must've been on the hidden side of the centre stairwell wall. Waiting. No way he could've scaled the steps that quickly.

'Fuck sake, Chib!' Archie said the name loudly.

'Been gettin' about, eh, Archie?'

'What d'ye mean?'

'Up the towers, over in Robroyston ... back tae the Great Eastern. A moonlit evening up the Necropolis.'

'Have you been followin' me, Chib?'

'Of course ah've been fucken followin' ye, ya daft cunt. How do ye think ah know where you've been?'

Chib strolled into the small living space. He flicked his cane around. Lifted two orange bed covers. Empty beer cans littered the floor underneath them. 'What a fucken midden!'

'What is this, man ... The Wigwam doin' home inspections?'

'Don't be fucken funny, son. I'll ram my fist intae yer neb.' Chib hunted on. Looking for something. He concluded his search.

'Fucken surprised this isnae cut off!' He said as he picked up the phone. He dialled some numbers, barely waiting for the metal ring to rotate back to its original position. 'Boss. Aye, it's me. He's here. Right. Ah'll wait then.' He replaced the receiver.

It took no more than half an hour for the distinctive rumbling sound of Wullie Dunne's Range Rover to pull up in the street outside. But it felt like a week to Archie. He'd bought three fish suppers. Chib had eaten two and a half of them.

Wullie tapped at the door. Chib had left it open for him but it was nice to be nice, nonetheless.

'Well, Archie ... here we are again, son.' Wullie waved a hand. Chib vacated the seat. Wullie occupied it.

'What's the script, Wullie? You gave me time off.'

'Ah did, son. That ah did.' Wullie leaned over and lifted a couple of yellowed, crunchy chips from the greasy paper of last night's *Evening Times*. 'But it appears you weren't entirely honest with me ... an' ah want tae know why.'

'Ye've lost me, boss. Ah don't know what ye mean.'

'Souness, son. Bobby fucken Souness. Ye've seen him, no?'

Archie didn't know how to respond. His thumbs tingled as if they knew their fate depended on his answer.

'There's a bounty out on the cunt ... an' ah'm a wee bit curious about that, y'know?'

Archie's imagination kicked in. 'Ah heard somebody talkin' in the bookies last week.'

'Aye. And?'

'Didnae know them, like. Ears just pricked up cos ae the name.' Archie gulped. 'They said he'd been battered.' The Wigwam's eyebrows raised. It seemed to be new information. It was also lies.

'That all?'

'Naw ... said that he'd had his thumbs cut off ... an' that...' Archie was sweating. They were playing chess. Archie needed to know if The

Wigwam *had* been responsible for the attack on Bobby Souness, or if, once again, his imagination had been busy drawing a picture. He gulped once more. 'And that it was you that done it tae him.'

There was a silence. It lasted a long time. Archie was only too aware of its significance. A new life beckoned. He loved his city, and especially the East End, but it was fast losing its appeal. He was now looking forward to waving at it fondly from almost five hundred miles away.

The Wigwam nodded to Chib. Chib left. Archie's mind raced to visions of Chib Charnley burning down Tennyson Drive. Hammering his cane into Geordie McCartney's ear using a mallet. Torturing Archie's dad. But Chib only went through to the back room.

'Look, Wullie ... ah dinnae ca—'

The Wigwam cut him off. 'How fucken long have you known me?' He wasn't angry. Wullie Dunne seemed genuinely hurt. 'Ah don't know what you think we dae here, but this is a respectable business ah've built. Souness ran up debts wi' me. And wi' other folk. He's a fucken mug punter. But ah offered him an opportunity. A way out ... for the *sake* ae his fucken kid!' Archie was confused. 'He was drivin' for me. Payin' it aw off. The same bloody job you've got now.' Wullie took another chip. And, surprisingly given the circumstances, offered Archie one too. 'One night, he's on a hire. Ah get a call ... middle ae the night. He's fucked off wi' the car an' left these big noises there. Up at The Balgarth. Senior polis, and some politicians. Next day, ah cannae get hold ae the cunt. The motor's been dumped an' he's disappeared. Don't know what the fuck happened, but the word's been out for him for months. An' now ah'm in the frame.'

It was plausibly delivered but Archie knew the next line before it was even uttered.

'So, ah'm tellin' ye, Archie. If you know anythin' about where he is, fucken tell me, right.'

'Look what ah found,' said Chib. He yanked Bobby Souness into the living room. Archie stumbled backwards.

'An' this baldy cunt was lying in the bath underneath him.' Geordie McCartney edged in, shame-faced.

'Who's this plank?' asked Wullie.

'Ah'm Geordie. Geordie McCartney, sir. Pleased tae meet you!' Geordie held out a hand.

Wullie looked at it as if it was a shitty stick. 'Ah don't give a fuck who you are, pal. It was rhetorical.' Puzzled faces. He looked at Chib and tutted. 'Dealin' with complete wallopers here!'

An hour passed, at the end of which Bobby Souness understood and accepted that his thumbs weren't packed in ice in the Dunne Driving HQ freezers.

Wullie Wigwam had a theory. But he was keeping it to himself for now.

Archie spent the hour deliberating over the envelope that was taped to the back of the Green Lady's frame. It was valuable, no doubt. But only if you knew how to trade. He didn't. But Wullie Wigwam did. Was there *really* that much left to lose?

Archie took the plunge and trailed his find.

It intrigued the bookie. Geordie McCartney was sent for more chips, the Wigwam giving him money.

With Geordie away, Archie revealed the hand they were holding.

He laid the pictures down – carefully and one by one.

Nobody spoke.

It was Jim Rockford who broke the silence:

Ah think you can trust these two fellas, Arch. Ah can tell from their eyes. They're not too far apart.

Ten more silent minutes passed.

'Where the fuck did you get these?' said Wullie finally. He'd looked at the pictures from every possible angle. He couldn't believe they were real. But they must be. They were on proper Kodak paper.

'Jesus!' Bobby Souness tried to pick up one of the photos. He gave up and pointed.

'What?'

'That's the boy ah dropped at the Royal. I recognise him now.'

Bobby Souness recounted the tale of woe he'd told Archie. Four simple minds struggled to work out what it all meant. How it was connected. And how any human's arse cavity could take a dildo the size and shape of a small elephant's trunk.

Half an hour after he left, Geordie McCartney returned.

'Who was for the *ashit* pie supper again?' He choked. 'Holy fuck!' Geordie had seen the photo. The one they had all been focusing on. 'That's the kid fae The Balgarth!'

Archie hadn't shown Geordie the pictures. Had tried to keep him out of it, given his friend's own domestic troubles. Too late for that now.

⏻

There was nothing left in Archie's larder. Even the Advocaat was finished. Wullie Wigwam had gone, but only to move the Range Rover out of the street. Now he'd come back to outline a plan. The lucrative one that had been assembling in his brain for more than an hour. Wullie Dunne lit cigars. He offered one to Chib, who took it, but to no one else.

'Right, what dae ye'se aw want tae get out ae this?'

It was a pretty straight question but one that they hadn't considered until The Wigwam had asked it of them.

After a long pause during which gormless looks were exchanged, the three answered simultaneously.

Archie: 'A shot at The Palladium.'

Geordie: 'Ma missus back.'

Bobby: 'Ma thumbs.'

Wullie looked at Chib, who shrugged contemptuously.

'Well, let's aim for one out ae three then, eh?' said Wullie.

The material that Archie had acquired was dynamite, there was no doubt about that. Wullie had suspected Heady Hendricks was into the sexually bizarre for well over a decade. A magistrate from Edinburgh had told him as much during a pro-am charity golf day that The Wigwam had partly sponsored. For Wullie, the opportunity of one last big pay day was what the contents of the envelope represented. He could get out of the game, and Chib could finally retire. It was just a pity the success of the embryonic plan rested on the shoulders of the three balloons in front of him.

'So, we've got these pictures, right?' Wullie began, Archie, Geordie and Bobby nodding in sync. 'They're worth a bundle tae the folk pictured in them.'

'Definitely,' added Archie, trying to calm his quavering voice.

'We've got them – they want them!' Wullie felt it was important to take this one slow step at a time, but not just for the benefit of the hard-of-thinking panel facing him; he was rehearsing it aloud for himself. 'We let them know we've got them, and that we want something in return.' So far, so obvious. 'When are ye meant tae be oan the show?' Wullie looked straight at Archie.

'December.'

'Ye sure? What date?' asked Wullie.

'Em…aye. Cannae remember the date but it's the first … naw, wait. It's the last week in November.' Archie blushed.

'For fuck's sake!' said Chib.

'Ah'm sorry. This is just aw a wee bit…' Archie farted. 'Ah get nervous when ah'm gettin' questioned like this.'

'Well, that's reassurin', int'it?' said Wullie. He drew deeply on his cigar then blew out a large cloud of smoke. Bobby Souness coughed. The Wigwam stood, scratched his chin and continued. 'We need tae go an' pay Hendricks a visit. We're gonnae blackmail the cunt, but no' for money. Which'll confuse the bastard. We'll do it way before the show. Let him know we've got pictures and that we know about him an' that daft fucken Heady Heights Hotel idea. That him an' Jamesie Campbell an' aw these other knobs are beastin' weans, an' that.' More smoke. He was on a roll now. 'Our demand is that your boys get through tae the Christmas final ae his show, or else we're goin' tae the papers wi' aw the stuff.'

Wullie sat back down. Chib was slowly shaking his head, as if not quite able to believe his boss was backing these imbeciles.

'While you an' the band are doon in London, we'll be back here making serious wedge on the bets.'

Wullie continued with the threads of the plan but it was important for him to know if they had all understood it sufficiently.

'Have ye'se aw got it?' Wullie said at last, looking at them all individually, including Chib Charnley.

'Aye,' said Archie nervously, before he too looked at Chib.

'Sure boss. Sure.' Chib shot Archie a look that laid blame.

Archie fidgeted anxiously. He let the look waft around him, missing its target. His thoughts swam with various possibilities. He was staggered at how relieved he'd been that The Wigwam was now in control. He felt safer, if not totally secure. Plus, he couldn't deny the excitement of appearing on *The Heady Heights* wasn't a massive adrenaline rush.

'So, how does it go then?' Wullie wasn't even looking up. He appeared to be filling in a medical prescription.

'Me?' asked Archie. Chib was the main man here surely? The one with the *real* threat.

'Aye. You. Sometime this week, eh?' Wullie was prescribing for more than one, it seemed. Archie looked closer. Betting slips. Archie had one part to play. And it was a big part.

'We're down in London an' ah go an' see Hendricks. Before the show, ah hand him a couple ae the pictures in the envelope. A sample. Ah tell him *sorry, but the rest ae these are gettin' circulated unless ye make sure The High Five win the show*. He says *aye*, the show goes on. The bets get laid. The vote gets fixed.

'An' whit if he says *naw*?'

'Ah get Chib tae phone him at the studio later that night, tae say he's a *Sun* reporter an would Heady like tae comment on pictures ae a highly compromisin' nature which had just been handed in tae him.'

'An' plan B?'

'If he contacts you, accusing you ae blackmailin' him, you say ye don't have a clue what he's on about. He gives you the gen, an' then you say it's aw down tae me. Ah only started wi' ye the week before he was in the city. Ah'm a rogue element. A lonely arsehole. Obsessed wi' the fame.'

'And?' asked Wullie.

'For seventy-five grand ye'll have me rubbed out.' Archie pointed two fingers at his temple.

'Rubbed out? Ya fanny. It's no' the fucken *Godfather*.' Wullie smirked.

Archie did too. Although it masked deepening concerns. From Archie's perspective, this plan seemed to have more holes than one of his dad's string vests. What if Heady just went straight to the cops? What if he simply denied it all and bluffed it out? How could The Wigwam even guarantee that Archie *had* been rubbed out or its *Weegie* equivalent? But when he started to ask these questions Wullie Wigwam dismissed them with the laconic waft of a gloved hand, like he was Alvin Stardust.

In the event, it was agreed that Wullie Dunne would have an anonymous contact connect with Heady immediately, tipping him off that a play was in motion. Wullie figured that an early warning would look far more professional. A threat with a forty-eight-hour expiry date might carry weight in Hollywood but not here, in real life. Chib would be the man to take care of the anonymous drop since he represented the far greater threat. And that way, Archie could feign total ignorance if challenged. He did have to appear on the show, after all, to promote the band. Chib would follow Heady home, remaining incognito, but ensuring that Heady was aware he was tailed – that the blackmail gang knew where he lived.

It initially seemed to Archie that Wullie was prepared to play high stakes for a relatively small return. But then it dawned on him. That was the key. Smallish, affordable sums leading to one bigger final sting. The Wigwam was banking on those implicated in the pictures considering themselves bullet-proof when it came to media scrutiny, and since the barons of Fleet Street and the lords of the Old Bailey also frequented many of the same 'clubs', protection did exist in the most vital of areas. It all added to a climate of care-free debauchery. Archie appreciated that Heady Hendricks was far from the only recognisable figure in those pictures who Wullie was considering extorting. In the dark perversions and uncontrollable covert urges of the seventies light-entertainment business, Archie wondered if Wullie Dunne had unearthed a growth industry.

⏻

Wullie glanced back up at the living room from the street outside as he waited for Chib to reach him.

'Ye really think this is gonnae work, boss?' Chib asked him.

'Mibbe. Mibbe naw, though,' Wullie Dunne replied. 'Thing is, there's nae fucken way five wee gadgies fae Bridgeton are gonnae get tae the London Palladium.' Chib was bemused. Wullie continued with his thesis. 'But if they can get through one round, an' we can score on the bets, then the following week's a different issue, know what ah mean, son?' The Wigwam winked.

Chib Charnley nodded. The three in the flat were probably too stupid to suspect The Wigwam's endgame. The lure of fame and financial security had blinded them, in any case. And, if, as was perhaps more likely, it all turned to shit down in London, The Wigwam and his faithful minder could remain at a distance, sauntering off into the midwinter sunset with their investment covered. Where was the risk, really?

Wullie glanced back up at the flat. The three faces stared back before hands reached around from the curtain and waved.

'Fucken morons,' muttered Chib.

⏻

'So ... what dae ye'se think?' Three Shettleston stooges deliberated. There were risks a-plenty, but the promised rewards also enticed them. The first hour of the evening following Wullie and Chib's departure consisted of the older man scribbling pros and cons for the benefit of the younger two, who largely didn't respond. The second hour saw a three-way discussion about the events of the last six months in between mouthfuls of the cold fish suppers. Bobby Souness – finding some surprising acceptance in his temporary lodgings – elaborated on the story of his last night in Wullie Wigwam's employ. All three were certain the ginger-haired boy was now dead.

By the third hour, they were back to some semblance of normality. Talking about football; about the state of Rangers. About whether Dalglish would go south or not; about whether he was even worth the half a million pounds the *Daily Record* was talking about. Reminiscing and telling jokes about workmates, about close – and not so close – friends. About Betty.

Over the course of three hours and seventeen cans of McEwan's lager between them, Archie explained the whole Heady Hendricks story. It remained astonishing to three working-class Glaswegians that they could be the principal players in a game that could ultimately bring the great showman down. Their thoughts returned to the plan.

Geordie and Bobby's jobs would be to stay in Glasgow. To help spread the bets far and wide across the city. Small amounts, initially, building to a final killing. The Wigwam would treat the direct blackmail opportunity separately. That might permit Hendricks to feel that he wasn't being specifically targeted. Following the initial tip-off, Chib was going to London alone, to lay the sting. As Archie lacked the necessary menace for such a task, his job was to play it straight. To get The High Five to the studios on time and to ensure they performed well.

'We'll need transport. Ah'm no' goin' tae London on the bus with they six dipsticks,' said Archie.

'Got any ideas, then?' asked Geordie.

'Ah dae, aye,' replied Archie. It might not have been the serving the community in the way that a probation order had envisaged, but Archie knew the very driver for the journey to London. And it would conveniently address another nagging *scunner* his conscience wouldn't let him ignore. His bladder needed emptying. He welcomed the calming reflection in the corner of his bathroom mirror.

You'll be fine, kid. You've dealt with bigger threats than this Hendricks cat. You're cool. You're made of ice. You're Jimmy Dean. You're Steve McQueen, man. I've got every faith in ya. Just keep to the plan we rehearsed and don't get drawn into anything that's not related, OK Archie? We need to be prepared, baby.

'Aye, Jim,' mumbled a sozzled Archie. 'Ah'm ready.'

23

October 1976

'Eh?'

'The Bar-L.'

'Aye? Ye got one gettin' out?'

'Aye. Somethin' like that.' The cab crawled through the developing football congestion. The driver said no more. He sensed a distracted man. Archie looked up at the imposing Barlinnie Prison gates and smiled ruefully. Archie was late. Fortunately for him, ineffectual administration at the prison held up the day's release schedule. He paid the driver and waited alongside a group of women of varying ages. The foreboding iron door slid open slowly. A familiar feeling returned to him. Guilt.

Archie Blunt had spilled a pint over another man. It was a routine bumping in a packed boozer. It happened all the time. He had quickly apologised, but something was being made of it. Some pushing, pulling; a pie in a face. Some spitting. Had it stopped there – with only the instigators getting thrown out – they'd have laughed at it for years. But Jimmy Rowntree was drunk, and insisted he had Archie's back. In an unnecessary demonstration of loyalty, Jimmy had taken his glass outside. Jimmy had waited. He stuck the glass in the face of Archie's aggressor. Five seconds of madness. Three years in jail. Reduced on good behaviour.

Archie wasn't sure what would come out of the prison gates. Regret, or retribution? He felt guilty, but only for being the catalyst. For his clumsiness. Geordie convinced him that if it hadn't been that pub, it would've been another one. It was Jimmy's hair-trigger temper that put him on a conveyor belt from school expulsion to courtroom sentencing. It could've easily been a murder. They both hoped prison would eventually sort Jimmy out. Time to find out.

He emerged fifth in line. The smallest, naturally. He looked like Jesus. Long, straggly ginger hair. Unkempt beard. Cherubic pale face. Like it hadn't experienced sunlight for all the time he'd been locked up.

With the first words spoken between them in six months Jimmy Rowntree informed Archie that he was now 'a fucking artist.'

'Conceptual, like,' he said proudly. As opposed to 'piss', Archie thought.

'Aye, OK *dude*.' Archie winced at his own use of the word. He sounded like a hippy.

The rest of the afternoon passed in a blur. Celtic won the local derby. Tension was in the air. So they steered clear of the city centre, and of the East End. They caught the shoogly Underground way up to Hillhead and headed towards Byres Road. It was Jimmy's suggestion. He'd never been there, but the inspirational art teacher who had become his guide and mentor in the earlier part of his sentence talked about it often.

It was bitterly cold. But the rain had abated substantially, and Jimmy suggested sitting outside a pub. Archie expected Jimmy to be gagging for a pint; *he* certainly was. But Jimmy ordered a coffee with a name that sounded like it belonged to a defender in the Italian World Cup squad. Fuck me, thought Archie, and then thought it again more forcibly when he saw the price. Forty-two pence ... you could get a pint *and* a short at the club for that! A fish completely out of water. It unnerved him that a man who'd spent the best part of two years in relative isolation could be more at home in these surroundings than he was. Archie carried the cup and his pint back to the outside table. He felt he owed Jimmy a future and now considered himself capable of providing it. He watched Jimmy expertly roll a fag, having turned down the offer of a ready-made one.

'So, any plans?' asked Archie. It was as good a place to start as any.

'Naw, no' really. Ah want tae catch up wi' Professor Gray. Just tae thank him for the help an' advice an' aw that. But beyond that, naw. Nothin' special.'

'Well, you can stay with me till ye get sorted out, like.' Archie heard the words differently in his head. He imagined how Jimmy might have interpreted them. 'What ah mean is, ah want ye tae come an' stay wi' me, Jim. No pressure.'

'Aye, thanks. Ah appreciate that, ah really dae.'

'Nae problem.'

'Cheers, Arch.' The awkwardness of the situation and the strangeness of the context exacerbated the significance of the offer. Both men felt it and didn't speak again for nearly an hour.

'Ye still got the van?' asked Archie.

'Aye. Thinkin' ae turnin' it into a mobile art studio. Maybe get involved with a few community groups an' that. Try an' put somethin' back into society.' Jimmy sounded like a different person altogether. Not necessarily an improved one; just unrecognisable.

'So, where's aw yer stuff. The art an' that?' asked Archie when they were in another taxi, heading back to Tennyson Drive.

'Ah flogged it aw, inside, about a year ago. The screws took stuff for birthdays an' Christmas presents an' that. It bought me fags ... an' peace. Ah wisnae allowed tae get any money.' Jimmy seemed remarkably calm about this. 'Ah'm no that bothered tae tell the truth. It got me through the sentence, an' ah can always dae more. Ah'm happy that somebody thought they were worth takin'.'

Archie admired Jimmy's sanguine attitude. There was none of the hardness Archie had witnessed on his occasional visits. None of the resentment that he'd anticipated. There were plenty of people Jimmy could feel bitterness towards – including, and perhaps especially, his friend – but he seemed uninterested in looking backwards. Over the course of the hours they had spent together since his release, Archie Blunt was forced to re-evaluate his initial perception of Jimmy Rowntree. Bolstered by this, Archie dived in head first.

'Fancy comin' tae London?'

'Aye. Why no', eh? When?' said Jimmy.

'A couple ae weeks yet.'

'Aw'right.'

'Would you drive ... an' take the van?' Archie ventured.

'Sure,' said Mr Positivity, his new devil-may-care attitude to life ignoring the pragmatic restrictions of his probationary freedom.

24

October 1976

The Circle didn't conform to many of society's accepted norms. It existed in a mahogany-lined plutocratic environment predicated on the anonymity of the Chatham House Rule. Freedom was its application – of opinion, expression and – most attractive to The Circle's members – predilection. Those who were granted entry to The Circle required three forms of personal recommendation, including testimonials from at least two existing members. The other criterion? Vast and immediately accessible wealth. In the early days of the secret organisation, location played a part. The founding members owned real estate in central London. They attended Eton or Oxford. They endured initiations and character-building humiliations to create the masters of men that they were.

Then the seventies broke, and the wealth shifted. Northerners infiltrated politics, culture and civil society. The Circle's founders resisted the trend but the tide swamped their leather Chesterfields. Even King Canute adapted once. And besides, uncouth new wealth had access. Better drugs. Higher thresholds. Rougher trades. Protection.

Scandals had skirted the edges of The Circle before, threatening exposure; even to destroy the clandestine activities. But the fear – such as it became – added to the excitement. The current investigation into the private life of The Dandy was intoxicating and frightening in equal measure. The Dandy was a founder member. Now leader of a major British political party, he was an exhibitionist and opportunist, who led parallel lives as a happily married family man and a closet homosexual. Characteristics shared with most of The Circle's fraternity. A botched attempt to shoot the man claiming to be his lover had resulted in the killing of the man's dog; a far worse crime in the eyes of *News of the World* readers. The Circle provided understanding, support and the highest level of connection. Up to a point. The Dandy was in danger of going beyond that point. He was too open. Too outré for the old guard. He'd been cast adrift. A fate that might well now await Heady Hendricks.

An extraordinary meeting of the Senate had been called. Its subject matter was far from extraordinary, however.

'Gentlemen, can we call to order please?' There were ten such 'gentle' men in attendance. More than adequate for a quorum. No strangers here. Still, real names were never used. Heady Hendricks, The Entertainer, was standing beside the fire. He swilled brandy in a glass the size of a goldfish bowl. Rotating the glass. Cupped it in the palm of a tense left hand. Hiding a barely detectable tremble. The Fixer, Vince Hillcock, stood on the other side of the fireplace.

A bell sounded. Double doors opened, and two young women entered the smoking room. Tight blouses. Fishnets and spiked heels. Short skirts. Painted smiles. All in black. All as instructed. They topped up glasses. Lit cigars. Dimmed lights. They had their bottoms patted or felt by almost everyone in the room. All habitual routine. It was 3 a.m. Time to address the purpose of the midweek gathering.

Eight dinner-suited members sat in their high-backed burgundy leather armchairs, adjusting their cummerbunds. They'd been called to the Mayfair eyrie from various parts of this sceptred isle. They were The Circle, in a circle. Clockwise from Vince, the others were The Scotsman, The Judge, The Inspector, The DJ, The Surgeon, The Magnate, The Actor and finally The Cleric. Two were serving members of Her Majesty's government. One had won a Best Actor Oscar. One had operated on several members of the royal family. Another had raised substantial funds for the hospitals in his region by running marathons. One had advanced stages of multiple sclerosis. And one had promoted an idea to eradicate homelessness in his home town by the end of the decade; a laudable idea for a socialist.

No minutes were taken. No notes written in code or confirmed agreements or decisions for absent members to inspect. A file rested on the glass table. The file was the problem. Its very existence had broken a central tenet.

'A difficulty has manifested itself,' said The Entertainer.

'...That affects us all?' asked The DJ. His carelessness had risked exposure on many occasions. He enjoyed the *Schadenfreude*.

'Not necessarily,' said The Fixer.

'So why the worried faces, hmm?' The Surgeon had a way of making a question seem simultaneously reassuring and threatening. The Surgeon was the oldest present. Only The Fixer was yet to reach fifty. The Surgeon had seen it all before. Stiff upper-lipped calmness personified.

'It's a blackmail proposition,' admitted The Entertainer. Expressions remained impassive. Few hadn't faced a similar awkwardness at one time or another.

'Well,' said The Surgeon. 'Take care of it then, hmm?'

'It's a little more complicated than normal,' said The Fixer.

'Explain,' invited The Surgeon.

The Fixer inhaled deeply. The Entertainer looked down. The Scotsman sunk deeper into the luxurious folds of his armchair.

'Photos and notes were taken,' said The Fixer, before adding, 'Stolen.' He paused. 'Private photos.'

'Yes. Hmm.'

'Incriminating photos, taken from the Northern Initiative file.' The Fixer looked at The Entertainer and then at The Scotsman. 'The ginger boy, the one we talked about before ... he's in the pictures.' There was no physical evidence of it, but the collective mood had cooled. As if the fire had suddenly gone out and chilled air was being forced through the Dickensian floor vents.

'Do we have proof that these people actually have them, hmm?'

'No,' replied The Fixer. 'Not as of yet, but the caller described the content quite accurately.' He shot a brief glance at The Scotsman, desperate to drop the fat, useless bastard right in it.

'And how did they get … loose, hmm?'

'We're not sure,' said The Fixer. 'A break-in, perhaps.' He was trying to shield The Scotsman's stupidity from the others, although he still wasn't sure why.

'Well, that does change things a bit, hmm?' The Surgeon was containing his anger. They were gentlemen, after all, not football hooligans reacting to a wrongful sending-off. 'And is the situation with the ginger boy now contained?'

'Yes,' said The Fixer. 'My men dealt with it. They picked him in front of a hospital. No one else saw him. We sent a message … via the driver. He won't be driving anywhere soon, that's for sure.'

'If he goes to the police, we'll intercept him.' The Inspector's calmness relaxed everyone.

'Dispose … just in case, hmm?'

'Already in play. He's gone to ground but I've got ways to flush him out.'

It was wrongly assumed that the meeting had been called to discuss progress on the Northern Initiative. Possibly with appeals to inject yet more cash. Most knew from their own fields of expertise that initial estimates rarely proved accurate.

The Northern Initiative had initially divided opinion within The Circle. It was The Scotsman's concept. And it was an intriguing one. He had prophesied that social deprivation caused by the government reaction to the 1973 banking crisis would see more and more people on the streets. Bleeding-heart liberals were making reputations with more documentaries like *Cathy Come Home*. The Scotsman had hypothesised that any ventures proposing to address this issue would be universally lauded. And thus he had drafted the Northern Initiative: a revolutionary plan to lift young, destitute men up from the mean streets of Glasgow, feed and clothe them in a refurbished building known as the Great Eastern Hotel and then have the members of The Circle and their acolytes use them for sex. The members who had once lambasted the entry of the crude northerners into their comfortable English Gentlemen's club, now saw this idea as going some way to addressing the decline in standards. The Scotsman's argument acknowledged the poor light in which politicians were viewed. Light-entertainment figures, on the other hand, were untouchable. A national children's television personality had recently been caught naked in the basement of a house belonging to an adult film star. His face was covered in so much white powder that he looked like Marcel Marceau. The public refused to believe that the hand that operated the country's best-loved puppet had also been knuckle-deep in Penis DeMilo's arsehole. The Fixer buried it. The Puppeteer survived. If the Northern Initiative was fronted by a public figure like Hank Hendricks, then The Circle could abuse, fuck and even exterminate the roughest of local trade with total freedom. The Circle had come to view it as an enlightened proposition.

'Who has the material now, hmm?'

'We're not sure, but local word suggests it's the man who provided us with security in Glasgow. A small-time bookie.' said The Fixer.

'That wasn't the cleverest of appointments, hmm?'

'These things are always a risk. You all know that.'

'I think a question has to be asked,' said The Magnate. 'Why were these photos taken from the safe-deposit box in the first place?'

The Scotsman knew this was coming. Beyond his own ego-driven hubris, he had no acceptable answer. Those private discussions held with the potential investor in The Scotsman's inner sanctum could easily have progressed without his compulsive desire to show off. He could well be blackballed for such a breach.

Providing photos such as these were a key requirement for any member of The Circle. They agreed to be captured on film in situations that would lead to criminal charges if discovered. This maintained the trust and equilibrium in the group. It was a form of mutually assured destruction that all involved understood. The Scotsman had abused a privilege and disclosed them to an outsider along with the Northern Initiative files. It was his failure, not that of The Entertainer.

'We'll return to that later, hmm?' The Surgeon's stern tone withered The Scotsman, making him feel childish and foolish. 'Meantime, what do they want? The usual, hmm?'

'No. Surprisingly,' said The Fixer. 'They seem to want fame.' He was still bemused by a demand that did not appear to be motivated by substantial financial gain.

'Don't we all, darling,' said The Cleric.

Titters filtered through the smoke.

'Well ah think we should hold out. This isn't our mess. Fuck 'em, ah say.' The DJ's rough cackle irritated those present.

No surprise, there. Many times, The Fixer had fixed it for The DJ to escape the front pages. His lack of affinity concerned all in the room. If they had no shared respect, no trust and understanding between them, then what was The Circle for?

'Is anyone else involved?'

'We think someone may have stolen the material,' said The Entertainer. It seemed such an obvious conclusion, but confirming it outright would've merely cemented the incompetence and culpability of those who were there when it was lost.

'There's also a young journalist. Scottish, a female,' The Scotsman injected. He had spotted an opportunity to mop up a few recurring annoyances with the one broom. The Entertainer glared at The Scotsman. Maintaining clarity for the assembly was proving to be hard enough.

'Specifics please, hmm...'

'The manager of those five young boys...' Puzzled looks. The Entertainer started again. 'There's an act ... rough young boys, five of them as a singing group ... on *The Heady Heights*,' he said. 'Their manager may have taken the material.'

Eyebrows were raised at this. None of the southerners had watched the programme, and Heady had to explain its premise regularly. 'They want to get to the Palladium show,' he added, to widespread apathy.

'Then let them,' said The Surgeon. 'But then you fix them, hmm? And not a re-run of that absolute fucking shambles with the unfortunate Mr Scott, hmm?' The Fixer bowed his head. 'No more family pets sanctioned, please ... hmm?'

'No sir,' said The Fixer. 'We have a new contractor.'

'One that can shoot straight this time,' said The DJ, sarcastically.

The Fixer imagined fixing this long-white-haired Yorkshire bastard to an upside-down burning cross. And then pissing on him as his blackening flesh stripped from the bone. It was a dream he was having more regularly.

'I can take care of it,' said The Fixer, glaring at the DJ. 'We just wanted everyone to be fully aware of the current situation.'

'Get the photos and the papers back, hmm? We don't care how you do it, hmm … but do it. Properly, hmm?' No further words on the subject were solicited. 'How is the Northern Initiative coming along, hmm?'

'Adequate progress,' said The Scotsman. 'Praise an' support from the media, thanks to The Magnate … an' strong protection being provided by The Inspector. Ultimately, when all's said an' done, nobody really cares about these poor spunks. They want them off the streets an' we're doin' that,' he said, to a round of *hya-hya's*; it was as if a favourable Budget was being delivered. 'An' the ones that surface further down the Clyde … well, folks probably think that's just the saps that didn't get intae the Heady Heights Hotel.'

'A special report in the papers last week called for even greater investment … for more Heady Heights Hotels to open up,' said The Fixer.

The assembled tipped their foreheads in the direction of The Magnate. If you could control the media, the police and the judiciary and make them compliant, what vices couldn't be satisfied? What then would be beyond the reach of The Circle?

'OK, enough of the business, can we get down to the entertainment, hmm?'

'Yes, let's,' said The Cleric.

A bell was rung. The Cleric disrobed, and the others removed their jackets. As they did so, The Scotsman prompted The Surgeon, who then drew The Fixer closer and whispered to the hidden side of his face. The briefest of nods was noticed by The Entertainer, whose left hand began to twitch ever so slightly. It felt like he was being excluded.

A troupe of naked young men from the Piccadilly main drag were marched in. They carried silver salvers bearing long lines of cocaine. They were blindfolded. The Circle chanted their oath.

25

October 1976

She had been very lucky. An ambulance on its way to the new Monklands Hospital had approached the bend ten minutes after the crash. The Mini was on its side, and the coach driver and several passengers had righted the small car with Gail still seat-belted into it. The ambulance crew admonished them for this, but thankfully no spinal damage appeared to have occurred. Astonishingly, given the speed the Mini was going when Gail lost control of it, a fractured ankle was the most serious damage she suffered. She also had painful facial bruising and a twisted wrist and was kept in hospital for four days. The car was written off, and with it Gail Proctor's resolve to pursue Big Jamesie Campbell further. It was utterly pointless going to the police with the bigger story, especially as the coach driver confirmed to them that no other vehicle was involved in the accident. She'd simply taken a notoriously dangerous bend a bit too aggressively. But if being run off the road was a pointed message, it was one Gail fully intended to heed.

She'd kept her head down and barely left the flat for a month after the cast had been cut off. She felt her novel was progressing well. With the working title *Songs for a Funeral*, it was an intense study of a professional man who had turned himself in to the police having killed a controversial right-wing politician, leaving the body to be found in the boot of his car. Not so much a whodunnit, as a *why*dunnit, she'd told an impressed Mrs Hubbard. The old woman regularly pleaded with Gail to get in touch with her mother, just to let her know she was fine. But Gail thought Mrs Hubbard was the only confidante she needed now. Gail rehearsed with the old woman her novel's shifts in direction, in tension and in emerging plot. Mrs Hubbard adored Agatha Christie's books. Gail booked out audio-cassettes of the crime writer's work and they spent evenings listening to them, Mrs Hubbard's ginger cat curled up at Gail's feet.

Gail descended the stairs carefully. She still walked with a limp. Still required the cane she'd brought home from the hospital. She was supposed to visit her doctor, but she wasn't registered with one.

Out in the Sunday morning sunlight, people strolled along the road to the big church at the end. Its bell rang, summoning them, and irritating any agnostics in the tenements who were trying to get some extra hours in bed. A pub and a newsagent bookended the church. Gail went into the shop, picking up the Sunday papers for her and Mrs Hubbard. Gail also selected some chocolate for herself. It would be a reward for completing a particularly difficult chapter. The central tenet of her book – the protagonist's motivation for the crime – had been tough work. But she'd cracked it, and last night it passed the old woman's scrutiny. Gail could see the rest of the book panning out more easily. The corrupt politician's ruthless pursuit of personal gain and his attempts to silence those who probed too closely was simply a way for Gail to express her personal frustrations. She knew this. It was pointless denying it to herself. But it made more sense to pursue a fictional prey than a dominant, protected, real-life one. The 'accident' had highlighted the foolishness of facing down an advancing tank, armed only with a whistle and a pea-shooter.

She walked home against the flow of the God-fearing, well-dressed worshippers, low-lying sunshine casting a long shadow behind her. The bells rang. She clambered awkwardly up the stone stairs and chided herself for having left the close door open. Trying to shut the door behind her, she dropped her cane. With the door closed, the sound of the bells outside was replaced by weeping coming from above her. It grew louder as she rose. It was Mrs Hubbard. She was at Gail's door.

'What is it, Mrs Hubbard? What's wrong?'

'Oh, my dear God,' she sobbed. 'Annie … what've they done tae ye?'

The old woman stepped back. Gail saw the lifeless cat, impaled on her doorframe by a foot-long serrated knife with a rusting blade. The cat's blood had dripped down the wood and was starting to make a thick red puddle on the concrete outside her door. Gail had only been away for twenty minutes.

⏻

'How could anybody dae this tae a poor wee thing?' Mrs Hubbard sobbed. She sipped the brandy as Gail talked quietly to the young WPC.

Gail's reluctance to deal with the police on any matter had to be overlooked this time. It wasn't fair on the old woman. She deserved to think that this horrible act was being properly investigated, even though Gail had no intention of telling WPC Sherman, or her uninterested male colleague, who she was convinced was behind it.

Gail had been wrong when she assumed that the previous warning was the end of it; the only one Big Jamesie Campbell needed to administer. She was now rethinking her future. Bringing him down might be the only way to make all this cease for good.

26

October 1976

'Tell that wee bastart ah'm no' comin' oot!'

It wasn't one of Dad's better days.

'He stole ma chocolate yesterday. Ma da got it wi' the last ae his vouchers, tae.' He started to cry. 'He's a wee bastart, so he is!'

'Mr Blunt?' Carol opened the door to the living room. Archie peeked over her shoulder. His dad was sat in the chair, thumping his fists on its arms. A plastic bib was wrapped around his neck; it was stained with soup from the bowl he was being fed from.

'Mr Blunt, Archie's here to see you.'

'Who the fuck's Archie? Ah'm dinnae know an Archie! Get him tae fuck!'

'Da ... it's me,' said Archie softly.

'Fuck off, ya cunt!' yelled Stanley Blunt. 'If you try and take ma stuff again, ah'll get ma big brother ontae ye!'

'Let me lift this out the way for ye, eh?' Carol carefully untied the bib and took the soup bowl through to the kitchen.

Stanley lifted his leg sharply and kicked the fold-up tray over.

'C'mon now, Da, yer aw'right.' Archie was stunned at the deterioration. His dad had seemed fine just days earlier. Now, he was like an actor playing the part of someone else. He closely resembled the man Archie knew but behaved like someone Archie had never met.

'Fuck off, you!' Stanley turned away. He faced the wall; a petulant child angry at a circumstance that only he was aware of. Archie had rarely heard his dad swear. He always displayed an even temper, even when Archie had informed him of his Bet's death. As a widower himself, Stanley's strength and fortitude were the examples that took his son through the worst period of his life. Now Archie simply couldn't process that the man upon whom he'd leaned so heavily was the agitated shell sitting in front of him.

'My God,' he said. Carol was washing the plates. Her calmness was of little comfort to him.

'Sorry, Archie,' she said. 'He didn't have a good night.'

'How d'you mean?' said Archie. The tears that had been welling in his eyes were now bursting.

'The warden caught him outside in the rain. He was in his pyjamas.'

'Fuck!' said Archie, before apologising. 'What was he doin'?'

'He thought he was goin' to work. The trams.'

It had been forty years since Stanley had last driven one. Archie's frustration gave way to anger.

'An' naebody thought tae phone me an' tell me?'

'The warden tried this morning, but he couldn't contact you. He said you had an answerphone thing an' that he'd left a message.' Archie's head bowed. 'When I came 'round your dad was still a bit disorientated.'

Stanley's distress was compounded by the conviction that he was being kept in the flat against his will; that it wasn't his home he was being forcibly imprisoned in. Carol left this detail out. She'd tell Archie later, when he was better prepared to here it. This morning had been a massive shock to him. Archie wept. Carol cuddled him.

'What ah'm ah gonnae dae, hen? He cannae stay here on his own, no' after this! What if he leaves the cooker on, or somethin'?'

Carol couldn't make those decisions for them. She could only offer her opinion. Archie knew the time had come for his dad to go into full-time residential care, but the type that he deserved cost more than Archie had access to.

'Da, ah'm gonnae go now. Ah'll come back in a wee while. We'll watch *Rockford*, eh?'

His dad was placid now; simply staring ahead. The fight had gone out of him.

'Look da,' said Archie. "'Member the time doon the water?' Desperate for some sign, some slim acknowledgment, he lifted a photo frame from the mantel. Him and his dad, on the *Waverley*. Years ago but remaining a vivid memory for Archie. There was a glimmer; a slight smile of recognition.

'Aye … that wis rerr.'

Archie smiled warmly at his dad.

'Me an' Hughie,' said Stanley. 'Do you know Hughie? Will ye go an' shout him for me? He'll be oot there kickin' a baw. Ma's got a piece an' jam made up for us. Ah'm eatin' his tae if he disnae hurry up.' Stanley tried to stand but he couldn't.

Archie stepped backwards. He was suffocating. He had to get out.

'It's OK, Archie,' said Carol. But it wasn't.

Archie left heartbroken, ashamed that he had abandoned his father. He went to The Marquis, desperate to stop the haunting sound of his father yelling for Hughie, his only brother, who had died in 1918 in one of the last battles of the Great War.

⏻

'Ah cannae dae it, mate. That's me. Ah'm done.'

Archie Blunt was broken. His eyes sunk into a skeletal face. He had barely eaten in the last two days. Geordie bought pie and chips for them, but it quickly became apparent that he'd be eating both.

'Look, Archie…' Geordie pulled his seat around the small table. He put an arm around his friend. 'Ah'll look in on yer da while yer away. Christ, ah'll even move in if ye want.'

'It's no' just that, though,' said Archie. 'This whole thing is completely fuckin' mental. Ah mean, look at us … sittin' here in The Marquis wi' barely enough copper tae buy a pint an' a mutton pie!'

Geordie looked at the handful of change he'd piled on the table.

'Goin' right square up against one ae the richest cunts in Britain … tryin' tae blackmail the bam wi' a couple ae fuckin' scud pictures?'

'It'll be aw'right…'

'Aw'right?' Archie was getting louder. He was unravelling. Fellow boozers were now watching. 'Fuckin' come ower here an' listen tae yerself!'

'Calm down, Arch.'

'Aye … fine for you tae say. You dinnae have tae go doon an' face the cunt off.'

'Right, ya prick, that's enough. Ah fuckin' get it. Yer life's pish … yer da's fucked, an' even if he wisnae, you're gonnae be a jail anyway.' Archie looked up. 'That whit ye want tae hear, is it?' said Geordie. He was leaning right in, his face almost touching Archie's ear.

The aggression shocked Archie into a silence. Geordie leaned back a bit and the interested onlookers returned to their conversations; the odds of a square go having diminished. The barmaid brought out their food.

'Ach, for fuck's sake!'

'Aw, ah'm awfy sorry, love.' The paper plate Archie's pie was on folded under the weight of the beans. It slid off, landing on his left shoe. A perfectly framed metaphor.

27

October 1976

'You shouldn't be doin' this, Sherman.'

They hadn't become friends; that would be a step too far. But Don Braithwaite admired his colleague's tenacity with the missing persons cases. And he'd come to respect Barbara's intelligence, her aptitude for understanding human nature; her ability to deal with the distraught old woman whose cat had been knifed. Don was used to dealing with the human victims of knives, not comforting elderly pet-owners. Empathy was a valuable skill for a police officer, regardless of gender. Privately, he thought she was being treated badly by the sergeant. He wouldn't speak up about it on her behalf. But he would cover for her when it only involved the odd hour here and there. This, though ... this was another level.

'I'm just going home for the weekend,' she replied, winking at him.

'And what if this boy's ma agrees tae speak tae ye? What then?'

'What's the problem, though?' asked Barbara. 'She filed a missing persons and I was asked to deal with it. Maybe if I had dealt with it properly at the time...' She tailed off. 'It seems only logical to speak to her in more detail.'

Barbara and Don knew that by dealing with it, she was being asked to tidy up the filing, not reopen investigations that were, to all intents and purposes, officially dormant. Some of these cases were more than two years old. Occasionally, a file would be taken from a box next to Barbara's desk. It would be returned later, with a red *CASE CLOSED* stamp across its front. A clipped photo of the subject, taken in the mortuary, would be inside the cover, the cause of death invariably recorded as suicide or misadventure. Barbara could then file that one in a different location. By the time the stamped copy reached her, relatives would've been informed. It didn't happen often though.

'It was a suicide. Cut an' dried. An' even if it wasn't, you can't just bloody wade in on another copper's patch. No' without permission,' said Don. He knew he sounded like a wee brother on the verge of jealously shopping a more adventurous sibling. 'Look, y'know what ah mean, right? Dodd's gonnae go Radio fucken Rental if he finds out you've spoken to a suspect in a case.'

'A suspect?'

'Well, aye. Fuck sake, Sherman, waken up, eh? Most MPs get found in their uncle's attic or buried under their da's tattie patch.' He sighed.

'But it was a suicide, you said so yourself. If the case is closed, this family can't be under suspicion, can they?'

Barbara and Don knew there was something strange about this case. A young man, understood to have been homeless, being fished out of the Clyde with a few signs that he may have been in a violent struggle. The post-mortem had detected an unusual substance in the body's bloodstream. It wasn't something the pathologist had regularly encountered. Following extensive testing, methylthioninium chloride was confirmed. Originally noted as misadventure, the death was then officially designated as a suicide. It made no sense at all. Lachlan Wylie wasn't even registered with the labour exchange, let alone a GP. So where would he get such a drug? And why would he self-administer a little-known treatment used for urinary-tract infections?

'Let it lie, Sherman,' Don had said. 'You're a good copper, but this just isnae worth the attention you're tryin' tae give it.' Don Braithwaite knew that when a suspicious case was closed by the homicide guys, it was because there was a higher purpose at work. Digging around for that purpose was not recommended.

'But nobody cares about these cases, Don. It's heartbreaking.'

'You sure it's no' just this one that's breakin' hearts?'

'I can't deny the personal interest, yes … but you'd be the same. Imagine a youngster from Tollcross Road was missing. That wouldn't get your attention?'

'Only if it was my case. This wasn't yours. It was assigned tae somebody else. Somebody way more bloody senior.'

⏻

Barbara Sherman reflected on this conversation regularly on the long journey from Glasgow up to Oban. She was headstrong, certainly. And unlike others on the shift, a bollocking from her sergeant now held little fear for her. And one from further up the division would simply prove she was right to be so inquisitive. She knew she had far more resolve than the tattooed hardmen who often crumbled in the muster room; more strength of character. If only they would give her an opportunity to demonstrate it.

She arrived an hour before the ferry set sail. She had forgotten how much she hated the five-hour crossing. There were shorter routes, but they added disproportionately to the drive time.

Once on board, the small vessel she'd always used bounced around on the volatile swells of the Hebridean Sea. A member of the crew calmed the family of a teenager who was vomiting violently as the horizon disappeared. Barbara smiled, remembering her own early voyages.

Darkness descended as the tiny harbour lights glinted through the fog. Questions jostled for attention. Would Esther Wylie be at the pier to meet her? Would she treat Barbara in the same curt way she had on the telephone? Why was she so indifferent to the strange circumstances of her son's death? If she didn't care about him, why did she report him missing?

It had been the strangest of phone conversations. Initially open, it had seemed to close down when Barbara had revealed their shared background. Attempts to understand more about where the Wylies had lived, or if Esther Wylie had known the Shermans were met with apathy, and then indignation when Barbara said she'd be returning. Well, here she was. Docked and disorientated. Home.

⏻

The following morning, a heavy grey had descended. Barbara had forgotten how quickly such oppressively low cloud cover could trigger a headache. It was as if the available air had been squeezed beyond the sides of the island and out to sea. Barbara found breathing a strain. She trembled as she approached the front door. She had checked the number with five people, desperately hoping that they'd got it wrong. She rang the bell. Minutes passed. A curtain twitched in an upper window. She noticed it. She chapped on the door this time. A proper police officer's chap. No fucking messing. The door opened. Just enough for both to glimpse into a shared past.

'Mrs McNeil?'

'It used to be.'

'Hello.'

'Hello Barbara.'

'Can I come in?'

'What good would that do now?'

'Look, I came up here to talk about Lachlan, nothing else.'

Mrs McNeil was taken aback by Barbara's directness. She had been a shy child, and they hadn't shared many words, even after the funerals of her parents. The McNeils were a reclusive family. None of the McNeil children were at school when Barbara was there. They didn't go to school at other times either. Mrs McNeil taught them at home. The blurred photo of Lachlan Wylie in his file in Glasgow was of a young man. Smiling. Taken in an Anderson Bus Station photo booth with a young woman on his knee. A girlfriend, Barbara had assumed. The investigation – such as it was – did not identify the young woman. And appropriate questions about the origins of such a personal photo appeared not to have been asked. As they sat together awkwardly in the McNeils' front room, it transpired that no one had contacted his mother in person either.

'I got two phone calls. That was it,' she said. 'One after I'd reported him gone, initially … it lasted ten minutes. And another, to tell me he was dead.'

'I'm sorry,' said Barbara, and meaning it.

'Why?'

'For Lachlan.'

'He was known as Lachie.'

'Why did he change his name?' asked Barbara. All the McNeils had changed their family name, not just the eldest son. When she lived here, Barbara had known the woman sitting in front of her as Mhairi McNeil. Esther was her middle name. Wylie was her maiden name. But Barbara concentrated on the boy.

'He left to see a bit of the place,' she said, seemingly ignoring the question. 'Why did *you* go?'

'It became too small for me. Memories at every turning. Too painful.'

'I think you have your answer,' said Esther.

'Did Lachie contact you regularly?'

'No.'

'Did you ever visit him in Glasgow?'

'He was in the city, but I didn't know where he was. That was the way he wanted it.'

Barbara was struggling. It occurred to her that she didn't know what she was trying to determine. But there was something indefinable. Esther was being awkward and obstreperous. Not because Barbara was a policewoman. Not because of the tragedy that connected them. But because there was something she was holding back.

'I never blamed Mr McNeil, you know. For the crash,' said Barbara.

Esther was affected by this. Like she'd been punched in the gut by Ken Buchanan. Barbara could see it. The older woman's resolve had crumbled.

But it wasn't true. Barbara Sherman hated Angus McNeil for what he had done. For his recklessness on the road. And for his determination – assisted by his local Catholic community – to cover it up. To shift blame. To avoid investigation. To absolve himself. Esther began to cry. Barbara stood to put a consoling hand on the woman's shoulder.

'Lachie left because his daddy was ab—' She stopped. She couldn't say it. She didn't need to. It was etched across her face. The pain, the guilt. A mother complicit in her husband's physical and sexual abuse of their children.

'I persuaded him to leave. To get away. He told me he'd kill his father if he touched him again. I couldn't cope with the thought of that happening ... of Lachie throwing his life away on such a f...' She stopped. Still mindful of the sins. She wiped her eyes. Composed herself. 'On such a fucking bastard of a man.'

Barbara cuddled her. She couldn't help herself. Esther Wylie tensed. Barbara now understood the whole family's desire to rid themselves of the McNeil name. Angus McNeil had ruined so many lives. It only made Lachie's death even more pointless.

They took a walk in the rain. Past the bend where the accident had happened. Past the pub where several people had lied about Angus's fitness to drive. Up the hillside to Heavel.

Halfway there they stopped. Barbara stared at the prominent white statue of the Madonna and Child. Esther had brought her here. Neither woman could speak at first. Barbara sensed the significance.

'He was found up here,' said Esther. 'He threw a fishing rope around the top and put the loop around his neck. Perhaps the only honest thing he ever did.'

Barbara reached out, but the former Mrs Angus McNeil pulled away. She sought no condolence. Not for him. Not for herself.

28

November 1976

Jimmy Rowntree loved this van. He had sacrificed a lot for it. He bought it legitimately from an Asian bloke he met at the cash and carry. Two days later, it was suggested to him that the van was not the Asian's to sell. An argument ensued, and Jimmy Rowntree, believing he had been stitched up, took it too far. Another fight. A rehearsal for the one that sent him down. He was out now. On probation and determined to go straight. He'd rethought the art plan. Glasgow wasn't ready to be a city of culture. Building a small enterprise selling fish and chips was Jimmy's new thing.

'Need tae stay clear ae the gangsters,' he'd told Archie. 'Do somethin' worthwhile with my life, man. Somethin' for the community!'

It was hard to see Jimmy Rowntree as the Mahatma Gandhi of the batter and the breadcrumbs, but Archie saw purpose where none previously existed.

The van reversed out of the lock-up. The driver's side scraped along the door jamb. But the new damage couldn't be seen, such was the proliferation of scars, welts and bumps in the bodywork.

'Fucken magic, man! Think its fryers are still workin'?' said an excited Marvin.

'Holy Christ, its tyres are baldier than McCartney!' complained Archie.

'How's that thing gonnae get us all tae London in one piece?' Sledge was unconvinced.

'Jesus, lighten up, eh? Have a bit ae faith,' said Jimmy. Archie's dark mood was a worry. Jimmy didn't yet know the reason for it, but the thought of sharing cab space for the long drive south with him in this form wasn't an exciting prospect.

Chib's advance party had landed. With the blackmail plot now in play, the *Heady Heights* production company had withdrawn their offer to pay The High Five's travel expenses and accommodation. The Glaswegians couldn't blame Heady Hendricks for that. They'd anticipated it. The whole scam sailed so close to the wind that board and lodging was an inevitable casualty. But The Wigwam had sorted this out. Archie just had to get them all there.

Archie wandered around the van, inspecting its rusting wheel arches. In its previous lives, the vehicle had been a mobile library, an ice-cream van and – immediately prior to his incarceration – Jimmy Rowntree's home. Its future activity as a mobile food outlet was betrayed by flaking gold-and-red livery, and the name emblazoned on its side panels: The Codfather.

⏻

'Fuck sake, man … this is total shite!' They hadn't reached Bellshill. The mood had changed.

'Ye might've got the bastard window fixed. It's fucken freezin' back here!' shouted Rich.

'It's the air-conditionin'. It's aw the rage.'

'Fuck off. It's caulder than yer ma's fanny!' Despite the conditions, the teenagers laughed. The word 'fanny' always had that effect, no matter the context.

'Put the oven on, then. That'll warm ye'se up,' yelled Jimmy Rowntree from the front. The front dashboard heating fired onto the legs of the two in the front before being sucked out of the open window, bypassing those chittering in the back.

Dobber searched for an oven that wasn't there.

The radio played. It had been turned up to the maximum to be heard over the whistling November wind.

'Think that'll be us soon?' said Smudge.

'Naw,' said Sledge, abruptly.

'Jesus Christ, wish we had a bus wi' beds an' that in it,' said Rich.

'Aye. An' groupies,' added Dobber.

'Can we no' stop an' get a box ae crisps or somethin'? Tape the fucken cardboard over the window?'

'Any more moanin' an' yer goin' in the boot,' said Archie from the heated front. Rich looked around.

'There's a boot in this thing? Where?'

'He's fucken kiddin' ye, ya dobber.'

'Hey ... ah'm the Dobber,' said Dobber. Sledge leaned over and punched Dobber's thigh.

'Ah ... fuck. Ye gave me a dead leg, man!'

'Anybody got any ae the Coke left?' asked Marvin.

'Hey, lay off that stuff,' said Archie, angrily. 'You've had enough already.'

'Christ, what the fuck's up wi' you, auld yin? Aw wisnae talkin' about the powder, man. Ma throat's as dry as a camel's arsehole back here!'

Archie passed a half-full bottle into the rear of the van.

Marvin glugged a mouthful. 'Christ, that ginger's aw warm, man.' He replaced the cap, shook the bottle and opened it over Smudge.

'Fuck off, you, ya cunt!' In the front, Jimmy laughed.

'Weans, eh?' It made Archie smile too. Being miserable wasn't his default setting. He reminded himself of his own personal motivation and, as well as comforting him, it forced the naturally upbeat demeanour back to the surface. The buoyancy of his fellow travellers was infectious. Despite the antics, these boys seemed far more streetwise than he had been at their age.

The time passed slowly. They were stopping every hour, once specifically to allow Marvin out to procure something that would block up the open window. He had returned with several alternatives.The teenagers couldn't countenance being trapped in the confines of the van for any length of time. Archie had hoped they would just sleep. But it seemed Manky Marvin never did. They crossed the border into England; a new experience for all of them.

'We're blazin' a trail here, boys,' said Archie. The others responded to his lightening mood. 'Nae other Glesga acts have been big in England for years.'

'No even Lulu?' asked Jimmy.

'Ma cousin shagged that Lulu once. She was singin' at the Springboig Bowlin' Club,' said Smudge, impressing everyone.

'Gen up?' asked Rich.

'Aye. It was just last spring ... at the openin' ae the bowls season do.'

'Last spring? Ya daft prick! Lulu's had two US number ones by last spring. She'd hardly be doin' a gig at the bastardin' Springboig Bowlin' Club, would she?"

'Well, she looked like her, an' sounded like her ... so my cousin Tommy said.' They laughed. 'Tommy paid her a fiver tae. Fucked her round the side, against a roughcast wall!'

'Aye he mighta made her *shout*, but that'd've been as close as he'd have got tae pumpin' the real yin!' laughed Sledge.

'Aw, fuck sake, man ... who's farted?' said Dobber. 'Was that you, Burkie, ya dirty wee bastard?'

'Jimmy ... stop, mate! Smudge has let off a fucken stink bomb!'

They pulled over. Piss stop number ten. They had reached Cumbria.

'Fucken hell ... must've seen about twenty *Jesus Is Coming* signs on this road in the last ten miles,' said Dobber.

'Wish he'd fucken hurry up, then. Ah'm starvin'.' Rich sniggered at Marvin's expression. 'Two melted Mars bars an' five cream crackers in the back here, an' that's about it, man! The cunt could have a field day!"

A brief silence. Archie read the paper. The radio played on, more decipherable now with a stolen bread board placed over the whistling gap: 'Oh Lori' by Alessi followed by Bowie's 'Young Americans'. Surprisingly, all aboard were in favour. Archie loved that their interest in music was genuine.

'Archie. It's about time we were swappin',' said Marvin hopefully.

'Naw,' replied Archie. 'Anyway, my turn tae drive soon.'

'S'awright for you'se, man. You're up the front wi' the heatin'. There's nae fucken room back here.'

'Well, ye shouldnae have nicked that bloody surf board then,' said Archie.

'It's for ma Granda,' said Marvin. 'For his Christmas.'

'Yer no' allowed intae Shettleston Baths wi' surf boards,' said Burkie.

'It's for the auld bastard tae sleep on. He's got a bad back. Plus, it's the only thing there is back here tae sit on.'

They all laughed again. The time was passing, Archie had to concede. Slowly, but at least there was some entertainment.

Ten minutes passed before Marvin said: 'An' he fucken loves they Beach Boys!'

29

November 1976

None of them could follow the old map. They got lost. Didn't make it to the meeting place. Didn't meet their contact, Eddie Bolton. They slept in the chip van. They turned up late at Teddington Lock, at the Thames Television Studios. They smelt like prop forwards who'd been locked in a week-long rugby scrum. The High Five's new haircuts – army regulation number-two buzzcuts all round – made them look like they had just been released from Vietnam War internment camps. Despite all this, they were here. Archie Blunt's heart was vaulting around in his chest cavity. He wished all this had been purely the result of raw talent. But once he'd entered the green room, met the other acts and their various hangers-on, partook of the free food and alcohol on offer, he compartmentalised the opportunistic theft and its role in propelling them here.

That familiar sound: 'Salute to the Thames' – a loud eight-note horn fanfare, piped into millions of homes nightly and accompanied by a graphic representation of St Paul's Cathedral flanked by the Tower Bridge. It sounded like a doorbell ... if your house was Buckingham Palace. Archie felt sick. The nerves were crawling all over him, constricting his breathing like a python crushing a monkey. He was stunned that the boys seemed unaffected by what they were about to do.

He stood in the wings, glimpsing the audience through a narrow gap in a velvet curtain. The set had the feel of a theatre. Not quite as archaic as the one on *The Good Old Days*, but with a fake proscenium, nonetheless. He'd watched earlier as the props were moved around, repositioned, camera angles tested. Rehearsals without the star. Heady Hendricks had turned up with less than an hour until showtime.

The embodiment of family values was in a foul mood. Another Chib Charnley visitation, no doubt. When he went into make-up, they'd locked eyes, Heady and Archie. The Celebrity and The Chauffeur. It could've been a ridiculous Alastair Sim film. Disgust poured out of Heady's eyes, and Archie shrank into his suit. He didn't have the character to see this scam through. That glare, hurt and hateful all at once, made Archie wanted to confess. To give up his dreams. To forget about stardom and go back to the turbulent but familiar turmoil of Shettleston. But then he remembered why he'd agreed to this madness. For his dear old dad. For one final chance at a comfortable last few years for him.

The acts were congregating. Their sponsors were herded into a pen in a dark corner. The director took charge. Vast cameras were moved around like daleks.

'Customers, welcome to television's top talent show, where your votes make the acts. You saw … Tiffany Lambert, The Bucking Broncos, Pammy St John, Lonnie Lo Bianco, and Dippy & The Sticks! Find out which has won this week, on *THE … HEADY … HEIGHTTTTTS*!' Heady's voice boomed around the set.

Archie couldn't see him. He was behind a curtain, orating like some omnipotent Oz. The familiar theme tune sounded, and an army of runners and stagehands kicked into gear. The sound dipped. And then another voice. Measured. Calm. Reassuring.

'And here he is … the dream-maker himself … Mister … Heady HENDRICKS!'

The horn fanfare concluded, and Heady peeked out from behind a blue curtain. Cue cards exhorted the audience to applaud. And they did. Heady made a face. An oblique wink to camera. A complete pro. Revelling in the spotlight. He sauntered across a low stage to a set that looked like a doctor's waiting room. Armchairs, glass table, a small flight of steps in the far corner that rose up to nowhere.

'Thank you tremendously…' Archie noted the return of Heady's mid-Atlantic twang, stronger now that he was back on home ground. 'I would like to say thank you to all those wunnerful folks that were kind and gracious enough to send all those get-well-soon cards to me. I really, really appreciate those cards, folks ... an' I'd like to quash all those rumours that I'm retiring. I'm not retiring...' Heady shot a melo-dramatic sideways look to a close-up camera. 'I can't afford to, hmmph!'

There was laughter, but Archie noted it wasn't as raucous as it was when he watched at home. Archie considered it polite, nothing more.

'So, friends, let's find out who you voted for.' There was a drum roll from a band of musicians over in the far corner. 'The winner in the studio last week was...' the drum roll peaked '...the wunnerful Lonnie Lo Bianco.'

This time, the studio audience clapped enthusiastically. It was still early in the recording. Their energy and collective will to live would be sapped by endless upfills and retakes. But for now, Lonnie – a dark-skinned Latin crooner, giving lie to Heady's drive for young boys – was their champion. He bounded out from the side curtain, arms aloft like a middleweight champ. He appeared to be crying. The singer draped his arms around the host's shoulders. Heady tried to shake him off. Joked about it not being that type of show. Lifted a leg and kicked it back, Larry Grayson-style. The audience lapped it up.

'So ... Lonnie. The folks at home really, really love you.' Lonnie smiled a goofy grin. He was only twenty-four but looked twenty years older. 'They've brought you back, because they love that velvet voice of yours, lemme tell ya!'

'Thanks, Heady ... ah'm, em, jus' so grateful to you.'

Heady smiled. Sanctimonious. Insincere, despite everything. 'Well, Lonnie ... tell the folks what you're gonna be singing for them tonight?'

'Eh ... ah'm em, going to do my new single—'

'That your Decca Records single, out in time for Christmas?' Heady interrupted. Screwed Popeye face winking down the lens. Protecting his percentage.

'Yes, that's right. My Decca single, 'I'm Dreaming of a White Christ-mas', Heady.'

'Aren't we all, Lonnie ... aren't we all! Off you go and get ready.' Heady patted Lonnie on the backside. 'Here he is, folks, for the third time ... your *Heady Heights* winner from last week ... Lonnie Lo Bianco!'

Lonnie sang beautifully, it had to be admitted. Archie could appreciate a good singer, regardless of their age. It was a safe choice of single, undoubtedly. But *The Heady Heights* always played it safe. Didn't rock the boat. Didn't get too loud, too risqué. Broad appeal. Saturday-night television, fronted by the master showman. He hoped his dad had remembered the time. Archie had left notes all over the house. If he missed it, Archie would be devastated. Their big moment, lost to history forever.

Archie watched three new acts try their hardest. Heady had cloying introductory chats with supporters of each one – a brother, a boss, and an old granny. The acts themselves were, to Archie's mind, dreadful; a ventriloquist with a puppet emu, two singing nuns, and a weird troupe of Cossack dancers. Archie was convinced that Lonnie Lo Bianco and little Scottish Amy from the Glasgow heats would've given The High Five trouble, if the fix hadn't been in.

Suddenly, it was their turn. Archie was up.

'C'mon over here, m'friend,' said Heady. Archie looked him in the eye. There was menace there.

'Tell me, m'friend ... what's your name and where have you come from?'

'Em ... my name's Archie Blunt, an' ah'm from Glasgow.'

'In Bonnie *Scod*-land. Archie; what a beautiful part of the world. I have many, many friends in Glasgow. You might even get to meet some of them after this.' It sounded like a threat. Heady wore a devilish smile.

Archie suppressed the urge to vomit.

'What a wunnerful, wunnerful place.' Heady put his arm around Archie's back. Archie could feel a sharp nip from Heady's thick fighter's fingers.

'Aaah!'

'You nervous, Archie? No need to be, m'friend. You're among folks who just want you to do well. Now, tell us, who are you with tonight?'

'Ah ... Ah'm with a young band ... The High Five.'

'And are they all your boys, Archie ... a father of five?' Heady side-winked again. 'Mrs Archie having a well-earned lie down, is she?'

'Naw. No. Ah'm no' their da, Heady.'

'They're just your *boys*, then ... ah right.' A salacious wink. 'Yessir, we get you, right folks?'

The studio audience laughed. Archie felt small. He looked at this man. That star quality sprinkled its anaesthetic everywhere, so much so that, despite having seen the photographic evidence of his depravity, Archie almost doubted his own two eyes. That was charisma. It was incredible. Intoxicating.

'Here they are, folks ... it's The High Five!'

The show's band struggled with the contemporary groove of 'Hot Love'. Bogart Bridlington conducted it while wearing glittery, star-shaped glasses. Like this was all just a joke; a comedy act. But The High Five were astounding. Relaxed, cool and effortlessly comfortable with the cameras. It was a revelation.

⏻

On the journey down, when Sledge was up front, and the others were asleep, he'd told Archie about his uncle Sammy. He lived with Sammy, who wasn't that much older than him. Sammy was a *bohemian*, Sledge had said. He sold imported records at the Barras Market. And imported drugs, under the counter. He played guitar and taught it to Sledge. He tuned him into Hendrix and Arthur Lee's Love. They smoked weed and scoured the late-night AM airwaves for cool shows. They played Stooges records, MC5 records, The Sonics, The Byrds. All of Sledge's impressive musical knowledge had been planted by an uncle who cared little for the normal conventions of daily life. And Sledge was keen to follow his lead and absorb his influence. Surprisingly, Sledge Strachan shared Archie's dreams of escaping the East End through music. He and the rest of The High Five had in fact been a band for three years. Archie hearing them hollering tunefully from a window that day of the Orange Walk had been serendipity, right enough.

⏻

'So, m'friends, you've seen all of the wunnerful acts tonight. What a fantastic show, dontcha agree?'

The studio audience did agree and warmed their hands in advance of the studio vote.

'Let's see just who the audience favourite is, shall we?'

Heady announced each act in the order that they appeared, accompanied by more dramatic drum rolling. Lonnie Lo Bianco came first, and his audience reaction, measured by the clap-o-meter, was a healthy seventy-six out of a possible one hundred. Healthy, but down on the previous week. The ventriloquist, the singing sisters from Dublin, and the Cossacks dancers all struggled to break the sixty marker. Little Amy hit eighty-one; a record score for the series. All over bar the shouting. Lonnie would be heading back to his truck-driving day job, his dream of a cruise-liner gig or a Butlins summer season shelved for the time being. The High Five would be heading back to the frozen north. To the dole, and lives illuminated only by fags, booze and the odd successful accumulator at Aintree. But then…

'Little Amy, that was a sensational audience response … but y'know, folks … those bright young men, The High Five, well I can't help but think *they* are headed for the Heady Heights.'

Archie acknowledged the fix but didn't really believe it would happen. Now, he was watching it with his own eyes. The clap-o-meter rocketed up. Seventy-six, seventy-seven, seventy-eight, seventy-nine. It hovered. Time seemed suspended. The dial wavered, and then finally jerked to eighty-three. It was incredible. Archie was overcome with anxiety. The boys were nonchalant. Heady smiled. It was an act. Little Amy was in tears. Behind Archie, her mother raged at a studio-floor attendant. Archie felt faint. He turned. He vomited. Straight into Little Amy's mum's plunging cleavage.

'You fucken bastard!' she yelled at him, before kneeing him in the balls.

He vomited again. Some blood in it this time, or else a residue of the tomato sauce he'd drowned all the free food in. He slumped to his knees like Otis Redding mid-encore. Heady wandered over. Similarly raging. Archie hadn't even heard him wrap up the show.

He grabbed Archie by the collar, pointing down at him like he was a misbehaving dog. 'Right, you listen to me you fucking cocksucker. One week, one win for these dirty little cunts, and that's us clear, right? You tell your bosses that the pictures get returned, and that's the deal done. Non-compliance ... an' anybody close to you is gonna get a fucking visit from some real mean motherfuckers. You understand me, you piece-a scum?' He didn't wait for an answer, seemingly satisfied with a nod. He let go and Archie dropped again. There were suddenly no bones inside his skin.

30

November 1976

'Whatta fackin' racket, eh, Eddie?'

'Ach, its aw'right Mike. At least it's no' fucken Queen, man.'

'Queen are the bizness, mate!'

'Aye, right! Awa' an' try dancin' tae them then.'

Eddie Bolton folded the *Sun* and put it back down on the bar. He despised the right-wing Tory rag, but it was all anybody ever seemed to read down here. He made a point of only reading about the football on the back pages, which was unfortunate, because today a man who was looking for him adorned the front. Eddie drained his pint. Waited until Johnny Rotten had finished yelling and then belligerently slotted coins in the jukebox to put 'Anarchy in the UK' on again. Just to annoy Mike the barman.

'Oi, Bolton, you *cunt!*' Mike laughed as Eddie prepared to leave The Winchester with two fingers extended.

Eddie Bolton had grown to despise London during this last eighteen months. Glasgow would've killed him, and literally not metaphorically, but there was still a predictability to it that you didn't get down in the smoke. The riots on the streets when the National Front fought with the anti-Nazis; IRA bombs going off all over the place and now, everyone getting up in arms about some *daft weans* with spiked hair and padlocks around their necks having a laugh and making some loud music. *In the name ae the wee man, why can't folk just let other folk dae their fucken thing in peace?*

'Eddie? Eddie Bolton?' A middle-aged Frank Worthington looka-like in tight-fitting white trousers approached.

'Who's askin'?'

'Sorry, pal. Ah'm Archie Blunt. Ah'd hoped Wullie Dunne might've been in touch about us.' Eddie Bolton exhaled. Relieved. His uncle *had* called. He just hadn't been specific about the reason.

'This is Jimmy.' Archie ushered his shifty sidekick forwards. 'We're down for *The Heady Heights* shows. Ah was hopin' we could aw maybe crash at yours for a few days. The Wigw— ... yer uncle Wullie said it would be aw'right.'

'Ah ... aye. It's cool, pal. Anythin' for my uncle.'

Hands were offered and shaken. Pints were bought. And quickly drunk. There wasn't room at Eddie's place for all of them, but following the call from The Wigwam, Eddie had sorted beds in a hostel closer to the studios for the boys and an increasingly irritated Chib Charnley.

The three men walked towards Eddie Bolton's flat near Hammer-smith Bridge. As they approached the detached deck-access block where Eddie lived, Archie began to feel a sense of doom. Heady's veiled threats, shrugged off in the euphoria of the clap-o-meter triumph, had now built steadily in his subconscious. But they were in too deep now.

Eddie Bolton shared this compact Hammersmith flat with three women. Once assembled in the living room, they were introduced by first name only and not by their relationship to Eddie. Their respective ages didn't shed further light on this either. Archie assumed that none of the four were related by blood or marriage.

Aberdonian Martha was to be the one most affected by Eddie accepting two interlopers into their group. She was asked to give up her single room and move in with Ange and Dee-Dee, the other two women. All three were annoyed but Martha continued the protest by making a racket and scowling venomously at the new duo for the best part of two hours. Archie made a mental note not to accept a cup of tea from her. Archie sipped tentatively from the can of Guinness that Eddie handed him. A Dubliners record was playing away on the record player. Archie picked up the *Sun* with its hysterical screaming 'Revie Out' headline and read the story again. The 2–0 defeat to Italy in the Stadio Olimpico capped a horrendous year for Revie. His two-year term as national manager was about to end abruptly, it seemed. When the tabloid press takes against you, you're totally fucking screwed, the three men agreed.

'Christ on a bike, Archie ... is that you?'

'Eh?' Archie thought Jimmy was asking if he'd farted. He shook his head while sniffing inquisitively.

'On the front ... there, on the cover ae the paper.'

Archie turned it round. It *was* him. A small picture, and a narrow column, but there nevertheless. A subtle headline, for the *Sun*: 'Heady Heights Show Winner Kidnapped by Manager'.

He read out the first of the three paragraphs: "'A sixteen-year-old band member of telly talent show winners The High Five has been abducted by the band's manager. Archie Blunt (sixty) vanished from the London studios where *The Heady Heights* is recorded with the child musician believed to be in the boot of his car."'

Archie panicked. Was there a chance his dad had seen this? Did they sell a different version up in Scotland? To make matters worse, Archie was beaming a big, dopey, straight-to-camera, *get-it-right-up-ye* smile. He couldn't even remember the picture being taken, but it must've been recently. Vince Hillcock didn't hang about; had to give him that. It was a non-story; a fabrication, yet there it was on the front page. He was being sent a coded message.

'Jesus fuck!'

Jimmy was confused. He understood the basics, but the developing nuances were roaring past him faster than the Red Arrows. 'Which yin are ye supposed tae have lifted?' he asked.

'Disnae say,' said Archie, his voice quavering. 'Dinnae think that's really the point ae this though, eh?'

They had just settled at Eddie Bolton's place. There had been a warm welcome from the host, and although it would be like climbing Mount Everest in his *sannies,* Jimmy had initially assessed that a ride off the Martha one wasn't totally out of the question.

Archie Blunt was irritated. He dearly wished he could stay here longer, but it now looked like that wouldn't be possible. *Fucken bastart tabloids!* Couldn't even get his age correct. He went out to the hall and made a call to The Wigwam. If the first part of the plan had gone well, Archie could expect to tap into some much-needed financial sustenance. The High Five were now holed up in the hostel with Chib Charnley monitoring them periodically; but keeping six teenage Bridgeton tearaways in pocket money in London was like feeding the electric meter powering Blackpool Illuminations.

Less than five minutes after Archie had returned, the telephone rang. Eddie Bolton was up, catching it after only two rings. Like he was expecting the call. Archie could hear him faintly:

'Aye. What did ye say yer name was again, pal?' A pause. 'Right, hold on an' ah'll get him.' Eddie came into the room. 'Archie, it's a lad called Geordie McCartney for ye.'

Archie was stunned. How did Geordie know they were here?

'Big man. What's up?' asked Archie into the phone, nervous of the response.

'Archie, it's your da!'

(¹)

Archie left early the next morning without saying goodbye to anyone. He thought that was best. He went home in much the same condition as he'd arrived only three days earlier; hungry, anxious and *skint*, and with his possessions inside a plastic Marks and Spencer's carrier bag. He boarded a train at Euston, finding a free table seat. When no one was looking, he tore up the four 'reserved' labels. He sat back and stretched out. He opened the first of a six-pack of Strongbow. It was 6.50 a.m. His dad was in the hospital. He was stable, Geordie had said. A chip-pan fire at the old man's house. An accident waiting to happen. Archie felt sick to his stomach. If Heady Hendricks had arsonists targeting his dad, he wouldn't be able to live with himself. This was total insanity; it was his fault. He couldn't be persuaded otherwise. Geordie told him not to worry. That Archie's dad was in the best place. Cathy, the young carer had been in the flat upstairs. Thank God for Cathy, his dad's guardian angel. She'd called the police, and they'd alerted the fire brigade. An ambulance followed swiftly. The city's emergency services all combining like a gang of underpaid superheroes. Archie now needed money more than ever. He'd have to pay for regular care for his father.

He wiped his moist eyes and tried to focus on other subjects. But everything dragged him back to the mess he'd made of his life. His unfulfilled life. He thought about Bet, as he had been doing regularly of late, and of their last weekend away, in Rothesay. The wind and the whisky; the shouting and the regret. Of how things were never really the same after it. He watched as the landscape became progressively greyer and grimmer, south becoming north. Hours passed. People came and went from his table. People he would never see again, brushing lightly against him. Preoccupied with their own stresses. No one spoke to him, and for this he was grateful. The raindrops intensified and exploded against the north-bound train carriage window. Archie knew there and then that the ludicrous dream of stardom was dead. Vince Hillcock was toying with them now. The *Sun* report would be just the beginning; a humorous hors d'ouevres to tide Heady Hendricks over until the photos were recovered and they could get to work on Archie and do some real damage. God knows what Vince Hillcock might concoct next, but whatever it was, Archie Blunt was certain he would be blamed for it. It was hard to assess the article's deeper meaning. 'A warnin', nothin' more,' Wullie Wigwam had reassured Archie, over the phone. 'Just them lettin' us know *they* know, y'know?'

Archie's inebriated thoughts danced with the only two outcomes he could now imagine: the scam didn't work and they were all arrested, or the scam didn't work and they all ended up supporting parts of the new M74 flyover. Either way, his dependant dad would be totally alone.

Someone sat down. Someone familiar. Someone who did speak.

Hey, boy … when you're hot, you're hot!

'Fuck sake, Jim. Put that away!' Archie glanced over the table. Jim Rockford had slid his brown leather bomber jacket back to let Archie know he was packing.

Relax, man.

'OK, where did you get it?'

What?

'The fucken gun, man!' Archie was angry but tried to contain it to a whisper.

Oh, that.

'Aye ... *that*! You're no' licensed tae carry a gun. No' over here, anyways.'

It's for protection, buddy. Yours, not mine. Wouldn't be doin' my job otherwise.

'Just ... keep it hidden, man. Or we're both fucked.'

Ah promised Rocky ... an' yer pop. Said ah'd look after ya!

'Ah know. Ah'm grateful. Really.'

Look, what d'ya really know about the Indian?

'Who?'

The Wigwam? Can ya trust him?

'Ah think so. Don't really know though. What options dae ah have?'

A man surged through the carriage with a young, crying child in tow. Looking for a toilet. Archie stopped momentarily. He didn't want him to hear the detail of their conversation.

A noisy group got on at Carlisle; a rugby crowd. Middle-class and high-spirited, as opposed to the negative way working-class football fans would be described when displaying the same behaviour. Surrounding him. Further chat with his *consigliere* would have to wait. But he felt reassured, nonetheless. For better or worse, Archie, Jimmy and even Bobby Souness had to trust The Wigwam's judgement. The boys would be fine. Fuck, they were having the time of their young lives. Two weeks. Three shows. And then hopefully it'd be over. The fake allure of showbusiness had faded faster than a Hollywood actress with stretch marks. Although it seemed like a slim chance, if he got out of this convoluted mess with his neck intact and a modest amount of cash with which to rehouse his old dad, then he'd have thought himself lucky and recounted the exaggerated tales from bar to street to bookie for the rest of his days.

He minded Jim Rockford's principal advice, every time he left the house; to avoid the dangerous city streets, which didn't leave many. But if he was to succumb to the worst of Heady Hendricks' menacing warnings, better to cop it back in the city he knew and loved than fade into nothing in a nowhere existence. That cyclical thought sustained the optimistic side of him through the depressing monochrome of Motherwell. Strange how the mind worked in times of stress, he acknowledged.

⏻

Chib Charnley paid another visit to Heady Hendricks' Hampstead home. This was the first time he'd approached the front door. The previous information had been handed to an assistant at the studios. Chib had tracked the vehicle carrying the star back to this address three times since. It was a hugely impressive artifice. Chib looked up at the four-storey façade, part of an elaborately constructed terrace that looked like it had been built as a film set. He wondered if Heady owned all four floors and the attic space above its Palladian portico, or if he lived in one large front room and sub-let the rest. His mental arithmetic capabilities worked overtime. A substantial wedge could've been earned from that venture. Chib rang the front doorbell.

'Can I help you, sir?'

'The man ae the house home, is he?'

'And who shall I say is enquiring?'

'So, he is in then? Good. Just gie him this. We'll be in touch soon.' Chib turned and, supported by his cane, edged carefully down the slippery concrete steps. The elderly, besuited manservant took the envelope and closed the door with no indication that the encounter was in any way unusual.

Four

The Final Curtain

31

December 1976 – Thursday

Archie went straight to the Royal from the train station. His dad was asleep. He'd suffered smoke inhalation, but the ward sister was sure he'd be fine.

Archie sat by his bed for a while. It was the middle of three on one side of the ward; there were another three on the other. All of them were occupied by pensioners. The ward smelled of piss. And dying flowers. Archie had to leave. It could've been the same ward his ma had died in. Maybe they all just looked depressingly similar.

A taxi dropped him off at the end of Tennyson Drive. A worrying thought had occurred to him. Geordie mentioned that some young guys were hanging about the close entry earlier in the week. They had jostled him as he tried to pass. Encounters like that weren't that unusual in the East End, but something about this one had prompted Geordie to recall it, and now Archie had construed it to be Heady's henchmen; the thugs who had surely set fire to his dad's place. But perhaps Archie wasn't thinking clearly. Perhaps he just needed a decent night's sleep. He'd contact the attending police officer in the morning. It was too late now.

He walked slowly along the drive. A black van was parked outside his entry. It could've been the TV Detector Squad. Rumour was they were now working nights to drop in on those, like Archie, with no television licence. He waited and watched. Eventually two figures – he assumed them to be men but couldn't be certain – emerged from the close and got in the van. Archie waited for five minutes after it turned right into Muiryfauld Road before progressing. There was other movement in the street, but it was the activity around his own block that unnerved him. He saw that the light in the flat was on. Geordie would be in. He was panicking for nothing.

Archie opened his front door. It was unlocked. It was a decent close – doors were regularly left that way to allow the neighbours to replenish sugar or milk or fags in the event of a sudden shortage. Archie was knackered. Too knackered to contemplate any remaining threat lying behind it.

'Geordie?' No response. He couldn't remember the shift patterns. Geordie was probably at work. He may have successfully appealed to Teresa. Either way, he wasn't here. And neither was Bobby Souness. But he came and went. Archie was glad about that. The flat was nowhere near big enough for the four of them when they were all home. Archie and Geordie had been sleeping uncomfortably in the double bed. Top and tailing. Faces may have been at opposite ends but neither valued foot hygiene as a priority. And that still left the bollocks-and-arse interface. Jimmy had taken the bath. He was the smallest, so it made sense. Souness – when he stayed – lay awkwardly on a sideboard. It had the same firmness as the pavements he'd been accustomed to prior to the Great Eastern.

The flat was now empty, but something didn't feel right. Of the four, Geordie was the tidiest by far, yet the living-room looked like he had vacated it in a hurry.

Ah think he's been taken, Arch, said Jim Rockford, casually.

'How?'

Don't know that, man ... but ah think you mean 'why?'

'Fuck off!' Archie was in no mood for a lesson in semantics.

Lighten up, buddy. You need to think clearly. Jim picked up a small card. It had numbers crudely written on it.

⏻

Archie searched for a coin. Fumbled with the ones he found. *Fucken decimalisation.* He still didn't get it. He dialled the number from the card he'd picked up the previous night. Got a ringing tone. Then a voice. One he didn't recognise.

'What?'

'Ah'm Archie Blunt.' Archie quivered as he spoke. This was all getting way out of hand.

'Coviello, can ye do the Fandango?' said the voice. The words seemed vaguely familiar, but Archie couldn't place it, or understand why they were being directed at him.

'Mate ... ah don't have a fucken clue what that means,' he said, flummoxed.

'Two men fae Carntyne, went tae mow ... went tae mow a meadow,' the voice sang. Archie wondered if he'd dialled wrongly, getting through to an inmate at Carstairs.

The voice continued: '...only they couldnae mow, cos one ae them had nae thumbs ... an' the other yin was a baldy cunt!' The smug voice let that sink in.

Archie couldn't focus. The illogical suggestion that a man was unable to properly mow a field because he had no hair was too difficult a chasm to cross.

'Look, ya cunt ... ah've got yer pals. You get here within the hour or they're both fuckin' gettin' it, right?'

After blurting some unintelligible rubbish in response to being given the location and being informed – American TV cop show-style – to 'come alone, or else', Archie phoned Wullie Wigwam.

'Look, dinnae panic,' said Wullie, in a way that only made Archie panic more. 'We're holdin' the aces, here. You just need tae hold your nerve, son.'

'That's easy for you tae say.' Archie raised his voice, but hearing its volume, made an immediate apology.

'Just calm down and breathe, Archie. We knew this could happen. These cunts'll no' mess about. There could be collateral damage. But Chib's just delivered the final threat. Just one more week an' then we're all home free, son.'

'Fucken collateral damage, Wullie ... Geordie McCartney's my best pal! He disnae deserve tae be caught up in aw this.'

'An' he'll get his cut, for all his trouble. Just like we agreed, remember?'

'What if these guys that've got him rub him out first, though?'

'For fuck's sake, son, will ye give it up wi' the gangster talk? Ah'm fairly sure it wasn't Ronnie or Reggie Kray that ye just spoke tae.'

There was a long pause, and Wullie knew he had to step into the silent void and fill it with something reassuring.

'Look ... we've got somethin' they want. An' now they've got some-thin' that we want back! Russian Roulette, eh?'

Archie wasn't entirely sure what that meant. He thought it might've been a type of vodka. But he sensed Wullie wasn't finished, so he kept the question to himself.

'When have you tae go again?' asked Wullie.

'Ah need tae be there within the hour,' Archie replied.

'Right, so go ... get the script off them, size them up ... an' we'll take it fae there. When dae ye need tae be back down south for the show?'

'Ah should've left this morning – on the early train. Ah cannae go back there now, though.'

'So ... plan B?'

'Jimmy'll go wi' the boys tae the studio. Because they're last week's winners, he'll no' need tae be on telly, talkin' tae Heady.'

'Ye sure about that?'

'Aye. Ah know this programme back tae front.'

'So ... we're cool then. Nae worries, pal.' Wullie Wigwam might've been calm, but he was sitting on the first week's winnings. Once again, Archie concerned himself about the level of trust he had placed in Wullie Dunne; Glaswegian bookie, security chief and loan shark. The phone line went dead. And Archie Blunt shivered.

'The Kelvin Hall, driver.'

Archie's mood was deteriorating, like the weather's gradual shift from windswept drizzle to angry downpour. He put off calling the police station. That could only be a last resort.

'Ah had that Brian Connolly off the Sweet in here last week. Nice guy.' The driver was trying to lighten the mood, although, he sensed a tip probably wasn't on the cards.

'Hmm.'

The rest of the journey to the city's West End was conducted in silence. The driver found the tension unsettling. He mulled over asking what his passenger was doing for Hogmanay. The words formed in his mouth, but he kept it zipped. The rain escalated as the cab drove the last mile along Argyle Street. They went beyond the Kelvin Hall's *porte-cochère*. Archie spied a shady figure at the precise location he was told to be.

'Ower there, pal.' Archie directed the driver towards him ... or her.

The taxi stopped suddenly. Archie passed some dross through the slot. He didn't count it. Just hoped it was enough. The rear door of the taxi was yanked open. Archie attempted to project hardness, but tripped on the loose, torn fabric of the rear seat. He tumbled out. His head bounced off the kerb. Pain ratcheted up through a potentially broken nose. The door shut, and the cab pulled away, u-turning sharply eastwards. Archie looked up from the gutter, seeing stars. His jaw slackened in disbelief.

'Susie ... Susie fucken *Mackintosh* ... is that you?'

'Get up, ya fucken twat.'

'Susie?'

'Don't fucken *Susie* me, ya bastart. Get up now, or ah'll fucken panel ye.'

Archie was totally confused by the whole turn of events. When they worked at the depot, their personal interactions could've been counted on the fingers of one hand; and now, Bobby Souness's. Where others were attracted like moths to a flame, Archie was always a bit scared of Susie. There was no comfort in realising his instincts had been right. His brain overtook his nose in aching like it had just been told the theory of relativity in Latin.

'Move it. Round the corner.' Susie grabbed Archie's left upper arm. She was a slim woman, but her grip was substantial. Hard-faced; a cow ... easy to see it now. To see beyond the tits and the mascara. Why were men such myopic arseholes? So easily manipulated.

Archie had no choice but to follow, mumbling pained questions that received no acknowledgement. They reached the entry to a dark, narrow close at the rear of the Kelvin Hall. It led to one of the few remaining tenements left in the area overlooking the River Kelvin. Most of its previous neighbours had been demolished to make way for the new Clydeside Expressway. Consequently, few people now lived in the area. It looked exactly as it was: the sad and broken detritus that was an inevitable consequence in a city that now appeared to value vehicles and infrastructure more than people and communities.

Archie and Susie moved swiftly now, she propelling him through the ground floor of the close entry, through the back court, past the rodent-infested middens and into the redundant railway arches behind. Only one arch was occupied. Susie Mackintosh pushed Archie Blunt towards it. He opened the rusting corrugated door. A man was inside. Heavyset, bearded. Sitting at a desk with a small lamp on it. Drinking tea from a mug. Reading from a newspaper that had Archie Blunt's smiling picture on its front page.

'Jesus, Suze … did you dae that tae him?'

'Naw. The plank fell out the fucken taxi. Stuck one right smack on the kerb!' Susie's stern face creased, and both laughed uncontrollably at Archie.

Archie wiped the blood on his sleeve. The flow had stemmed, but he was sure the crusting dam forming inside his nostrils could burst at any minute.

'So … you're *Mister* Susie, then?' said Archie. This was a conundrum. Was he pleased that his life wasn't being threatened by brutal fire-raisers on the Vince Hillcock payroll? Or dismayed that this Mackintosh family opportunism was just a coincidental starter before the inevitable main course?

'Naw … naw, please. Nae fucken more. Ah dinnae fucken know anythin' … ah'm fucken tellin' ye. Ya bastart!'

Archie looked to his left. These tortured wails were coming from a side room in the darkness of the vaults.

A crack, and then: 'AAAAAAAHHHHH! … ya fucken cunt, ye!

Stop. STOP!' Familiar screams, but not those of Geordie McCartney. Not unless they'd cauterised his vocal cords first.

'It's like this,' said Mackintosh. 'There's nae big trip here. It's aw about the money, plain an' simple.' He slurped from a mug. Archie noticed a tiny kettle. *PG Tips, appropriate for a fucking chimp like him.* 'So, the baldy boy ... he's been dippin' my missus.'

'What's that got tae do with me?'

'Well, he's got tae pay!'

'An' what about her? Ye gonnae skelp her about a bit too?' asked Archie. 'Or is she part ae the scam?' Bravado had overtaken him. It was this parallel life he'd been living since those boiling days of summer. He didn't recognise himself anymore.

'You a gallus cunt, pal? You want tae take me on here?' Mackintosh stood. Trying to make himself seem bigger.

Susie lit another cigarette. Archie noted that their menace seemed fragile. Amateurs. Just like him. It didn't prompt any alternative options for him, but it did make him confident that no lives were in danger from these opportunists. Everyone was on the make. Blackmail was the only game in town. It was like a cheap soap-opera script gone awry.

'Ah don't know what ye mean by "the money"?' said Archie.

'You're on the fucken telly, pal. An' the front page ae the *Sun*. You're a celebrity. Rakin' it in, eh? Ah want the winnings ... or else?'

Archie surprised himself by pondering aloud, 'Or else what?'

'You're gonnae pay me five grand, or Yul fucken Brynner's out on his arse at the Corporation ... an' the wee gadgie loses more fingers.'

Susie stood suddenly. 'Five grand? We agreed on ten, Benny!'

'For Christ sake, Susie ... ah told ye no' tae use my real name!'

'What? He fucken knows us! Ah worked wi' him on the buses.'

A domestic argument seemed imminent. The tuppence ha'penny scams directed at dopes like McCartney and all those other desperate middle-aged men with frigid wives just about covered the rent. But since Susie had been fired from The Balgarth for cheating the punters, things had been tougher. This was a potential retirement fund; a nest egg. Unfortunately, they hadn't thought it through properly.

'Ten grand is just bein' fucken greedy, hen,' said Benny. 'We wrote a list, remember ... telly, fridge, a week at Blackpool, somethin' for the boys ... the bookies.'

'You didnae have tae suck a pile ae stinkin' boabys, though did ye?' She turned to Archie, taking control. 'It's ten grand. An' ye've got a week tae get it!'

Some deductions could be made from this. That Susie Mackintosh was a Glasgow Corporation piranha. That Geordie McCartney wasn't the only mark led penis-first into Susie and Benny's honey trap. And that they – like everyone else in this freezing cold, brick-vaulted chamber – were totally and completely out of their depth.

'What about Souness?' asked Archie. He cared far less what happened to him, but since he'd been lifted from Archie's flat, a strange form of collective responsibility enveloped him.

'Who? The thumbs? He's just extra security. If ye don't dae whit ah'm gonnae tell ye tae dae, he's headin' fur the deep water in a bag wi' nothin' but a tonne ae bricks for company.' Benny took his right hand and inverted the thumb, like a Roman emperor at the Colosseum.

'Fuck sake.' Archie sighed. He had enough problems without having to deal with these comedians.

'Aye, fuck sake,' echoed Benny. Believing he held all the aces.

'AAAAAAAAAAAAHHHHHHHHH! Jesus fucken Christ, man.' The sudden terrifying noise from the other room visibly jolted both men. Susie Mackintosh hid it better.

'Right. Whit's yer plan, then?' Archie was up the Clyde without a paddle-steamer; bent police and gangsters to the left of him, sex-obsessed light entertainers to the right. Stuck here in the middle with Mr and Mrs Mackintosh.

'The money, the fi— ... the *ten* grand in used bank notes, In a suitcase. In a left-luggage locker at Central Station, by next Sunday ... or the wee yin'll be deid before the *Morecambe and Wise Christmas Special*.'

'Look, ye need tae listen, son. There's nae prize money for the show. It's just about the opportunities that come fae it. Where ah'm ah gonnae get ten grand, eh?'

'Ah don't fucken know, dae ah? That's what you need tae work out. Aw ah care about is the dosh.'

Archie needed to get back to Wullie Wigwam. He'd know what to do. He was the type of *gadgie* who could have got off the *Titanic* by persuading some poor cunt to carve him a lifeboat out of fragments of the iceberg.

'An' one final thing. You go tae the polis an' both ae them are gettin' it, obviously.'

'*Obviously.*'

'Don't get fucken fly, ya cunt. There's other ways ah could've gone here.'

Benny Mackintosh ushered Archie towards the side door. He pushed it open. Through the gloom, Archie saw a bearded man hanging upside down from a meat hook by feet tied together with heavy rope. Bobby Souness. He was naked. Four large, angry red blotches pockmarked his dirty, pale skin; three on his torso and one on his thigh. A young man stood to the left-hand side holding a bag of American baseballs. He casually lobbed one to another man, who rattled it straight at the hanging man. It hit him right in the balls.

'AAAAAAAAAAAAAAHHHHHHHHHHHHH! FUCKEN BAST— AAAAAAAHHHHHH!'

'See that, Da? Ah'm gettin' fucken good at this daft game. Have Scotland no' got a national baseball team?'

'Fuck sake,' said Benny. 'Dealin' with fucken morons, here! Now he knows who *you* are tae!'

'Sorry, Da!' said the pitcher.

'Jesus Christ!' sighed Benny.

He pulled Archie back into the main shed. With the heavy door closed, Bobby Souness's screams became muted whimpers.

'Where's Geordie?' said Archie.

'Never you mind that, pal!' Archie turned to Susie.

'So, yer dain' it, right?' asked Benny.

'Look, there's nae need for all that surely,' said Archie, nodding backwards.

'Just a bit ae harmless fun for the boys. Yer dain' it?'

'Aye.' What else was there to say at this point? Archie needed to be somewhere else. 'Aye. Right.'

Archie got up and left. Geordie McCartney would be tied to a heating pipe at Susie and Benny's place, no doubt. He was sure their imagination would've stretched no further. He headed for an emergency meeting with The Wigwam. The rest of his mounting considerations would have to wait. At least the angular stair-rod rain had abated, and the sun was back out to play.

32

December 1976 – Friday

'Where's the big yin? That *Manky* cunt?'

Chib Charnley was annoyed. His loyalty to his boss was being sorely tested. He was being forced to trail around a city he didn't know well and disliked more. His hip felt like it was making a play to burst out of its socket. And worst of all, he was being expected to shepherd six short-attention-span idiots – and a kilted ex-con – around the edges of their own individual social parameters. He fixed things, collected debts and occasionally threatened a battering or two. It had been a while since he'd administered one, but in doing this impromptu head count, he now desperately wanted to hand out six simultaneously.

'Fuck knows. Haven't seen him since the start ae the week. Marvin's a free spirit; he does what he likes. He's maybe got a burd,' said Sledge.

'What, in the space ae two days?' said Chib.

'Fuck sake, grandad. Lighten up, eh?'

Neither the boys nor Jimmy could remember the last time they'd seen Marvin. He'd been at the studio for the first show. Dobber had seen him heading outside with the young girl who brought trays of food to the green room. But he didn't reappear after the recording, or when they'd all been preparing to leave. Chib questioned them further, but all he received in response was apathetic shrugs. Chib imagined taking all six of these disrespectful gadgies out with one rotational swing of his cane.

'Switch that fucken telly off, an' listen tae me,' he ordered.

'Gonnae just gie's a wee minute,' asked Sledge. 'These guys are fucken brilliant. Let us watch it, eh?'

Chib Charnley breathed deeply. The tiny television set with the flickering picture showed a middle-aged man in a grey suit with a sheaf of papers, struggling to keep pace with eight youngsters all dressed like the Guy on Bonfire Night. The four in the front row were seated, the four behind standing. A potent mix of attitude and boredom. Their hair was outrageous, their language was atrocious. It was a live television interview and it was teatime. Chib focused and listened. Not much shocked him, but this did.

'Well keep going, chief, keep going. Go on, you've got another five seconds. Say something outrageous.' The host of this primetime current affairs show was goading these kids. Encouraging them.

'You dirty bastard!' said one seated at the front. The others behind him laughed. The host did too but he was losing control.

'Go on, again.'

'You dirty fucker!'

'What a clever boy.'

'What a fucking rotter.'

'Well, that's it for tonight. The other rocker, Eamonn – and I'm saying nothing else about him – will be back tomorrow. I'll be seeing you soon, I hope I'm not seeing you again. *From me though, goodnight.'*

The closing music and credits ran. Chib and Jimmy were stunned. The boys were exhilarated. As if they had just glimpsed a future they never knew could be theirs.

'Fucken hell,' said a breathless Sledge. 'Ye see that there! That's was fucken outstandin', man.' There was a glint in Sledge's eye. Chib knew what he was thinking. It was as if the youngster had twigged the grand plan. With Wullie's instructions for the second show still fresh, Chib could use The High Five singer's mischievous demeanour to their collective advantage.

'Stay here,' said Chib. 'Ah need tae make a quick phone call an' then ah'll be back. We need tae talk.'

⏻

The large double doors opened, throwing sharp and sudden light into the dark interior.

'Mr Hillcock to see you, sir.'

'That's fine, Albert. Leave us.' Vince Hillcock walked into the most private space in Heady's life. A space that no one beyond Albert was ever granted entry to. But this was an emergency. The doors closed. Heady waited until Albert would have reached a different floor.

'What the utter fuck is happening here, Vince?' shouted Heady.

Vince was disorientated. He'd known and represented Heady Hendricks for more than a decade yet knew nothing of Heady's true love: Hornby railways. He looked at his client, standing in the middle of the largest and most elaborate model railway set he could've imagined. It filled the entire room; a room capable of hosting a small wedding. Heady was wearing what looked like a conductor's uniform, complete with hat and whistle. Vince edged forwards, marvelling at the incredible detail assembled in front of him. As he did, he saw that Heady was wearing nothing below the waist. A big, dangling cock hung down below his shirt front. The only light was provided by minute spots located on the black ceiling, which resembled a blanket of stars shining down on the night-time papier-mâché countryside. Vince was grateful for its small mercies.

'We've got it under control, Heady,' said Vince.

'With all due respect, no, you fucking don't!' Heady was livid. He was still highly suspicious of Vince. The dynamic of their relationship had shifted since that night in Mayfair. 'These Glaswegian motherfuckers are running rings around you. Do you know I had one of 'em at the door, hassling Albert? Making demands.'

'We're dealing with it, calm down.'

'You cheeky little cunt!'

Heady was on the verge of spontaneous combustion. He lifted an engine and threw it across the room. It was still harnessed to three carriages. Heady's incandescent rage was being fanned by the fear that The Circle had instructed Vince to sanction him. All that whispering at the recent meetings. It was happening more often, but Vince was evasive when Heady probed him about his suspicious side chats with The Surgeon.

'I brought you into this group. I put all that money and influence and power in your fucking pockets, you ungrateful little shit!'

'I'm not ungrateful. I'm *very* grateful … but you need to remain calm. This is a betting scam, nothing more. It's about money for them – and not even yours. They only wanted exposure on television. They wanted you to fix a shock win one week, and then a major loss the next. Think about it, Heady. Do what they ask, an' we'll get the files back, I'm sure of it. If there's one thing I know about, its people. Especially desperate ones. I've got this.'

Heady bent down, pulling his underpants up in the process. He crawled out from under the painted plywood world. He took Vince's arm and they left the room.

Back in the bright daylight of the upper sitting room, Heady apologised for his tantrum.

'No need, man,' Vince assured him. 'I understand the stress all this is putting you under.'

'That fat Scotch bastard an' his necrophilia fantasies. It's a fucking step too far, Vince, it really is. I told everybody it had to stop. I'm all for free expression, you know I am, but we have to have some boundaries.'

'I know. I've had a word with him. It won't happen again.'

'It *can't* happen, again!' Heady's hand was shaking. The whisky in his glass was spilling over the rim and onto a white sheepskin rug. He didn't seem to be aware of it. 'What he must fucking realise is that it's my name on that bastard building, not his!'

'Heady, we're following these kids everywhere. We've got one of them held until this is all over. And I've got the papers running the cover story that Archie Blunt kidnapped him. We know where they all live. If the material doesn't come back to us after this weekend, there's nowhere for them to hide that we won't find. You *know* this.'

Heady was finally calmed by Vince's reassurances.

'And if it did come close to you, Heady, well we've got the Daryl.'

Heady knew it would be an admission of defeat if they got to that point, but since keeping his good public name intact – and keeping him out of jail in the process – had always been Vince's brief, Heady knew that invoking it was always a possibility.

33

December 1976 – Friday

'Braithwaite, Sherman ... there's a disturbance down at the Great Eastern. Some woman shoutin' the odds. Sounds like a bloody domestic again. Get down there, sort it out.'

The desk sergeant had spoken. It was pointless to argue. Don Braithwaite was annoyed. Being partnered with Sherman meant his own career was stalling. He was beginning to understand how Barbara felt, and he didn't like it one bit.

'Aye, Sarge ... right. Come on you!'

Barbara Sherman was pouring over the missing persons boxes again. Her colleagues indulged this madness. The novelty of the practical jokes had worn off, so they now had a different game. If shagging the more attractive WPCs was the subject of one type of sweepstake, making Sherman cry was another. But the chart of named competitors had been up on the wall for over six months. The prize fund was now a whopping fifty quid. Almost all had given up. Barbara Sherman was made of fucking stone, it seemed. Except that she wasn't. She regularly cried off duty for the multitude of forgotten people the files contained. She had compassion, and for more than just poor Lachie Wylie and his broken mother. She couldn't erase the memory of seeing his black gravestone on that cold, wet walk with Esther. And of knowing that his brutal father was buried close by in the tiny island cemetery. Family pride and Catholic guilt finding an uneasy compromise that avoided the one plot, the one stone, but preserved a veneer of normality.

'You can drive,' said Don Braithwaite.

'Really?' said Barbara.

'Aye. Fuck it!' Don's willingness to ignore protocol for the WPC was the clearest indication of his indignation with his gaffers.

Barbara pulled the big Triumph saloon out of the car pool and down London Road, heading west. Such was her shock at being in the driver's seat, she had forgotten to turn the headlamps on. Horns peeped until she flicked them on.

The Great Eastern towered into view. It was the type of building that seemed to expand in mass at night, like a compulsive eater. Blocking out the light; solid and impenetrable. Only the rooms around the entrance were lit, the regular inhabitants not yet returned from their daily for-aging in the city centre. Friday nights were ripe with profligate punters out after work, drunk and in love with everybody. The downward slide into hate and aggression happened around ten-thirty. You could set your watch by it. Those lucky enough to have somewhere to be, like the Great Eastern, would be off the streets by then. The others, the unlucky ones – the prostitutes, the destitute – just had to ride their luck.

She pulled up outside the monolith. A commotion was still going on just inside the main doors. Don Braithwaite stayed seated, in an apparent huff.

'Well, ye wanted more responsibility. On ye go then. I'll be right here, behind ye.'

Barbara got out, feeling unusually empowered to be walking any-where in uniform alone. She pushed at the open doors. Those involved in the scene inside froze. A mix of the uniform, the surprise of it being a woman inside it, and the disconcerting realisation of her apparently being on her own.

Barbara recognised one of them. The female.

'Fuck good ae you, hen?' asked the man behind the desk.

'My colleague is outside,' she responded, defensively. She hadn't taken her eyes off the young woman, who didn't return her gaze. She continued to stare down at her shoes.

'What's going on here?' Barbara cursed herself for using the ulti-mate police cliché. From *Dock Green* to *Z-Cars*, the opening words of every fictional copper.

'This fucken lassie is causin' aggro. Told her tae fuck off three times, an' she'll no' dae it,' said the man.

A younger, smaller man stood over the tiny woman. Barbara struggled to see the need for police intervention.

'Miss?' she asked. 'Is everything OK?'

This question took the three by surprise. It seemed to imply that the men were the aggressors, and that she might have been at risk from them.

'Fuck d'ye mean by that, hen?' The older man moved towards Barbara, the object of his anger shifting focus.

'Back away, sir,' said Barbara. 'I'm just trying to establish that everyone is fine, and that there will be no more trouble.'

'I'm fine, honestly,' said the woman. 'I'm a journalist – Gail Proctor. I'm researching a story.'

'Fucken hasslin' us, more like,' said the man. He glanced outside, waiting for the male to join them and put an end to this sensitivity bollocks.

'I broke a window, I'm sorry,' said the woman. 'I apologise. I'll pay for it.'

'Fucken right, ye will,' said the man.

'Did you approach these men and ask permission first?' asked Barbara.

'No, I didn't. The story ... the thread makes that difficult. You know how it is?'

'Well, not really,' said Barbara. 'This is a potential breach of the peace.'

'I appreciate that, officer. I'm sorry.' Gail reached into her bag. She opened her purse and counted out thirty pounds. She handed it to the older man.

'Aye, well ... dinnae fucken come back an' we'll say nae more about the windae, right?'

'Yes, right.' Gail grabbed her bag and coat and limped outside.

Barbara Sherman followed her.

'What's the crack?' Don Braithwaite was leaning against the car, smoking.

'Nothing. I've got this.' Barbara walked down the pavement with the young journalist. 'I remember you from the incident with the old woman's cat. Is this connected, Gail?'

Gail didn't answer.

'Did they do that to you?' asked Barbara, pointing downward.

'My ankle? No. That was a car accident. I got run off the road a few months ago.'

'Did you report it?'

'Yeah. But nobody followed it up. A witness said he'd not seen the other car,' said Gail. 'Guess I'm not important enough.'

'Who do you work for?'

'Nobody. I'm freelance.'

'And what's the story you're working on?'

'Is that an official police enquiry?'

'Well, it will be if you break the law again.'

Gail Proctor sized Barbara up. She didn't trust the police. Knew senior-level officers were deeply involved in the sinister activities she was investigating. Knew that a loose word to the wrong junior officer would have dire consequences. This one seemed different though. But she'd have no power, no leverage. She'd get stamped on with a state-supported, steel-toe-capped Doc Marten boot just as quickly as a young female journalist. Then again, Gail had reached a pivotal point. After the cat's killing, there could be no turning back. She had to make it all stop somehow. Maybe it was time to trust someone. Maybe it was worth the risk. Maybe.

34

December 1976 – Saturday

'What will you have?' Gail felt she should at least offer.

'A tea, please,' said Barbara, before adding, '...and a doughnut.' They looked so tempting. Sugar-coated, shouting at her. Diets were for *Playboy* models, not plump policewomen.

Gail came back. With the teas, nothing more. The broken window had cost her all the notes in her purse. She only had enough change for the drinks but wasn't going to admit that to Barbara.

Barbara was disappointed, but decided not to say anything. She examined Gail. The best way to describe her was elfin, Barbara thought. Not a word used much around the East End of Glasgow. But, nonetheless, if Gail Proctor had been listed in the *Oxford English Dictionary*, that definition would sit adjacent. She had short black hair. Piercing green eyes that darted about constantly, hunting for something, or wary of something different. It was hard to tell. She was a journalist. Or so she claimed. Barbara asked who she wrote for. *No one*, she'd said during the previous night's fractured introductions. *Freelance*. Barbara wasn't even sure what that meant in the context of a normal job that provided wages to pay rent. For food. Gail Proctor was pretty but made little of it. No make-up; worn, baggy clothes two sizes too big for her. A flat cap like an extra from the Hovis advert. It was a strange persona for a young woman in a very male city. Glasgow women wore pinnies, hairnets, lipstick applied sparingly to the middle of their lips. It was regularly said that you'd have more fun at a Glasgow funeral than at an Edinburgh wedding. Gail Proctor, from the capital city, highlighted the gulf between west and east.

'Are you married?' It was a stupid question. No ring ridges, no suggestion that her life was shared with anyone else.

Gail smirked.

'I just meant, does anyone know you're here?' From bad to worse. Coming across like a veiled threat from an off-duty copper. 'Look, I'm sorry. I'm a bit nervous,' said Barbara. 'I want to help, and I think you want me to. I'm new at this. We don't get much opportunity to get directly involved.'

'We?'

'The female officers. We're treated like servants. Kept downstairs, if you know what I mean.'

'Hmm.'

'Unless you've got the big tits and a slim waist, of course. Then you're allowed upstairs. To sit on the boss's lap.'

Gail smiled at this. Had they made a connection? Shared frustrations?

People came and went. The cafe was very busy, bustling with customers of all ages. Most heading on to the Barras Market across the street. Traders. Punters. All looking for a deal or a bargain.

'Did you file the report on Annie?'

Barbara was temporarily lost. 'Oh, sorry ... the cat? Yes, I did.'

'And?'

'Well ... it's still on file. Still open.'

'I'll bet,' said Gail, scornfully.

'Do you know more than you told me?'

Gail didn't answer. She looked away. Barbara knew now that there was more. A few minutes passed without words between them. Barbara felt it better to wait until Gail was ready.

'I'm sorry about last night,' said Gail at last. 'I really didn't mean to be so short with you.'

'It's fine. But I genuinely do want to help. I thought a lot about some of the things you said.'

'Such as?' She was so guarded. Barbara thought that unusual for a journalist. Then again, this was the only one she'd spoken to directly.

'What did you mean when you called Mr Campbell an abuser?'

'When did I say that?'

'Last night. Just before you got into the car.'

Barbara was keen to let Gail know that this wasn't an official chat, without specifically stating it. 'Look, you can trust me. Honestly.'

There was a look on Gail's face. It was as if she was calculating the risk level of every potential word. She had waited such a long time to be in this position. Two years, on and off, logging information, comments, observations. Never knowing how many of them were relevant. How many were taking her away from what she thought the truth was. It was a strange feeling.

'I think...' Gail paused and breathed deeply. And then she said nothing more. She lit a cigarette. She blew out the smoke. Side of the mouth. And then leaned back in the seat.

It would've been so easy for Barbara to have avoided this meeting. To have used her day off more productively. Only there wasn't much for a single woman far from home to do in Glasgow. Argyle Street; but the limited joys of shopping for something personal had been sucked out and spat into the gutter by Maude Campbell. There were the walks. Glasgow Green. Kelvingrove. But the nocturnal activities of the pimps and prostitutes, dealers and addicts, made them tough places to enjoy in daylight. Disassociation was difficult.

Barbara leaned forwards. 'I've been in the city for a year. And I hate it. I hate the grey. I hate the soot-stained buildings. I hate the smog that gets everywhere. Your hair, your lungs. I hate the job ... that nobody values me as a human being. I hate that no one is interested in my opinion. And I hate that no one I work with trusts me.' Barbara lifted the teacup to her mouth.

Gail Proctor's expression hadn't changed.

Barbara refocused. 'If you have any information relevant to a crime, then you need to hand it over, Gail.' It sounded too formal.

But Gail leaned down and into her bag. She brought out a notepad. She sat it in front of her, unopened. Taunting. This was a game of chess. Barbara's move.

'That for me?' asked Barbara.

'Not a chance,' said Gail.

'So, what?' Barbara was getting frustrated.

'Tell me what you know about the Heady Heights Hotel.'

'Erm, not much,' said Barbara. 'Only what I've read in the newspapers. An initiative to reduce homelessness. The TV personality Heady Hendricks is behind it, I understand.'

Gail looked around. The rattling noises from the kitchen and the counters were loud but she leaned in to whisper anyway.

'What if … I told you that it's all just a cover?' Gail was edgy. She looked over at the counter. At a man. He'd turned and was looking at them. 'Let's go.'

They paid and left. The man wasn't a threat. Just staring at the two women while waiting for his roll and chips. Barbara and Gail walked through the rain. The summer's prolonged heatwave was a very distant memory.

'Look, the Great Eastern is a front. It's a scam for rich, privileged men taking advantage of vulnerable young people, mainly boys. They get them off the streets, offer them a bed, some food … warmth, but in return for all sorts of deviant, fucked-up behaviour. They're taken across to The Balgarth Inn,' said Gail.

'How do you know this?'

'I just do. You asked for trust … well you need to trust *me*.'

'OK, let's say I do, what do you expect me to do with this information? Do you have any evidence?' Gail looked away.

'I've spoken to someone. Seen things myself.'

'That wasn't what I asked.'

'No.'

'Where did you witness this?'

'Does it matter?'

'Of course, it matters. Gail, I can't help you unless you give me something to work with.'

They stepped into a tenement close recess. The rain was lashing down. Bouncing off the street. A van drenched a group of pensioners stood stooped at a bus stop across the road. Their clamour was distracting.

'I paid a man. A hundred pounds. His wife worked at The Balgarth Inn. He got me some information.' Gail looked away. Her face reddened. 'I had to fuck him once on top of that. Jamesie Campbell...' she trailed off.

Barbara didn't know what to make of this girl. Her anxious, awkward demeanour. There was nothing on microfiche. No record. She'd never been in trouble. Then again, as Barbara knew only too well, the new Strathclyde police filing system made about as much sense to her as the offside rule. Was Gail Proctor a fantasist?

'The MP?'

'Yeah. Do you know him?'

'No. Not really. I had to drive his wife around recently. He's friendly with our super. That's the kinda shit jobs a WPC gets.'

'Jamesie Campbell takes people – *famous* people – to The Balgarth. Entertains them. Then, after a lock-in, they abuse young men there.'

'Under-eighteens?' said Barbara.

Gail ignored the question although she knew the answer. 'You know he's a fucking crook, then?'

'Well, he's a politician. Aren't they all?' said Barbara. Was this merely a grudge? A personal grievance? Perhaps Gail had had sex with a man who hadn't respected her, or paid *her*.

'Jamesie Campbell is part of a secret organisation in London. A private club. Many well-known VIPs are part of it. They pay massive sums to be allowed to exploit young kids, protected by Scotland Yard and the judiciary. Some of the most well-loved celebrities in Britain are part of it.'

'You said "kids". That's hard to believe.'

'And that's how they fucking well get away with it.'

There was a rage to Gail Porter. Barbara could tell it was always there. Constantly simmering below the surface.

'But if you're a journalist, why not run a story?'

'Because...' Gail took a deep breath '...they are protected by Fleet Street too.'

Barbara could see the frustration rising. Gail Proctor's head slumped forwards a little.

Gail was exasperated – she thought Barbara would brand her another conspiracy nutcase. She'd seen it so many times before. No editor wanted this story. Freelance was just an alternate word for unemployable. A story without facts, evidence or people prepared to go on the record was only of use to the *News of the World*. And they didn't smear the establishment; only those fallen, or without the means or the mentality to defend themselves.

'Who do you think butchered that poor wee cat? And they almost killed me by forcing me to crash my car.'

Gail was angry. She'd tried to walk away from Big Jamesie Campbell's world, but after Annie the cat had been killed, she knew proving his complicity was the only way for her to leave it all behind.

Her breathing grew heavy. 'Jamesie Campbell killed my uncle.'

Barbara leaned in. Gail had whispered it. It was barely audible in the clatter of diesel engines and barking dogs and loud Glaswegian patter. But she'd said it.

'What? Your uncle was murdered? How long ago was this? The police will be investigating—'

'The police don't care.'

'About a murder? What are you *talking* about?' It was Barbara's turn now to be exasperated.

'He was a journalist ... a *real* journalist. Working in England. He did undercover stories. Political ones. His name didn't appear on these pieces. He investigated government activity. A couple of years ago, he got a tip-off that MI5 were planning a military takeover of the Wilson government...'

'Wait ... aren't we heading off the subject a bit?' Gail looked at Barbara contemptuously.

'Three years ago, the army occupied Heathrow Airport. It was claimed that it was a training preparation for possible IRA action. But it was a dry run for a coup. Jamesie Campbell was behind it. My uncle knew this.'

'But in that case, the Met would be all over it.'

Gail laughed sarcastically.

Barbara was annoyed. 'How did your uncle die?'

'An old woman out walking her dog found him dead in a public park. The official verdict was suicide.'

Barbara recalled something of this story.

'The newspapers reported that he had money problems, addiction issues and a secret affair he was having. All of it was fabricated bullshit, smearing his name. And Campbell's secret organisation was behind it all. I've been pursuing this for two years. And I stumbled on his plans for Glasgow. I was at the Great Eastern to speak to a source ... someone I thought would maybe go on the record. A former driver of Campbell's. Those clowns at the door wouldn't tell me if he was there or not.'

'What happened at The Balgarth?'

'Men, mostly ... famous men. Big Jamesie Campbell and his cronies. Wearing masks. Acting obnoxiously. Throwing money around.'

'None of that sounds illegal though. And you had sex with the source of this information ... willingly, I assume?'

'His wife told him that one night, after midnight, some went to an upper floor. Although the music was loud, she heard shouts and then some screams. A young guy wrapped in a towel ran along the corridor past her. His skin was blue. He jumped out of a window.'

Barbara's eyebrows rose at this. 'His skin was blue? What do you mean?'

'It had a blue tinge to it, she said. But he'd been hurt. She could see it in his eyes. And there was blood on the towel.' Gail paused. 'That same night, I saw him running up the road, being chased by three gangsters. He made it to a car at the end of the street and it drove off.'

'Were you there too?'

'I had followed Campbell to The Balgarth. I was watching from across the street.'

Barbara drew in breath and sat back in the seat. 'What happened to him ... the young guy?'

'I don't know. I've been trying to find out. The man I paid ... the one I had sex with, – he won't say anything more about what happened. The last time I saw him he told me his wife had been threatened, and that they were finished with The Balgarth. But he did say that the "boys" all came from the Great Eastern.'

'So, what are you going to do next?' said Barbara. It was an incredible story. She could understand why it would be hard for a paper to run it, unverified.

'I need to find this driver ... the Great Eastern guy. I was told he'd been involved. He was the guy in the car the ginger-haired boy ran to. And he'd know what happened to him.'

Everything was hearsay, Barbara thought. Even if it had substance, it would be like completing a thousand-piece jigsaw puzzle without any clue about the picture the pieces formed. And Barbara was sure Gail didn't even have all the pieces. But now two of them were potentially significant. Barbara shuddered at the possibility it was Lachie Wylie they were discussing.

'You never mentioned he had ginger hair before. What was the name of the man you paid?'

'No chance. We're not that close, you an' me...'

'How can I help you then, if you won't give me something else to go on?'

'That kid, the ginger one, I heard him shout a few words. He had a strange accent, like he was a Highlander.'

The colour drained from Barbara's face. Gail could see it happening. 'Do you know anything about this? If you do, fucking tell me!'

'I might,' Barbara said.

35

December 1976 – Saturday

'Wullie, this is gettin' totally fucked up.' Archie Blunt was highly stressed. A pulsing vein in his forehead was only the latest tell. 'Folk at the club are gonnae think ah'm some kind ae bloody paedophile, wi' aw this newspaper shite that's flyin' about!'

'Just a few days, an' then we're aw in the clear, son. Ye've done nothin' wrong, so ye cannae be guilty ae anythin'. Calm it, eh? For your own health if nothin' else.'

'Easier fucken said than done. Ah come crashin' back up here, thinkin' these bastards have torched my da's place ... an' then ah find my mate's bein' held tae fucken ransom, aw in the space ae a few hours.' Archie was pacing. If he continued Wullie Wigwam's rug would need replacing before the day was out.

Archie looked up. He'd never been in Wullie's house before. It was a nice place. Nowhere near as ostentatiously garish as Jamesie Campbell's, but a more comfortable living environment as a result. He spotted the picture on the wall; of the Green Lady. This was a few steps up from Archie's flat, but it reassured him to know that someone considerably better off than him shared his taste in art. She smiled, still beguiling.

'Look, son. Sit down an' let's watch the fucken show, eh?' The Wigwam poured Archie a whisky. Three fat fingers' worth.

Archie couldn't sit.

'Ah phoned Chib earlier at the hostel. Everythin's fine down there, an' he's on his way back tae sort out your mate's domestic situation.'

It was noticeable that The Wigwam was distancing himself from the Mackintosh kidnapping. Archie had hoped the money being scammed from countless small registered bookies via *The Heady Heights* show results fix would accommodate the necessary ransom. But Wullie Wigwam had other ideas; a Chibbing primarily.

Archie finally sat down. But he fidgeted. There was so much to be apprehensive about right now. He still couldn't visualise an outcome that didn't involve all of them at the bottom of the Clyde, ankle-deep in concrete. He downed the whisky in one, and then coughed. The show began.

Heady Hendricks appeared from the side of the stage as he always did. But there was a marked difference this week. The star was dressed head to toe in black. As if going to – or presiding over – a mass.

'Ladeez an' gennulmen, we have something happening which has never occurred in nearly thirty years of my time with this show...'

Archie's heart pounded like an undercover cop in a prison shower block. What was happening?

'Last week, the resounding winners in the studio were those singing Artful Dodgers, The High Five. Now, folks ... you may be aware of an ongoing police operation to trace the boys' manager, Mr Blunt. He appeared on the show last week, an' has now disappeared along with one of the boys...'

'Jesus fucken Christ!' Archie protested. 'Naw, ah didnae!' It was bad enough to be falsely accused in the newspapers, but Archie had been unprepared for Heady Hendricks to elaborate on the lie on national prime-time television.

'We've taken some legal advice, m'friends ... an' despite this, I don't wanna let the situation stand in the way of these boys' dreams. It's not their fault they were duped by this ruthless Scottish Fagin.'

'What the fuck is this, now?' Archie was shaking. 'Ah still don't even know if any ae them are actually missin'!'

'Calm doon, fuck sake. It's no' even one ae the important yins, accordin' tae Chib. It's that heidcase, Marvin Mountjoy.' Wullie made it sound like losing track of Marvin was an unexpected bonus. 'Look, it's probably just a tactic, son. Another safety net in case they don't get the files back,' said Wullie.

'That's fine for you tae say. It's no' your name being branded about as a bloody criminal on the telly, or your picture on the front page ae the papers.'

They stared at the television set. A series of lorries passed the front of The Wigwam's house and the horizontal hold went. When it, and the sound returned, Heady Hendricks was standing with a tiny girl dressed in a short, sequined, pale-blue dress. Heavily applied make-up concealed her age. She looked like a disproportionately sized hooker, next to Heady's slicked-back, stuffed-suited Dracula. It was little Amy, last week's beaten act. The sound from the TV set remained intermittent, but Wullie and Archie understood that the week-long public vote had produced – melodramatic drum roll, courtesy of Bogart Bridlington – a dead heat between the precocious child star, and the unruly East End High Fivers.

By Christ, Heady Hendricks was good, thought Archie. He had manipulated this whole fucked-up and ill-considered scam to his own ends. Archie experienced a palpable mix of admiration and fear.

'*So, now folks … let's hear it for this outstanding young talent … an' lemme say this most sincerely, I think she's headed for the Heady Heights. It's Little Amy!*'

The studio audience went crazy. Given his recent experience of it though, he doubted the rapturous applause was genuine.

Little Amy was a consummate professional. Archie had to admit she deserved to go forward to the following week's Christmas all-winners special. And, although he still yearned for a life lit by the arc lights, its appeal had gone forever. Even if The High Five pulled off a miracle and won tonight's show, he had decided he was finished. With the tabloids now on his case, he may be forced to vanish, but regardless, he was done with showbusiness.

'Archie. Archie? Fuck sake, son!' Wullie Wigwam's insistent voice. 'You're a fucken dreamer, pal. A right Billy Liar. Wake up … that's them on.'

Archie had been staring at the Green Lady. For half an hour, according to the bookie. He'd missed the five acts between the opening act and The High Five, who were on last. Wullie dismissed the other five as 'shite.' Heady gave no elaborate introduction to The High Five, and they ambled on stage lackadaisically, as if part of a staged counter-culture protest.

Archie was stunned. They were dressed like tramps. Unrecognisable from last week. The white suits were gone, replaced by ripped T-shirts and what looked like shiny, skin-tight latex trousers. The garish colours of The Wigwam's TV couldn't hide the brutal orange and yellow dyed hair and scalps. And, in the biggest shock of all, they were set like a proper band. With instruments plugged in, wires trailing, drums, guitars and a keyboard. And there were five of them. But Archie knew the next day's papers wouldn't retract the planted story. The damage had been done.

Dobber used his drumsticks to count them in. And then Sledge's guitar line sounded like he was sawing the instrument in half. Smudge's bass made Wullie Wigwam's set vibrate from more than five hundred miles away. Archie watched open-mouthed, while a slight but notice-able smile manifested itself on Wullie Wigwam's face.

'You know anythin' about this?' said Archie, stunned at the violence and the volume.

'Just watch them, fuck sake. They're your boys.'

No fun to be alone, walking by myself
No fun to be alone, in love with nobody else.'

Archie didn't know the song, beyond these lines, which Sledge had been singing periodically in the van on the journey to London. Despite this, it was a riveting performance. Not suitable for prime-time, Saturday-night family television, certainly, especially when Sledge shifted the final refrain, over a dirty groove, to:

'This is no fun ... no fucking fun ... at all!
Get it right up ye ... English cu—'

The screen went black. The test card appeared after a few seconds. A young girl, not unlike an unmade-up Little Amy, surrounded by con-fusing graphics and playing noughts and crosses with a boss-eyed doll, stared back at the two Glaswegians.

As surreal experiences went, Archie knew this one topped the lot. Five minutes passed. Archie sat staring at the technicolour test card. Wullie Wigwam was at the phone table in the hall, speaking quietly. Arranging collections. After a well-spoken continuity announcer made an apology for a technical fault, *The Heady Heights* was back.

Six acts were lined up on stage in anticipation of the clap-o-meter. The High Five were, unsurprisingly, absent from the scene. Archie visualised Mary Whitehouse writing apoplectic letters to the head of the BBC and the Queen, demanding they be beheaded. The *Daily Mirror* reprising their recent 'The Filth and the Fury' headline for the second time in three days.

Heady Hendricks made no reference to the performance when calling for the audience responses. All six remaining acts scored in the seventies, apart from Little Amy, who was way out in front with a staggering ninety-two percent.

'An' now, m'friends, let's hear it for the final act ... The High Five!'

There was silence in the studio, apart from some clearly orchestrated boo-ing, which built to a crescendo. The clap-o-meter, strangely, detected only applause; another indication to Archie that the whole show was rigged from the outset. The High Five scored three percent.

'Looks like we've seen the last of those lewd, objectionable yobbos, folks!' said Heady.

A velvet curtain ruffled behind the personality. Like a Tommy Cooper comedy routine. Two hands reached out from below and behind it to grab at Heady's ankles before the body they were attached to was yanked back. Before Heady Hendricks could signal to his musical director to strike up the band, a muffled voice yelled: *'Heady Hendricks sucked ma boaby!'*

Wullie Wigwam switched off the set. Smug and self-satisfied, he raised a glass to Archie.

'Well, we've done it, son. The big time, eh?'

'What dae ye mean, Wullie?'

'The fix was in. Ye fucken twigged that we planned it aw, no?' Wullie was toying with Archie. He knew that Archie was in the dark. In fact, The Wigwam's grand plan relied on it.

'Aye … but bettin' us aw the way tae the winners show … they've fucked that up now!'

'Naw. Naw, they haven't,' said Wullie, smugness transforming into a big cheesy grin. 'We bet hundreds ae wee sums on the first show … low odds, laid by loads ae different plants. Aw over the city. Nae suspicions. Then we did the same for the cunts tae *lose*. An' even bigger bets tae *win* on that daft wee lassie fae Auchen-fucken-shoogle or whether the fuck she's from!'

Archie was stunned. No one had told him about this *volte-face*. Wullie explained that it was to protect him. If cornered, he could legitimately act dumb, although he was proving to be quite adept at that in any case.

'Chib laid the trap. Telt the bam that he had tae get the wee Amy yin back on the show somehow. An' for The High Five to fucken sink without a trace.' Wullie smiled contentedly. 'Fair play tae the daft bastards … couldnae have gone any better.'

'Jesus Christ,' said Archie. 'Did they know?'

'No' tae start wi', but Chib phones the other night wi' a peach ae an idea. They'd aw spotted these clowns on the telly … the Six fucken Pistols or somethin'. He tells me they want tae go on the show as punks. *Fucken magic,* ah tells him.'

Archie was drained.

'So, what happens now?' he said.

'We collect the winnings, divvy up, hand the scud photos an' aw the other shite back. Go on our merry way.'

'You think it's gonna be that simple? You really think Hendricks's mob will let this go?'

'Aye. Ah do. They dinnae want aw the palaver. Ah knew the minute ah saw that dirty cunt at the Great Eastern. They're fucken shysters, Archie, just like us. Ah mean, it's no' as if we've robbed their bloody money, is it? Heady's probably knobbin' that wee lassie's maw. This'll make it easier for him. He should be fucken thankin' us, the cunt!'

Archie walked home. Briskly, and steering clear of the streetlights where possible. He was beginning to suspect that looking over his shoulder would be an hourly occurrence for the rest of his life, regardless of how brief that might be. Tomorrow was another day though. A day in which Chib's intervention would see Geordie free of the Mackintosh shackles. His dad's health improving and Archie's meeting with WPC Sherman confirming the blaze was accidental, and not the work of hired Cockney hitmen. And Bobby Souness freed from the baseball target practice routines, poor bastard. Next week, Jimmy would return with the van, and at least five of the boys ... and this whole ill-advised descent into fame-curdled madness would finally be over.

36

December 1976 – Saturday

Chib came home on the overnight train. He hadn't gone to Teddington Lock with Jimmy and the boys. He'd watch the televised chaos unfold on multiple sets in a Granada TV Rental shop window near Euston. He then bought a ticket for the sleeper.

He was unaware that The High Five had been detained in a local police cell, coppers demanding to know where the sixth member – Manky Marvin – was and what Archie Blunt had done to him.

In Glasgow, Archie was only aware of this because Jimmy had used his one permitted phone call to ring his friend in Tennyson Drive. Archie instinctively knew that this was the Vince Hillcock plan reaching a conclusion. Hold on to Jimmy and the boys on a trumped-up charge until the incriminating evidence of The Circle's shocking activities had been retrieved, and then probably dispose of them all.

Archie was in a similar position. Even with the material back in the hands of the perpetrators, how could they know additional copies hadn't been made, or if it had been shown to other people? Vince was using the media to close these avenues off. If Archie went public now, the papers would be more interested in his 'kidnapping' of Marvin, and in the connotations of a single, fifty-something man in charge of a group of male teenage singers. Archie Blunt, after all, was no Tam Paton, and as had been publicly demonstrated, The High Five were no Bay City Rollers. No one would cry for Archie Blunt.

⏻

Chib looked out at the car lot. The only vehicle available was a Hillman

Imp. He reluctantly grabbed the keys. Squeezed into it, he looked like he was wearing the vehicle like a tight waistcoat. Chib headed for the arches under the Expressway.

He wasn't surprised to find them vacant. The lock had been jemmied, and there were signs of a struggle inside. But the place hadn't been used for days. Tiny mould spores were emerging in the abandoned dregs of more than one teacup. The milk in the small fridge was off. But a two-day-old newspaper was lying on the desk in the main space. It had a scribbled address on the top right corner. A new paperboy, most likely. *Fucken morons,* thought Chib. He left and headed back to the car.

The Mackintosh flat was in a densely populated deck-access concrete slab. A big mass of horizontal ugliness, like an old, square grey warship run aground in Dennistoun. Laundry wafted like tiny sails from improvisational rigging on every level. Steam billowed out of air vents and rooftop flues, and crag-faced women leaned over the decks, gossiping and moaning to their doppelgangers on lower and upper levels. Chib looked up at the scene. Block Four, 3/D. It could've been worse, he thought. He climbed the steps, his cane of more use than a loose, unsafe handrail. Three children stopped eating their jammy pieces when he walked past them. His massive frame, clad totally in black, and his skinned head the stuff of their future nightmares. Even at their tender age, they knew he was an enforcer. Here to give some poor walloper a doing. Rather than follow, they headed into the safety of the shadows, hoping and praying it wasn't their da.

Chib reached the door. He lifted the letterbox and peered in. No signs of activity inside. A radio played 'Stuck in the Middle with You'. Chib fixed the dusters on each hand. He tried the doorhandle. The door opened silently. He stepped inside. A bedroom on the right. As untidy as fuck, but empty. Another bedroom. Then the kitchen, with a kettle starting to boil. Someone was here. Another door opened. A bald, middle-aged man emerged. Chib raised the cane. Geordie McCartney squealed in shock.

'Fuck sake, man!'

'McCartney?'

'Ahhh ... em ... aye. It's me. Dinnae hit me!'

'Anybody else here?'

'Eh ... naw. They've just nipped out. Went a message.'

Chib peered into the living room. A heavy rope was tied to a heating pipe. Apart from that, the scene was normal.

'Ah'm meant tae be here tae free you, ya diddy. What the fuck's goin' on?' Chib was bemused.

'Ah. Right. Cheers.'

'Fucken spill, Kojak!'

'Well, they brought me here on Friday. After Archie turned up at those garages.'

'And?'

'They've been aw'right tae me. Ah cannae really complain, ye know?'

'Look son, ah'm no Esther fucken Rantzen. Ah'm no' askin' ye for a consumer ratin' for *That's Life.*'

'Ah know that ... ah'm just sayin', ah began tae feel sorry for them. It was weird. They were feedin' me, an' they let me untie the rope an' go tae the bog on my own, an' that.'

'They left the front door open, for fuck's sake. What are ye still dain' here?'

'Ah dunno. It's warm in here. An' there's a big tin ae corned beef through there. Haven't had that for years. The wife widnae buy it for us.'

'Christ on a fucken bike! How many ae them are there?'

'Four. One ae them's a woman tae.'

'Right. Fucken beat it ... before ah panel you tae!'

Geordie gathered his cigarettes, his jacket and the tin of corned beef and left. Chib took a seat on the bed in the first room after the front door. He sat on the piles of clothes and waited. He was finished after this. Enforcement was a young man's game. Chib lived frugally. He could retire and disappear into the anonymity of the smog.

It was nearly two hours before they came back. Chib could hear them out on the deck. An older man and his son, arguing. Souness had escaped, it transpired. Stealing the younger man's bike.

'Ah'll head back out an' look for him after ma tea,' said the son.

'Shouldnae be that tough tae track down a middle-age jakey ridin' about on a chopper in the scud!'

The door opened.

'Telt you no' tae let him down. Even for a fag. We should have kept the prick hangin' there,' said the dad.

'Sorry, Da,' said the son.

'You need tae sharpen up, son.'

The bedroom door opened. The younger man had only taken a step over the threshold before Chib's cane hit him right on the Adam's apple. He went down immediately. His father came running. Straight into Chib Charnley's metal-lined fist as it swung around the door jamb into his path. Blood spurted from a nose that was split in two. A bit of bone fragment protruded. The man was out cold. Chib's boot smashed into the younger man's jaw. He too now was no threat.

Minutes later, another young man walked straight into a piledriver right as Chib punched through the frosted glass of the front door. Another one down like Liston in the rematch, an eye socket fractured this time. A woman screamed. Susie Mackintosh. She dropped the fish suppers and the carry-out. Chib stormed out, a black stormtrooper hunting her down. She turned, but he grabbed her long hair and dragged her back in. Doors along the deck shut. No one would be interfering. No police would be summoned. She wasn't that close a neighbour, they'd rationalise.

Susie screamed. Chib covered her mouth. She bit his palm. Chib laughed. He lifted her head back and rammed his fist into her mouth. Broken teeth flew as she collapsed.

It had been a long time since he'd administered a beating to anyone, and one to a woman was a new entry for the CV. A rage had taken him over just like it did in the old days. He was breathing heavily. Getting too old for this. He walked along the deck, swearing, as he had done many times before, that this would be the last. The concrete stairs were cold. Rain that had fallen through the open access was starting to freeze. Not easy for a man with a dodgy hip. He used the cane, but still the segs on his brogues made the downward journey precarious.

On the last flight, a voice called out: 'Ye got the time, mister?' One of the kids from earlier.

Chib stopped. The top of the flight. He looked at his watch. It had stopped.

'Naw,' he replied. 'Time you were in yer bed, wee man.'

He moved his weight forwards. The cane caught in a ridge on the concrete. Chib's free hand shot out for the rail, but the rail wasn't where he expected it to be. He tumbled forwards like a Hollywood stunt man without the padding. Seventeen cold concrete steps. The one that killed him was the last.

37

December 1976 – Sunday

The double doors opened, flooding the otherwise blacked-out room with light.

Albert retreated briefly and reappeared holding a golden breakfast tray with ornate legs. His master looked as if he was lying in state. Propped up on pillows, sporting a gold lamé blindfold and monogrammed pyjamas. Albert approached cautiously.

'Sir?'

Heady didn't respond. His cheek and hand twitched. Albert knew he was awake.

'There was a call for you earlier, sir. I told them you were not to be disturbed.' Albert paused. Heady hadn't moved. 'The gentleman left a message, sir.' Albert noticed Heady swallow hard. 'I was asked to inform you that ... it's a long way to Tipperary.' Heady Hendricks was breathing harder.

Without moving, he croaked, 'Take it away. I'm not hungry.'

⏻

'Jimmy? Is that you, mate? Where are ye, now? What the fuck's goin' on, man?'

Archie had been wakened by the telephone ringing. He'd pulled the answerphone out from the wall. Hearing his own voice telling the caller he was out was disorientating him. And besides, he figured that hired English hitmen wouldn't bother calling him first.

'Ah cannae speak for long, bud. Ah'm on the run!' said Jimmy.

'Eh? On the run fae what?' Archie wiped his eyes to ensure he wasn't dreaming again.

'The coppers, for fuck's sake! Keep up, son.' Jimmy was frazzled.

'Hey. Haud on a minute. What's happened?' asked Archie, frantically.

'We aw got nicked, remember? Did ye no' see the fucken show?'

'Aye. Ah did but...' Archie was having trouble distinguishing fact from fiction, and Jimmy hadn't elaborated on the charges against them during his previous, brief phone call.

'Gross indecency, it was. They daft laddies effin' and fucken blindin' live on the telly. They got let go, but ah got detained ... cos ae the bastardin' proby.'

'So...' Archie was still missing a few links.

'The boys came back. That daft cunt Marvin sets fire tae the cop shop ... alarms are goin' off aw'roads. An' wi' us all out on the street, the boys nabbed me.'

'Jesus Christ, Jimmy!'

'Naebody knew where he was but turns out Marvin had been gettin' held in a locked cupboard in that studio for nigh on a week. He breaks out, batters some cunt, follows us tae this daft wee polis station. The other yins get out, an' then he comes back an' torches the arse out the place,' Jimmy laughs, as if unable to believe his own account. 'The total state ae this polis station, man ... like a wee village hall run by the Keystone fucken Cops!'

'So where are ye now?'

'Fuck knows. Some tiny wee service station on a B-road.'

'Why...?'

'Cos drivin' up the M6 in a fish an' chip van wi' *The Codfather* painted aw over it would be pretty fucken easy tae spot.'

'Hmm. Aye, ah suppose so.'

'Look, Archie ... ah'll need tae scram here. Ah've nae more change left anyways. Ah just wanted tae make sure we're still on for the business.'

'Aye. Sure Jimmy, sure.' Archie had almost forgotten the promise he'd made to Jimmy in return for driving them to the shows.

'Right. We'll drop the van off. You an' McCartney are in charge, an' ah'll disappear tae the heat dies down.'

Archie couldn't help thinking Scotland Yard might have more serious things to do than chase his pal. He was Jimmy Rowntree after all, not Jimmy Cagney.

'Geordie? Is that you? Fuck sake, man ... are you aw'right?' Two phone calls. Both unexpected. A couple of hours apart.

'Aye ... em, ah'm no' sure!'

'Geordie, what is it? Where are ye?'

'Chib Charnley's dead!'

'Jesus Johnny ... how?'

'Fell down a flight ae stairs.'

'Christ ... the polis got tae him, then, aye?'

'Naw. He fell down a flight ae *actual* steps. Concrete yins. It was an accident. Smashed his own head in. He'd just freed me fae the Mackintosh gang.'

'Did you see it?'

'Aye. Ah was sittin' on a bench over the road. Eatin' a meat pie. Ah'd fuck all else tae dae, so ah just thought ah'd wait an' watch.'

'What about the Mackintoshs?' Archie couldn't bring himself to call them a gang. That sounded way too melodramatic.

'Dunno, but five went in ... an' one came out...' Geordie McCartney had watched too many Clint Eastwood films. 'An' then went arse over tit, an' killed himself!'

'Where are you?'

'Ah'm pickin' up some clothes, pal. Then ah'm hightailin' outta here. Ah'm done, man. If ah dinnae get away, it's gonnae be a fast black tae heart-attack central!'

'Where can ah get a hold ae ye?'

'Ah'll be at Deek's ... out in Cumbernauld.' Archie was sure he had Geordie's brother's address written down somewhere. He'd find it later.

'Wullie, is that you?' A third call. Archie Blunt making it this time.

'Aye. Look ah've nae time, son. Chib's been found dead.'

Archie didn't want to admit he knew this in case it opened more worm-filled cans. 'Fucken jokin'! How?'

'Still gettin' tae the bottom ae that.'

'Look, Wullie ah appreciate this might no' be a good time ... but have ye done the collections yet? Ah'm fucken brassic, an' ah need tae sort out ma da's situation.'

'Did ye no' hear me? Chib's fucken broon breid! Ye know how long he's been wi' me, eh? Show some fucken respect, Archie!'

'Ah'm sorry.' Archie *was* sorry. Chib was a harder than a demolition ball hitting a derelict tenement, but everybody knew what he meant to The Wigwam. And it sounded like the bookie was in tears.

'Come round the cabin on Tuesday. Ah'll square ye up, then.' The line went dead.

⏻

'Hello. Heady? Are you on the private line?'

'Yes. What do you want, Vince?'

'I need to come over.'

'No. I'm not seeing anyone.'

'Heady, it's important.'

'Have you been told to kill me, Vince?'

'What? What the fuck are you talking about, Heady. You're the closest thing to a father I have.'

There was a long silence.

'All those little side chats with Circle members recently...'

'The Surgeon?'

'They were about me, weren't they?'

'No ... God's honest, Heady. That vile fucking Scots prick wanted some stupid, inconsequential female journalist dealt with. She's been asking questions about him for months. I've been asked to fix it. It's nothing to do with you.'

Vince was convincing, Heady had to acknowledge that, but since the slimy bastard was a professional liar, the jury was still out.

'So, what are you calling me here for?' asked Heady.

'It's Operation DWS ... just as a precaution.'

'For fuck's sake, you promised me this wouldn't happen. Mother-*fucker*!'

'The tall kid broke out of the holding store. He'd fucking shit all over it and smeared it on the door handle! Someone thought he was ill. Thought they should check on him ... an', well ... you can guess the rest.'

'Jesus Christ ... is it *only* fucking halfwits that you hire?' Heady sighed. 'What about the rest of them?'

'Well ... that's the thing...'

'Oh, for the love of Christ, don't tell me...'

'They got away. They're loose ... but we're on their tail, Heady, don't—'

'Don't what? Worry? Panic? Shoot my fucking load? Tell me, what in the name of sweet suffering fucksticks don't you want me to do, eh?'

'Don't answer anything by your own name. From now on, you must be Daryl W. Seberg. Any time there's a call ... the door rings ... even in front of Albert.'

'You little prick!'

'It might not come to it, but it's only for a few months, *max* ... until the papers lose interest.'

'They won't lose interest in me goin' to fucking Wormwood Scrubs, you bloody clown!'

'It won't reach that point. I promise you.'

'Well, that's about as comforting as Mick McGahey being put in charge of my personal fucking taxation! We'd be better off dead!'

Heady Hendricks was certain that the whole pack of cards was going to collapse. His career, his reputation, his freedom. The Circle would survive though. Too many invested interests.

'I'll call you later,' said Vince.

He was putting out fires all over the place. Tracking the movements of Glaswegian wasters and young female journalists – crooks and opportunists – and all because of a handful of overprivileged, preening wankers who considered themselves above and beyond the law. He hated these disgusting, deviant cunts, but their money was plentiful. His growing business was built on its foundations. He had long since learned to sup with a very long spoon.

'Get some rest, Heady. I need to go to Manchester for a week or so. But you keep your head down ... and remember ... it's Daryl W. Seberg.'

38

December 1976 – Tuesday

He saw shapes in the shadows. Snakes in the grass. Threats around every corner. The subconscious was a powerful foe when it chose to take arms against its host. He had no respite. He hadn't properly slept since ... well, that night at Eddie's place in London. Archie Blunt was running on empty. The cool release of the bampot's blade might even have been welcome.

The rain battered down. That damp, stale smell of clothes only washed by smog-infused water stuck to him. Hung around him like a stench of decay. He had no money for food, never mind the steamie.

He turned the corner. A line of men stretched out from the Dunne Driving compound. Bets being squared, or debts recovered? It was hard to tell from this distance. Archie joined the end of the queue.

'What's the score, pal?' he asked the man in front of him.

'You work wi' The Wigwam?'

'Aye. Well ... an associate, more like,' said Archie. It sounded better.

'He's emigrated,' the man said. 'Sold up, an' fucked off. Sunny Spain, ah heard. Lucky bastart.'

Archie's mouth gaped open. He felt the little colour there was drain out of him. It was like the atomic bomb strike on Nagasaki. All that would be left of him after this shocking truth hit home was a shadow.

'Gone? But ... but how?'

'Dunno. Just had enough probably. Chib dyin' hit him hard. Chib was like a son tae him, y'know?'

Archie stood motionless. Nothingness.

'Know him, did ye? Chib, ah mean?'

Archie didn't answer. The man shrugged to his colleagues and the queue edged closer to the cabin door. He didn't feel his feet moving. Didn't feel anything. But somehow, eventually, Archie was inside the cabin.

'You are?' The serious man behind the desk that used to be The Wigwam's was taking names, ticking them off like an administrator shutting down the Parkhead Forge Steelworks. The room was bare, Archie noticed. Celebrity pictures; gone. Sledgehammer; gone. His own future; all gone.

'Erm, Blunt. Archie Blunt.' Drool was running out of a mouth that seemed to be incapable of closing.

'Here,' said the man. He handed Archie an envelope. 'Next!'

Archie walked away. He felt he might cry. Not from the shock of the betrayal from a wide Glaswegian bookie. No, from the knowledge of what was inside this envelope. He didn't even need to open the fucking thing.

⏻

It was a discombobulated Archie who met WPC Sherman later that December afternoon. With everywhere on early closing, they walked in the bitter cold towards Celtic Park. Once over the unusual coincidence surrounding their first meeting, Barbara reassured Archie that the fire at his dad's home had been a complete accident; nothing more suspicious. Had his dad been in one of the old tenements, the spread of it might have been less rapid. The internal walls of his new home were made out combustible timbers and a flammable boarded lining. The kitchen was a burned-out shell and had affected those above and either side too. Barbara only told him of the extent of the blaze to reinforce how lucky his father had been.

Archie was ashamed as he told the off-duty policewoman of his guilt. They sat on the wet park bench. He wept uncontrollably. She put a comforting arm around him. He was embarrassed. The policewoman could be his daughter, she was so young. A clichéd indication of advancing age. He suddenly felt very old. Distraught and vulnerable too.

She could see it. She knew there was more to his emotional pain than met the eye. She detected his need to confide. She'd make a proper police officer, one day. One that understood the perspective of others, and didn't rush to judgement.

And Archie told her. Far more than he perhaps should have. He told her about Heady Hendricks. About Jimmy Rowntree and the young boys from Bridgeton on the run in a busted fish-and-chip van. About Geordie McCartney, and his descent into darkness at The Balgarth; hopefully he was now out of the direct line of fire. About Wullie Wigwam, the thieving bastard, uprooted and sunning himself on the Costa del Sol. Only Archie was left, still holding photographs and evidence that would shock the telly-watching nation. He dearly wished he'd just thrown the fucking things in the Clyde; or had never taken them in the first place. What had he got out of them? A preposterous shot at being someone famous; someone his dad might be proud of.

Barbara listened. It was all that she could do at this point. But she was joining the dots. The many, many threads – random when examined individually, but wound together, they began to make sense. The Balgarth, Jamesie Campbell, Heady Hendricks. Lachie Wylie.

She asked, but Archie wouldn't give her the material. He said it would only endanger her life.

Archie didn't know what to do next. He felt a noose tightening slowly around his neck.

Barbara had an idea. She left him. She needed time to think it through. To confide in a trusted contact. She told him to stay safe and she'd be back in touch soon. She kissed him gently on the cheek.

He watched her until she was out of sight. Archie was shaking. A sudden fear that they'd been observed from a distance. That this considerate young woman would be found floating face down in the river before the day was out. The thought of his actions having such finite consequences for others was too much for him to bear. He suddenly had a desperate urge to anaesthetise his agony with booze.

39

December 1976 - Christmas Eve

Archie Blunt was home. Alone. The compact flat, which, only three weeks before, was alive with the anxious anticipation of four men, all dreaming of a better life, was now silent. A small artificial Christmas tree, bought and carelessly erected when the collective optimism was at its peak, now just emphasised how irrational and stupid they had been. Its few lights blinked, winked. Taunting him. The pittance left to him by a duplicitous, double-crossing cunt of a man was gone. Blown on a day-long bender. Archie was still drunk; had almost drunk himself sober. Almost, but not quite. His da remained in hospital, delirious and demented. Geordie McCartney had gone too. Implemented a voluntary redundancy option and been accepted for a council flat in Cumbernauld. Agreeing to such a location arguably made him as demented as Archie's da. But the speed with which that turn of events had occurred meant it had been in the works for some time. Maybe Archie deserved Geordie's lack of trust.

Jimmy Rowntree was still on the run in an antiquated van; fuck knows where. His planned business venture had about as much hope and viability as a spaceship launched from Sauchiehall Street.

And Archie still had these fucking photographs. The only thing currently saving him, he assumed, was the erroneous belief that The Wigwam had them, and that, in the *Heady Heights* scam, Archie Blunt was merely an ignorant foot soldier.

Archie fiddled with the bent coat-hanger. The TV picture stabilised sufficiently for him to see Jimmy *fixing it* for a buck-toothed brat from Hull to meet Freddie Mercury. He looked thin, did Mercury. Archie had given up hating him and his pretentious pomposity. That song, the *bismallah* bollocks one, was still everywhere over a year after it first came out. Too late for jealousy now. Freddie Mercury would never have given his only taped copy of 'Bohemian Rhapsody' to the local gangsters with no collateral. But, ostensibly, that's exactly what Archie had done three months ago. He had trusted Wullie Wigwam, who had first employed him, then took advantage of him, and had now ground his dreams into the Glasgow whindust.

Archie got up slowly. The alcohol in his system limited his pace. He flicked the switch; telly off, radio on. Better for drowning the sorrows … and there were *many* sorrows. He poured a Chivas, and for old time's sake, paired it with a Vat 69. Archie was drunk and depressed, travelling through a three-day tunnel of blackness with no light in sight. Music drifted in and out through the jaggy maze of his tangled brain.

Gazin' at yer navel through the bottom of a glass wi' yer head up yer arse is quite a scatological feat, Archie the cunt!

Archie registered the voice; a high-pitched one. It sounded familiar. He picked up the radio and shook it.

'Wireless pickin' up the fucken taxis again,' he muttered to himself.

Even Jim Rockford had deserted him. The gaudy tinsel shivered as he aimed a wayward kick at one of the tree's low-hanging baubles.

Naw, ya clown, behind ye. That high-pitched squeak. *Ye fucked it up, Blunt, just like you always dae. Nearly feel sorry for ye. Couldnae just drop it, could ye? No point greetin' about it now, son...* Chib Charnley leaned against the narrow fireplace. He was in front of the mirror hanging above it, but the mirror wasn't doing its job. *Don't beat yerself up … there's a queue here waitin' tae dae that for ye!* And with a lopsided, gumsy grin, Chib – the Carntyne Cat – was gone.

Cold sweat rolled down Archie's neck. He stared at the wall, its damp, peeling, flowered brown wallpaper. The Green Lady, frowning, not smiling. The pitch to The Wigwam was a ludicrous dream, he could see that now. But it had been one conceived with his da in mind. He couldn't find the words to explain that. And now, he was alone. In a purgatory of his own construction.

Archie flopped onto the couch, exhausted. He dozed. His eyes opened, and he was uneasy; he could smell Chanel No 5. Bet's. But some other lass in a Mary Quant dress appeared and smiled lovingly at him. He didn't recognise her. At first.

Hello. That familiar voice.

'Bet, is that you?'

Oh, aye darlin'... an' we're goin' dancin'. She took his hand and they whirled. When they stopped, they were in the Barrowland Ballroom. It was Christmas Eve 1960, and Jimmy Rowntree was on the bell. Archie saw his young self and Betty dancing. She wasn't Betty Blunt back then. Not yet. He'd cut in and taken her back from some other, older walloper whose hands were wandering. Proud of himself for taking the initiative, for plucking up the courage in the face of potential aggro, and that she'd allowed him to escort her home afterwards. Weeks after they'd first met. They'd circled around each other. Courted. But that was the night he knew she was the one. She was the prize.

'Can we stay here awhile?' he asked.

No!

Archie turned to see Bet changing. She was beautiful and wearing her mother's wedding dress. Grasping Archie's sweaty hand, they revisited scene after scene of Archie letting her down, him always ending with the broken-record plea: 'It'll be different, next time, Bet ... ah promise ye!'

Archie Blunt, distressed and teary. He howled like a starving baby deprived of the tit.

'Jeez, Bet, what dae ah need tae do, hen? Gie's a fucken clue!'

The radio was now playing 'Sammy and the Radio Man'. His song. What kind of fucked-up practical joke was this? It was like a concrete boot to Archie's aching balls. He flicked the switch, back to the telly. Val Doonican was there, rocking back and forth ... back and forth. Back and forth. Archie, alone again. Just him and the drink. The drink and him. And this fucking Doonican joker murdering *his* song. All canines and cardigan, soft light and sincerity. Killing him softly. Val's rendition of Archie Blunt's song. How was that even possible?

Archie, remember the best Christmas? Archie knew immediately. 1969. Beautiful. Perfect. The woman on the tiny TV screen was speaking directly to Archie. It was Val Doonican's special guest, Brenda Lee. She dedicated her song to him; 'Sweet Nothings'.

That's all we'll ever have, Archie, sweet nothings.

'But Bet, ah always loved ye. Always.'

Mibbes aye, mibbes naw. Sweet nothings.

Archie stood on shaking legs. The Vat 69 took a fall. Betty was gone, forever. It was still only half past ten. His song suddenly played on the radio. That fucking radio! Archie heaved it, shot-putt style. It smashed against the fireplace. But still, the song played on; like the catalyst of all his pain. Archie vomited. What the fuck was happening to him? Mental breakdown? Only an excuse. He looked at the clock. Ten minutes to midnight. Maybe there was still time.

December 1976 – Hogmanay

The clarity of purpose that followed the weirdest night of his previous fifty-odd years evaporated gradually over the subsequent days. Archie Blunt spent Christmas Day alone. It hadn't been the first time, but it was certainly the worst time. The loneliness of his life was now more painful than anything he had previously encountered. He was in a holding pattern where the bottle temporarily assuaged his remorse before the brutal hangovers brought it all back, and more viscerally with every passing day. Archie considered himself to be a fundamentally decent man, but the bad things he'd either been responsible for – or had been easily led towards – were returning to haunt him. In his more lucid moments, he was grateful that his conscience forced him to remember them. Rank evil bastards like Wullie Wigwam evidently had no such remorse. If any consolation was to be had now, it's that he had never veered down the road that those types had ultimately chosen.

Archie sat in The Horseshoe Bar staring at his glass, as the bells tolled in another time zone on a television set above the bar. He wanted to be out of the East End and away from the need to lie. There was exaggerated happiness in the air. *For auld lang syne, my friend.* It would most likely dissipate into violence once the bampots that frequented the city centre's cobbled lanes and sheltered doorways got to work. A&E would see visitor numbers soar to levels only normally experienced in the aftermath of an Old Firm match. It'd be a two-day shift since there was another Glasgow derby the following day. Revellers, prostitutes and innocent bystanders were the typical post-Hogmanay casualties.

Archie was determined not to be one of them. It had felt like he'd been under self-imposed house arrest this last week and he was now glad of the temporary freedom of a day release into the city. But when the sounds of Big Ben rang, it would only remind him of how lost he was without Bet to kiss and make daft, irrational resolutions for the year ahead with. And even his da, to reminisce about the good old days of the music halls.

'Excuse me … can I buy you a drink, mister?' Archie heard the voice but didn't turn; naturally assuming it was addressing someone else. 'Happy New Year, when it comes, by the way.' A fragile hand with bony fingers reached around from behind Archie. He turned to face the person it was attached to.

'Eh … aye, you tae, hen.' Archie shook the young woman's hand. She looked familiar, but Archie couldn't place her.

'Can I get you a drink?'

Archie was confused. He'd almost forgotten the anxiety of being approached in a Glasgow pub by a stranger who appeared to know him.

'Eh … aye, aw'right. Whisky.'

Archie watched the young woman order. He quickly scanned the heaving bar for signs of any interested associates. It was unheard of for a young woman to be in a city-centre bar alone. Most of the East End pubs still didn't admit women at all, not unless they were going to be behind the bar. She must be with someone else. The Horseshoe had the longest bar of any pub in Europe but on Hogmanay, there was barely room to stand, let alone sit. The woman seemed – like Archie – to be on her own. She bought two drinks; one for each of them.

Archie lit two Benson & Hedges. He instinctively passed one to his new drinking buddy.

'Ah, cheers but I've given up. Those things'll kill you.' It was an attempt at humour, but Archie didn't laugh.

'Fuck ye, then,' said Archie, as if he had just sacrificed his last ever cigarette. They clinked glasses. 'Cheers,' he offered.

'Your good health, sir,' said the young woman. They finished their drinks in silence but mainly because the singing had started in their corner of the pub, making conversation virtually impossible.

Archie ushered the young woman outside. 'Listen hen, ah appreciate the drink an' that, but ah'm ah supposed tae know you?'

'You were on *The Heady Heights* show ... with those young guys, the punks.' Archie was immediately on guard.

'So, what ... are ye after an autograph, like?' asked Archie, trying to face it off.

'No. That's definitely not what I want...'

'Look love, ah'm sorry. Just goin' through a rough time at the minute, y'know? Ah need tae get goin'.'

'Can you come round into the lane with me first?' Archie was stunned. Prostitutes blatantly soliciting inside the pubs now? Buying punters drinks as enticement? *Jesus Christ, trade must really be tough!*

'Ye jokin'?' said Archie, barely able to believe such open entrapment.

'There's somebody who needs a word with you.' The words were spoken with a directness, and a coldness, that rocked Archie on his heels. She didn't look dangerous, or deadly, like she was here on Hillcock's business. She looked kind, and compassionate. Then again, Mata Hari's success was primarily down to seductive looks and evocative mascara. Archie weighed it up. She was slight in stature and while he would've struggled to fight his way out of a wet paper bag, he couldn't conceive of mobsters hiring female hitmen ... hitwomen. Nonetheless, his hands shook as he followed her along the street in the freezing fog.

Archie saw the car through the mist. It was jammed into a dark service access with no through exit. A moving outline was in the car. His knees buckled. He was going to die tonight, right here in a wet Glasgow city-centre lane. He would be gagged, knifed and dumped down behind the bins. He'd be classed as a casualty of the overexuberance. Perhaps even assumed to be the aggressor. No way out, this time.

His tense shoulders relaxed. His breathing was suddenly calm. He was so tired of being scared. *Fuck it,* he thought. He was ready to walk willingly onto the end of the cold sharp steel. There was nothing left to live for.

'Don't be worried, Archie,' said the young woman as they headed towards the darkness.

He was exhausted. He couldn't resist even if he wanted to. The car window wound down.

'It's you,' he said, almost tearful now.

Barbara Sherman smiled and slid across the back seat, simultaneously opening the door for him to get in. He stood motionless. His knees had locked. The young woman took his arm and helped him get in. He couldn't tell if he was being arrested.

'Archie, Gail here needs the information you have. The files and the photographs. It's the only way to bring Hendricks and Campbell and the rest of them down.'

'Aw fuck, not this again,' he muttered. Still no end in sight.

Gail Proctor got in the front. Archie sighed. The agony was being prolonged. This was worse than a quick death.

'Jesus, hen, did you tell this wee lassie? Christ, ah thought ah told you tae keep this tae yersell. For your own good as much as mine.'

'This is bigger than my status at the station,' she said.

'That bastard Hillcock's got the papers sewn up. They'll fucken bury you an'me. And her, if she ends up involved.' said Archie.

'I *am* involved,' said Gail. 'And far more than you!'

'Seriously doubt that, hen,' said Archie.

'Archie, Gail's been investigating Jamesie Campbell for nearly two years. She hasn't been able to get a break ... until now,' said Barbara.

'Listen, ah'm no' her break. Ah'm done wi' aw this, so ah am. Ah shouldnae have told you about the stuff. Ye caught me at a bad time.'

'Is it any better now?' asked Barbara.

'That's no' the point.' Archie wasn't sure what the point was anymore.

'Mr Blunt, two years ago, Jamesie Campbell had my uncle Alec murdered because he got too close to the truth on a story. The photographs Barbara said you had will send him down. It won't be justice for my uncle Alec, but it'll be what the bastard deserves.'

For what seemed to Archie like an hour, Gail and Barbara elaborated, filling in blanks and answering the questions forming in Archie's head before he could ask them. Still, Archie seemed unconvinced by the young woman. He had seen the evidence of it, but it remained hard to believe that Hank Hendricks was involved with people so diabolical. He also couldn't conceive that murderers would get away with an act so public and obvious that this young woman had worked it all out.

Just as he reached this conclusion, he understood how naïve he'd been. And not only about the pursuit of fame.

'Someone got in touch. An editor at the *Guardian*,' said Gail. 'Barbara ran a check. Phoned him too. He's legit. He's researching a story on my uncle's work and wanted to know if I had any information that might help him. He confirmed all the things I'd suspected about Big Jamesie Campbell's involvement. When Barbara told me about the photos and files you had, I knew they would be the proof I'd need to be taken seriously. Pinning the murder on him would be difficult but this guy thinks those would seal his fate. Either way, Big Jamesie Campbell will be finished for good.' She was sounding desperate. 'You're my only hope of getting any type of conclusion to all this. To make it all stop.'

'And for all those poor kids like Lachie Wylie that they've been abusing for decades,' Barbara added.

Gail Proctor's eyes were pleading. 'I'm on a train down to Manchester to meet this editor tomorrow. Please, Archie.'

Archie sighed. Making it all stop was all he wanted too. If he handed over the material, there was a chance of that. It may not save him, ultimately, but at least he'd be free of the fucking things. If these two wouldn't heed a warning, then what subsequently happened wouldn't be on his conscience. He'd done his best to keep as many people as possible out of the developing madness, but according to Barbara, Gail was already in up to her eyebrows. It couldn't get any worse for her.

'How dae ye really know ye'se can trust this guy?' said Archie, wearily, almost like a father enquiring about a new boyfriend.

'I don't. *We* don't,' Gail admitted. 'But I'm just so tired chasing the dead-ends now. Almost every avenue gets closed off.'

'Aye ... they're fucken good at coverin' tracks, ah'll give them that.'

'Lachie Wylie was injected with a chemical substance ... methylene blue. It makes people's skin grey with a bluish tinge.'

Archie was confused. His brain ached like a hundred migraines had descended at once.

Barbara continued. 'Anyone injected with it looks ... dead. They had drugged Lachlan and then injected this stuff into him to make him look deceased. Then Jamesie Campbell sodomised him.'

'Fuck sakes,' said Archie. 'How dae you two know this?'

'I was at The Balgarth the night it happened. Outside. Lachlan broke away from them and got out of the building. Your friend Bobby Souness drove him to the hospital. He didn't make it inside, though,' said Gail, calmly.

'His body was dumped in the Clyde,' said Barbara. 'Made to look like suicide.'

'The same as my uncle,' Gail added.

'That's the kind of people they are, Archie,' said Barbara. 'Senior police protect them, and Campbell's thugs hoover up the mess. This is the only way.'

⏻

Archie directed the car to the road that skirted the Necropolis. All three got out and climbed the slopes guided only by the full moon shining down on a city revelling and resolving to be better in the year ahead. It would fail, as it always did. But at least it made the effort, annually, to acknowledge its deficits.

Archie knelt by a small headstone. Its inscription didn't seem to be ironic or relevant; just a simple name: *ROBERT ROSS. BORN 1934*. One that he would remember easily. He took out a penknife and scraped away at the soil to the left of the stone. Twenty minutes later, he had excavated enough to pull a polythene bag out. The photographs and incriminating papers were in it. He handed them to Gail.

'Thank you, Archie. It means a lot that you trust me with these,' she said. She finally had all the pieces in place; the roadmap that led to Manchester.

'Aye, well ... that's some pretty fucken dangerous stuff in there. You watch yer back, hen!'

'I will.'

'You two go on, eh ... ah'll wait an' clear up here! An' good luck tae the two ae ye'se.'

'You too, Archie,' said Barbara.

'I'm meeting the *Guardian* editor tomorrow, so the story should be out by Sunday. You won't be named at all. It'll all be over soon.'

'Aye ... maybe.'

Archie watched them all the way back down to the car. It drove off and he leaned back on Robert Ross's gravestone and wept. He couldn't stop. The pain. The loss. The release. The relief. All of it.

41

January 1977

She'd bought the *Guardian* every day for ten days straight. She knew it wouldn't appear immediately. Facts would have to be checked and double-checked. A scandal that blew the lid off the UK's political and light-entertainment fraternities would be agonised over by lawyers and newspaper owners. She knew this, but still the delays were concerning. The beat cops now called her Mrs Slocombe. Her paper had big words in it. There were no tits on page three, and its football coverage was virtually nonexistent. Another chasm that separated them.

Davy Dodd had been in closed-door conference with one of the bosses from upstairs for over an hour. Whispers circulated, but no one knew the reason for it. The door opened. The superintendent left, staring over at Barbara. The squad saw it, but she didn't.

'Sherman!' She looked up.

'Yes, sarge.'

'Get in here.' Davy Dodd wasn't shouting. There were none of the usual histrionics from her colleagues. It was as if they all had knowledge of a secret that she wasn't yet in on. 'Close the door.' That request was highly unusual. Two closed-door meetings in one morning. 'You're being transferred.'

Davy Dodd sat back and folded his arms. The body language said many things: that it was a done deal. That it wasn't going to be reversed. And that it was a decision reached much higher than his level.

'But I didn't ask for a transfer,' said Barbara. But she knew that, while on probation, the police reserved the right to move people around, particularly single people. Nevertheless, it wasn't the army. Surely there were the formalities of interviews. Assessments. Some fucking inter-personal discussion about it.

'Think of it as a promotion,' said Dodd.

'Why?'

'Because you're bein' fucken promoted ... tae a higher grade. Fuck sake, Sherman. Thought you were supposed tae be clever?'

'Where am I being sent?' she asked, with as much disdain as she could muster.

'Ye've caught the eye ae the super. Christ knows how ... but yer goin' back home. Fucken Teuchterville.'

'Where?'

'The Hebrides. The Islands beat. Some auld duffer's just copped his whack! You're the new sergeant, God help them.'

Barbara didn't know what to say. It was true that she'd had it with Glasgow, and Glaswegians. Only Don Braithwaite was tolerable among the apes that passed for her East End peers.

'How long, sir?'

'They need you up there end ae next week. That'll no' be a problem, will it?'

As rhetorical questions went, it was a doozy. She turned, opened the door and walked back out, glancing only at Don, who shrugged as if to indicate the futility of any protest his beat partner might be contemplating.

WPC Barbara Sherman stared at her desk. It remained in the same position that she initially found it. She'd learned to live with the gents' lavatories. She'd become accustomed to its odours. She wouldn't miss it, that would be going too far. But this was her personalised workplace. People looking for her knew to locate her here. They left notes, or instructions, or files. The missing persons detail – that was universally recognised as her job. Admittedly, it wasn't the solving of these cases ... more the organisation of them. But many's the time a murder-squad detective requested her attendance on the floor above them. To quote details from an MP file that might rule out – or rule in – a possible lead. It wasn't vital work in the wider scheme of things, but it made her feel significant. And that sense of belonging was important to her. Maybe she wouldn't have that opportunity in a place where the regularity and pace of crime moved at a slower speed.

She lifted a new batch of files. A fresh set of misplaced lives all reduced to as many details as would fit on a single A4 sheet. Barbara placed the files in the box. They wouldn't be her concern for much longer. The stories that she had concocted for the disappeared while sitting in her flat alone at nights would be someone else's responsibility. She hoped it would be a woman. Someone who might nurture a maternal instinct towards them and care about their outcomes. Someone to pray for their lost souls.

She dropped a file. It was the last one to be added. She was sure it wasn't there when she'd gone into her sergeant's office ten minutes ago. She picked it up from the floor. Opened it.

Tears rolled instantly. Whoever spotted them first would claim the responsibility for it and claim the sweepstake money.

But they weren't down to any man. A small, rectangular photograph of Gail Proctor, paper-clipped to the single-sheet report, stared back at her.

42

April 1977

'Ye right, well?'

'Aye. Roll her out.' Geordie McCartney reversed the van backwards. The spring sunlight glinted off gleaming headlamps and chrome wheel arches.

'Looks fucken magic, mate,' said Archie. And it did. Jimmy Rowntree's ramshackle van, transformed and refurbished into *The Codfather II*.

Just like the film, Archie had said, *the sequel's fucken much better than the original.*

Geordie agreed. The van was a business, and ready to take its licence-approved place among the street vendors of Shettleston and beyond.

'Jimmy'll be chuffed as fuck when he gets out, eh?'

'Aye, Archie. He will, mate!'

Geordie enjoyed these trips back to the East End to see his pals. He still had the Corporation pass so the trips cost him nothing beyond a few pints for old chums, which he was more than happy to stand. Cumbernauld had cleaner air but, by Christ, the people were as fucking dull and lifeless as the concrete everything was built out of.

''Mon we'll take it out, eh? Ah've got aw the stuff. Let's go an' sell some chips!'

Jimmy Rowntree had another month left to serve. When he'd returned to Glasgow with The High Five plus one, he'd holed up in the roofspace of an old acquaintance. He'd been up there for six weeks when he finally thought, *Fuck this ... Barlinnie's a better option.*

Some of Geordie's redundancy money paid for the van's body

work, and Archie acquired the business permits and the stock. It was to be a three-way partnership, but Geordie McCartney didn't want the responsibility. He was just happy to help and be involved. Teresa had come back, and although what little grass there was in Cumbernauld wasn't exactly greener, they were giving it another go. Like all of them, Geordie had learned his lesson; the quiet life was the one for him.

Their first circuits were temperamental. Archie was glad that they'd waited until after the Easter holidays, until the schools had returned. Coping with hundreds of tiny starving gannets, all yelling and screaming for all sorts of bizarre battered fry-ups would have been a deep end he'd have drowned in. But by the end of the first week, he'd become adept at dealing with the boiling oil. He'd mastered the batter consistency and the preparation of the food prior to frying. A few complaints gradually gave way to more queues and longer hours. More money. Life was good. The radio blared: *...we gotta get right back to where we started from.*

Archie smiled. Not this time.

'Haw, big yin...'

Archie looked up. A familiar voice.

'Nice fucken hat, by the way.'

Archie laughed, and extended a hand through the window. He was genuinely pleased to see him; to see them *all*. Although the brief time they'd shared was surreal, he couldn't say it didn't make him laugh when he recalled it.

'So, can we get a *High Five* supper, then?'

'Aye, lads. On the house, boys!' Archie prepared the double-fish and a pie special he'd named after them.

They looked like a band. A *real* band. But a cool one. Not one with daft white suits. Black leathers, ripped T-shirts. Dyed, spiky hair. Like they had a purpose. Archie reached down for a spare newspaper to wrap the food in. He retrieved one from a drawer. It was an old copy that he'd saved from a few weeks earlier. This felt like the right occasion to use it.

'What's the story, Arch?' asked Sledge.

'This fuckin' disgrace.' Archie held up the page. Above a series of adverts, there were two stories, unrelated in any way other than what Archie and Sledge knew to be true. The first story had a picture of Heady Hendricks leaving what was described as 'a rehabilitation centre'. The text told of Heady having been cured of the personality disorder that cursed *The Heady Heights All-Winners Show* on Christmas Day, when the star had sworn at the show's tearful winner, Little Amy, insisting on live television that he wasn't Heady Hendricks, but Daryl W. Seberg, an American movie mogul, and not the fictional agent many associated with the name. Since then, Heady – or rather, Daryl – had been treated for nervous exhaustion, brought on by overwork and the stress of fulfilling his many charity obligations.

The second article confirmed the retirement of Jamesie Campbell MP, following his recent knighthood in the Queen's New Year's honours list. He was 'drawing back from public life'. Vince Hillcock, the orchestrator tying up all the loose ends, still earning his exorbitant hourly rate, Archie thought.

'Fucken cunts,' said Sledge. 'Fuck 'em aw, eh?'

'Aye. Too right, son.'

Sledge took the food and reached into his pocket.

'It's fine, son. As I said, on me, just tae say thanks for everythin'.'

'An' this is on me … fae all ae us. Just tae say thanks … for everythin'.' Sledge handed Archie a brown paper bag. There was a thick wad of notes in it. And most of them were fifties.

'The fuck's this, son? Ye'se rob a bloody bank, or what?'

'We've been signed. By EMI. A three-album deal. They want a band like The Sex Pistols or The Buzzcocks, or The Damned. That's your cut, Archie. We widnae be in this position if it wisnae for you, man.'

Archie felt tears welling. He couldn't believe it. He had no idea they had been approached.

'It's ten grand, Archie. Away an' have a good time, pal. Ye deserve it.'

They turned and strolled away; five gallus Glaswegian lads with the world at their feet. Archie couldn't have been prouder had they been his own children.

'Haw, Sledge,' he shouted after them. 'Where's Marvin?'
'He's away doin' a deal. He's our new manager!'
'Holy fuck … God help the music business!'

'When I was a boy I was a Catholic.
I paid the fine and got out.'

—*Billy Connolly*

July 1977

Archie Blunt went to Mass. To say sorry, but also to say goodbye for the final time. His relationship with Catholicism was tenuous at best, but this was a day for drawing a line under it. There had been too much guilt. Too much retrospection. Far too much looking over the shoulder, although that had been driven by a different emotion during these past six months. It was time to move on.

He walked from the chapel in glorious sunshine. The Dear Green Place of St Mungo was truly beautiful in sunshine. People smiled. They relaxed. They looked up, seeing the angels and gargoyles in the Victorian architecture that remained unnoticed when they were cowering against the wind and the rain. Even the soot stains glinted in summer. Connolly claimed there were only two seasons in Scotland: June and winter. But it was just a joke. A deferential way of looking at the country that was part self-preservation, part acceptance of the general lot of being Scottish.

Archie Blunt was choosing to leave that all behind. To follow a new course. One of forward-looking optimism. It was always inside him, waiting to get out, but his dream-state procrastination held him back from a better future.

With the van business expanding, Archie's partnership with Jimmy Rowntree would soon see the addition of a shop unit. Jimmy was happiest being mobile. Archie craved the anchor of a base. It suited both and part of The High Five's cash had allowed him to secure a new lease on Tollcross Road.

He walked up the slope of the Necropolis. An old couple

approaching him may have assumed he was talking to himself, but he was saying farewell to another significant part of his past.

You know what, boy ... ah think you're gonna be just fine. Just fine, man!

'Ah think ye might be right, Jim.'

⏻

Archie reached the plot. He sat on the grass and unwrapped his sandwich. The carved, beige masonry faced south-west. It was gleaming. It had one word on the stone: *BLUNT.* When the paperwork and the bureaucracy was finally concluded, his mother would rejoin his father here. Lying eternally on the peaceful, quiet upper quartile. Gazing out forever at the wondrous, ever-changing metropolis below them.

Playlist

That gallus mid-seventies vibe was lovingly recreated using the following:

Theme from *The Rockford Files*
Mike Post
(Written by Mike Post and Pete Carpenter)
Available on MGM Records, 1975

'Wake Up Little Susie'
The Everly Brothers
(Written by Felice and Boudleaux Bryant)
Available on Cadence Records, 1957

'Sweet Nothings'
Brenda Lee
(Written by Ronnie Self)
Available on Decca Records, 1959

'Summer Wind'
Frank Sinatra
(Written by Heinz Meier and Johnny Mercer)
Available on Capitol Records, 1965

'Here Comes the Sun'
The Beatles
(Written by George Harrison)
Available on Apple Records, 1969

'All the Young Dudes'
Mott The Hoople
(Written by David Bowie)
Available on Columbia Records, 1972

'Just Dropped In (To See What Condition My Condition Was In)'
Kenny Rogers & The First Edition
(Written by Mickey Newbury)
Available on Reprise Records, 1968

'I'm Not in Love'
10CC
(Written by Eric Stewart and Graham Gouldman)
Available on Mercury Records, 1975

'I Think I Love You'
The Partridge Family
(Written by Tony Romeo)
Available on Bell Records, 1970

'Sugar Baby Love'
The Rubettes
(Written by Wayne Bickerton and Tony Waddington)
Available on Polydor Records, 1974

'Hot Love'
T. Rex
(Written by Marc Bolan)
Available on Fly Records, 1971

'These Boots Are Made for Walkin''
Nancy Sinatra
(Written by Lee Hazlewood)
Available on Reprise Records, 1966

'To Sir with Love'
Lulu
(Written by Don Black, Mark London, Mike Leander)
Available on Epic Records, 1967

'Silly Love Songs'
Wings
(Written by Paul and Linda McCartney)
Available on MPL Communications, 1976

'Afternoon Delight'
Starland Vocal Band
(Written by Bill Danoff)
Available on RCA Records, 1976

'Folsom Prison Blues'
Johnny Cash
(Written by Johnny Cash)
Available on Sun Records, 1955

'Last Train to Clarksville'
The Monkees
(Written by Tommy Boyce and Bobby Hart)
Available on Colgems Records, 1966

'Oh Lori'
Alessi
(Written by Billy and Bobby Alessi)
Available on A&M Records, 1976

'The Year of Decision'
The Three Degrees
(Written by Kenneth Gamble and Leon Huff)
Available on Philadelphia International, 1973

'Golden Years'
David Bowie
(Written by David Bowie)
Available on RCA Records, 1975

'The Faith Healer'
The Sensational Alex Harvey Band
(Written by Alex Harvey and Hugh McKenna)
Available on Vertigo Records, 1973

'Stuck in the Middle with You'
Stealers Wheel
(Written by Gerry Rafferty, Joe Egan)
Available on A&M Records, 1973

'Anarchy in the UK'
Sex Pistols
(Written by Matlock, Lydon, Cook, Jones)
Available on Virgin Records, 1976

'No Fun'
The Stooges
(Written by Alexander, Asheton, Asheton, Pop)
Available on Elektra Records, 1969

'Right Back where We Started From'
Maxine Nightingale
(Written by Pierre Tubbs and J. Vincent Edwards)
Available on United Artists Records, 1975

Acknowledgements

Elaine, Nathan and Nadia.

To all the dudes I've thanked before. Once again, I'm totally in your debt.

Much love and gratitude to Karen Sullivan and West Camel, for their patience and forbearance. Kevin Toner for Shettleston vibes. John Carnochan for the police procedures, and to James Semple for introducing me to methylene blue.

Thanks to David Stirling, Robin Johnston, Graham Nolan and Robert Hodgens for the short film clip. And especially to Chris McQueer for the narration. I wish I had a fraction of his talent.

The character of Bobby (or *Boaby*, as he was then...) Souness originally began life as a month-long collaborative story on Twitter. It developed beyond that first story into something special with incredibly talented guest contributors keeping it fresh.

Thanks to everyone who directly contributed to those tales, but particularly Paul Thomson and Hugh Mulholland.

⏻

This book is also dedicated to Billy Connolly: Genius, and Knight of the Glaswegian Realm.

⏻

Bobby Souness will return, when the author
considers it safe for him to do so.

Other titles by David F. Ross, available from Orenda Books...

'Full of comedy, pathos
and great tunes'
HARDEEP SINGH KOHLI

'Warm, funny and
evocative'
CHRIS BROOKMYRE

'Dark, hilarious and heart-breaking'
MURIEL GRAY

David F. Ross

THE LAST DAYS OF DISCO

David F. Ross

THE RISE & Fall OF THE MIRACULOUS VESPAS

'A great white-knuckle read set in the
world of hope, dreams and DIY pop'
Stuart Cosgrove

'An astonishing tour de force'
John Niven

THE MAN WHO LOVED ISLANDS

DAVID F. ROSS

'A real new talent on the
Scottish literary scene'
Press & Journal

'An astonishing tour de force'
JOHN NIVEN